Advanced Reviews

"You'll laugh. You'll cry. You'll love it."

—Susan Yanguas, author of *Bluff*

"*New Normal* is the story of the life-altering, tragic loss of a spouse told in a way that turns grief on its head. The toughest events of the novel are injected with a dose of humor and humanity that turns tears to a comforting smile. The plucky main character has something to teach anyone about how to pull yourself up with not only grit, but grace."

—LR Trovillion, author of *False Gods*

"Main character Emilie Russell is the kind of friend you wish you had in real life. She is strong, smart, funny and very relatable. You'll want to hold her hand in the rough times and cheer for her as she reinvents herself after loss. Paris' dialogue is witty and sharp; her characters authentic and memorable. I was sorry when the story ended, and if there's ever a sequel, I'll be first in line!"

— Cari Scribner, author of *A Girl Like You* and *A Place Like This*

"How can a young widow properly mourn the loss of the husband she adored and overcome the grief that now defines her life? In *New Normal*, Emilie Russell does it with a sense of humor, a spirit of adventure, a little help from her shrink, and a lot of help from her friends. With witty dialogue and a keen eye for cultural touchstones, author Michelle Paris tells a story—both her heroine's and her own - of resilience, community, and love."

— Dian Seidel, author of *Kindergarten at 60: A Memoir of Teaching in Thailand*

"*New Normal* is a story about navigating life after the sudden loss of a beloved spouse. It touches on healing, hope, and finding love again. It will make you cry, laugh, and cheer for the main character on the journey to happiness until the very end."

—Deliah Lawrence, author of *Gotta Let It Go*

New Normal

New Normal

Michelle Paris

Apprentice
House Press
Loyola University Maryland

First Edition

Library of Congress Control Number: 2022950404

Hardcover ISBN: 978-1-62720-451-4
Paperback ISBN: 978-1-62720-452-1
Ebook ISBN: 978-1-62720-453-8

Design by Riley Kamm
Promotional Development by Natalie Misyak
Editorial Development by Sienna Whalen

Published by Apprentice House Press

Apprentice
House Press
Loyola University Maryland

Loyola University Maryland
4501 N. Charles Street, Baltimore, MD 21210
410.617.5265
www.ApprenticeHouse.com
info@ApprenticeHouse.com

This book is dedicated to anyone who has suffered loss and is searching for a new normal.

"Have enough courage to trust love
one more time and always one more time."
---Maya Angelou

1

Emilie tilted the rearview mirror to assess the damage. It was worse than she expected. Chocolate on her chin and even her nose—it had been a bumpy ride. Using an old napkin she found in the glovebox, she wiped away the evidence she'd scarfed down a brownie on the short drive to Viv's. Satisfied she no longer looked like Augustus Gloop from Willy Wonka, she balled the napkin up and threw it at the dashboard in a failed attempt to block the blinking digital clock. Eight thirty. Sigh. The party began more than an hour earlier. "Just stay until the fireworks—thirty minutes tops," she said to herself, giving a pep talk of sorts to summon the courage to leave the safety of her car.

It had been almost five months since she began her self-imposed exile. She couldn't hibernate forever, even if that's what she really wanted to do. Attending Viv's annual Fourth of July party tonight would be a baby step in the right direction. A baby step.

She tugged the collar of her T-shirt to get it close to her nose, hoping to catch a trace of his scent—Hugo Boss cologne mixed with an occasional cigar—but only the scent of lavender fabric softener remained. Memories would have to suffice. She thought of the last time Rob, her late husband, wore the shirt a year ago to the day. Trying to soften Viv's overreaction to a tiny yellow stain on her white linen blouse, he had said, "Colonel Mustard did it on the rooftop with a hot dog." She smiled fondly at the memory. Going to parties with Rob was fun—hell, just being married to him was fun.

After letting go of the T-shirt, she took a deep breath and forced herself out of the car. Baby steps.

A few baby steps later, it became painfully apparent the three-inch, high-heeled strappy sandals were a bad idea. Looking down at her unpolished toes made her wish she wore the red canvas flats instead. By this time last summer, there would have been at least two or three mani-pedis. The canvas flats would have not only been more comfortable, but they would also have covered her un-pampered and neglected toes.

After entering Viv's house, she scanned the small crowd gathered in the narrow living room. Hearing Viv's familiar cackle coming from the kitchen, Emilie headed there.

Viv's kitchen was tiny, as was the case in most Baltimore Federal Hill row houses, with exposed brick walls that fit the French farmhouse style decor. The blue and white square marble floor tiles matched the drapes that adorned a small window, which opened out to the alley behind the house.

Upon seeing Emilie, Viv put a tray of cheese and crackers down on the granite countertop and grabbed both of Emilie's hands. "I'm so glad you came," she said. The woman Viv was talking to excused herself and left the room. Viv stepped back and looked at Emilie. "You look great."

Although Viv sounded sincere, Emilie did not believe her. Sleepless nights had formed dark circles under her eyes, and stress eating had added a few obvious pounds to her petite frame.

"I have a surprise for you," Viv said. Her Botoxed forehead made her eyebrows arch in a constant state of mock shock. "There's a new neighbor I want you to meet. His name is Colin, he's a lawyer, and he recently moved from Philadelphia. He'd be perfect for you." Her voice became sing-songy at the end.

The brownie Emilie ate in the car started to make its reappearance. Her first instinct was to take off those stupid heels and run. Yes, break free of Viv's grasp and hightail it out of there. Viv's glassy eyes and more than a hint of gin on her breath gave Emilie the confidence she could outrun Viv, the onetime Maryland State cross country champion.

Quickly, she realized her plan had flaws. If she did make it to her car and home without getting caught, Viv would, undoubtedly, check up on her after hours, or days of unanswered calls and find her sprawled on her bed, a dark sticky goo covering her face and the linens. Ben and Jerry would be the likely culprits. Death by chocolate, indeed, a fate Emilie surprisingly decided was more embarrassing than her current predicament. Instead of running away, she gritted her teeth and said, "Viv, have you lost your mind?"

"No, I haven't. I'm only thinking of you when I say you gotta get out there." Viv shimmied her hips and shoulders as she spoke. The wink she added suggested "get out there'" meant something naughty. "Have I ever steered you wrong?"

Emilie nodded.

"Let me rephrase that. Have I ever steered you wrong when it came to men?"

"Yes!"

Viv pursed her lips. "Oh, pshaw! You aren't still blaming me for setting you up with Sarah's cousin, are you? That was fifteen years ago."

"He was a convicted felon."

"It was only white-collar," Viv said.

Emilie tilted her head to one side. "Really? *Only* white-collar?"

"I mean, it wasn't anything violent like robbing a 7-Eleven or something like that. Embezzlement, I think." Viv looked as if she was deep in thought. "At least, I'm pretty sure."

"Oh, *now* I see your point," Emilie said with a hint of sarcasm. "Please don't do this to me."

"Aw, c'mon. It'll be good for you. And don't worry, I don't think this guy, Colin, has ever been to jail." Viv shrugged and added, "I take that back. He's a lawyer, so he's probably been to jail plenty of times, but on the other side of the bars. Besides, that doesn't matter. What does is that he looks exactly like George Clooney—the Ocean's Eleven version—only with longer and grayer hair and a mustache. And taller and thinner."

Emilie tried to imagine this comparison, but couldn't.

"Why, if I weren't married, I'd go for him myself. C'mon. Let's go find him before one of my cougar neighbors starts pawing him," Viv said.

"You can't be serious." Emilie squeezed Viv's hand hard. "Criminal or not, I don't think I'm ready."

"Ow." Viv pulled her hand away and shook it. "Yes, I am serious. Look, Em, I'm worried if I don't intervene, you'll become a reclusive cat lady."

"That's not going to happen. I don't even own a cat," Emilie said.

"Yet. You don't own a cat yet. Soon you'll be telling me, 'Guess what? I got a cat.' And then, 'Guess what? Fluffy has the cutest meow.' And then, 'Guess what? Fluffy sits on my lap, and I spoon-feed him albacore tuna while we're wearing matching sweaters I crocheted from his shedding fur.'"

That made Emilie laugh.

"Aw, that's the Em I know. I miss that laugh." Viv leaned in close. "You're too young to be a cat lady," she whispered in Emilie's ear.

"I don't want that either," Emilie whispered back.

A man entered the kitchen and put his glass down on the counter. "Sorry, didn't mean to interrupt. I think you're out of ice upstairs." He was about six feet tall and lean. He had bluish-gray eyes, salt-and-pepper hair, and a thin mustache. Emilie thought he might have been the most handsome man she had ever seen—well, at least in the past five months.

"Oh, there you are. Colin, this is my friend Emilie. You know, the one I've told you about." Viv turned toward Emilie and winked.

Colin reached out his hand and gave Emilie a firm handshake. "I'm Colin Meyer, nice to meet you." His cheeks displayed dimples when he smiled.

"Emilie, Emilie Russell. So nice to meet you too," she managed to say, averting her eyes toward the brick wall so that she did not look directly at him when she spoke.

"Okay, I'll let you two get to know each other." Viv put her arms around both of them, forcing them closer together. She picked up the cheese platter from the counter and left the room yelling, "Andrew! Andrew! I thought I told you to watch the ice!" Her voice trailed off as she went up the stairs.

"Hamilton," Colin said, pointing to Emilie's shirt. "Cute. And very appropriate for the Fourth of July. I wish I would have thought of that. Broadway fan, I take."

"What, this?" She tugged at the knotted tee. "Yeah, kind of." Emilie swallowed hard in an attempt to rid her throat of the lump forming. "It's my husband's. Was. Was my husband's. He wore it here last year."

"Oh, I see. Clever," Colin said. His words lingered as he turned toward the refrigerator.

"So, Viv tells me you moved here from Philadelphia. How long have you been here?" Emilie's voice cracked loudly, displaying her nerves.

He opened the freezer and took out ice cubes, which made a loud clink when they hit his glass. "Three weeks. I'm working for Miller and Schmidt on Charles Street. Hopefully, soon it will be Miller, Schmidt, and Meyer. What do you do?" he asked.

"I work for American Communications—the cable company. Doing PR."

He turned on the faucet and filled his glass with water. After taking a sip and turning back toward Emilie, he said, "Viv told me about your husband."

She did? The brownie taunted her once again.

"I'm sorry for your loss." He drank some more water. "I know how it feels. I lost my partner a few years ago. Even though we weren't married yet, I considered him my husband."

Instantly, a wave of calmness swept through her body, and she let out an audible but pleasant sigh.

"Yes, I'm gay," he said. "And, if you want, we can tell Viv we made out to get her off both of our backs."

Emilie smiled. "I like the way you think."

"Viv is only trying to help," Colin said. "My good friends did the same thing."

"Yes, I know. She just doesn't know what it's like."

He nodded. "I understand your husband had a heart attack. I can't imagine the suddenness. Howard, my partner, had pancreatic cancer. So, I had a few months to prepare. I'm not saying it was easy. I still feel cheated. But I'm happy to say, we made the most of those months. I told him how much I loved him every morning when I woke up and every night when we went to sleep." He finished his water and put the glass in the sink. "Your husband, he must have been young."

"Forty-two."

Colin shook his head. "Howard was forty-five. He would have

been fifty this year. It's been hard. Lots of memories." He shook his head again. "Lots of emotions. I decided to move to Baltimore for a new start. Should have done it years ago. I guess I'm a slow learner. Unfortunately, there's no widow's guide for dummies."

"I have to admit, I'm pretty lost. I guess I'm a slow learner too. At least when it comes to this, I am. It's still so hard for me to believe he's gone."

"Yep. I know. It was, and at times still is, hard for me to believe Howard's dead. For a long time, I only kept pictures of him around my house from when he was well. I didn't want to be reminded of how sick he was in the end. I wanted to remember him in the good days." There was a long pause, and then Colin said, "Emilie, you're going to be fine. It may not feel that way now, but you will. Soon you'll think about him less and less. It's all too new for you now. It takes time, and you have to do it at your own pace."

"I hope so. People tell me all the time how well I'm doing, but I don't feel it myself. I didn't expect to feel so conflicted—feeling lonely, but moving on seems like such a betrayal. And not to mention the thought of dating again at forty . . . awkward." She scrunched her face up and then asked, "Have you dated since Howard died?"

"Yes, I've done quite a bit of dating. I'm quite a catch if I do say so myself—no baggage, just a dead partner. But I do understand what you're saying. It was rough for me. Not just because I thought I'd spend the rest of my life with Howard, but because dating is much different now—everything is digital. It's like online shopping but for someone to kiss," he said with a raised eyebrow.

"To be completely honest, online dating is too scary." A pop and crack came from the alley behind the house, followed by some laughter. Emilie could hear people from the living room climbing the stairs, making their way to the rooftop.

"Yes, it is. But, when your fear of being alone outweighs your fear of online dating, you'll give it a try. Now, I do have to warn you, being swiped left does take some getting used to."

"Swiped left? Sounds awful."

Colin laughed. "It's the newest form of rejection. Swipe right if you're interested, swipe left if you're not."

"Oh, I see." She felt herself cringing on the inside and was sure it showed on the outside too. She never did have a poker face.

"You'll get used to it. Let me see, cute redhead—I predict lots of right swipes in your future."

"Glad you think so. Viv thinks if I don't start dating, I'm going to turn into a cat lady."

"Avoid the cat lady status—I think that is a Match.com slogan." His smile faded slightly as he added, "You'll know when you're ready to date. But I can tell you aren't ready yet."

"I'm not? How can you tell?" She imagined there was a black "W" emblazoned on her chest.

Colin pointed to her left hand. "You're still wearing your wedding ring. That's a sure sign you aren't ready. When you can accept and admit you are no longer married, the ring will come off. It'll be hard and may take a few attempts—you'll take it off, feel weird about it, put it back on, only to take it off again. Howard and I had matching diamond engagement bands. It took me three attempts, but when I finally got it off, I knew my heart was ready to let someone else in."

Emilie self-consciously used her pinky to twist the modest emerald cut diamond engagement ring toward her palm and out of sight. The ring and her platinum wedding band had become so much a part of her she didn't realize they were there. Removing them would feel like cutting off a finger. She started to cry. Embarrassed, she covered her face with her hands. "I just wish it never happened."

He wrapped his arms around her and pulled her in close. "If we want it to, life goes on. And you have a choice to go on with it, without him. But make the most of that choice. He would want that."

For the first time in what seemed like a lifetime, her head rested on a man's chest. She could feel and hear his heartbeat, and she smelled the faint hint of Hugo Boss cologne. And it felt good.

A loud pop was followed by a chorus of "oohs."

Colin broke the embrace and took out his cell phone from his pants pocket. "Now, give me your number so I can prevent Viv from fixing me, or you, up with anyone else tonight. And here's mine. Call anytime." He looked intently into her eyes. "I mean it. Call me anytime."

2

Opening the July fifth *Baltimore Sun*, Emilie gasped. "Oh, God, No!" The full-page ad she'd taken out for the Nature Channel's new series on Antarctica—the one she reviewed the copy from several times—had the typo all PR professionals dread. In bold it read, "Penguins: A Cold Reality, premiering on the Nature Channel this fall, for more information contact Emilie Russell, Pubic Relations Manager, American Communications." There it was, as big as day, her pube exposed for all of Baltimore—maybe even the world—to see. She envisioned herself becoming fodder for late-night television, the internet, oh and the cruel world of social media. Can't forget that! Pube-gate.

She thought hard about what to do. Maybe she could buy all the newspapers and handwrite an *l* in all of them. How many papers could there be? A hundred thousand or so? Doing the math not only did she not have forty or fifty thousand dollars to spare, and it would be physically impossible, nor would it solve the problem entirely. What about the deliveries? Her heart sank. She could hear the shrieks of laughter now.

She pounded her fist to her head and said, "Shoot, shoot, shoot!"

Just then, the phone in her office rang.

On the third ring, she answered, "Public Relations, this is Emilie Russell."

"Hi, Emilie. This is Tina Jenkins from the Inner Harbor Hotel."

Oh, dear God! Tina saw my pube! Emilie cringed at the thought.

Emilie decided to play it cool. "Yes, hi, Tina. What's up?" Emilie had been working with Tina on a black-tie event in conjunction with the Nature Channel show. It was an opportunity for the cable company's largest ad buyers, and members of the media, to preview the series before it aired on the fall schedule.

"Emilie, I think I know the answer to this question, but here goes. Last week, you emailed me that Perry and Penny Penguin needed a hotel room. I'm just checking to make sure they aren't, well, you know, real penguins."

"Yes, they're real birds." Emilie laughed. "I'm sorry. I thought I told you we were getting penguins on loan from Arctic Land in New York. They're going to greet people and provide a photo op. I can see where it may not be a request you get every day."

"Hmm," Tina said. "Well then, I see. I thought Perry and Penny were costumed characters . . . like Mickey and Minnie Mouse. Since they are real, we have a problem. Our hotel has a strict no-pet policy. None at all."

"What?" Emilie felt her heart begin to beat faster. "Tina, can you hold on for a second?" She pressed the hold button and opened the "Penguin Event" folder. In the file, she found the contract. Hoping she had written something about live penguins in it, Emilie scaled her finger down the first page. Nothing. The second page. Nothing. Midway down the third page, under the subject "Other Considerations" was typed "none." She closed her eyes and muttered, "No. No. No." Then she looked on the last page to see when the contract was signed. February twenty-eighth, three weeks after Rob died. Seeing the red blinking hold light, she put her head in her hands and tried to think quickly. Arctic Land was an eight-hour drive from Baltimore. The owners had insisted the penguins have premium housing before they would lend them to the event. Not really knowing what to do, she decided to wing it. She removed the call from hold and said, "Tina, these aren't pets, they're actors—show birds," she said, trying hard not to let her voice crack.

Tina said nothing.

"If the issue is cleanliness," Emilie continued, "we will pay to have room fumigated."

Still, nothing came from the other end.

"Honestly, I think they just stand in the bathtub—on dry ice. They won't be walking around and getting on the beds or anything." Emilie was throwing spaghetti on the wall, seeing if anything she said would make Tina change her mind.

"I'm sorry, Emilie," Tina said. "I wish I could be flexible. Last month, we told Oprah she couldn't bring her dogs, even though she had the Dog Whisperer as a character reference. My general manager is insistent that we cannot break this rule. I think he hates animals or something." Tina whispered the last part, which was barely audible.

What? As Tina's words began to sink in, Emilie started to feel sick. Perry and Penny were going to make the event special—they were the gimmick that she came up with and the Nature Channel loved the idea.

"Will we at least be allowed to have them at the event? I don't think we can do it without them there." Emilie rubbed her throbbing temple.

"Do they walk on their own or are they in cages?"

"I don't know. Walk, I guess."

"Oh, that's too bad. Once I had a client sneak a parrot in through the kitchen. We covered the cage like a room service cart. But then the stupid bird started squawking something about bringing sexy back in this creepy Justin Timberlake-like voice. So, we quickly got him out of the hotel before the manager found out. Penguins don't talk, do they?"

"No. I'm pretty sure they don't," Emilie said, feeling a little hopeful.

"Okay, good. Maybe we could sneak them in and have the event in the garden out back. That's technically not the hotel. I'm willing to work with you on the event, but I'm sure they'll have to sleep somewhere else."

Suddenly, an exposed pube was now the least of Emilie's worries. "Thank you, Tina. You're the best. I'll try and sort out where they will stay." After hanging the phone up, Emilie composed herself. Fearing this problem wouldn't be easily resolved, she knew she had to brief Carl, her boss—and he was not going to be happy.

When she reached his office, she tapped lightly on the metal frame that surrounded the fabric cube wall. Carl had worked for American Communications for twenty-five years—twenty-five years too long, by most people's assessment. As Director of PR, he loathed fixing issues and lacked the positive attitude that was necessary for the industry. PR was all about slapping on a smile and making even bad news seem good. Carl would often say, "If the people of Baltimore don't like it, tell them to turn off their cable." That may have worked ten years ago when American Communications was the only cable provider in the city, but now with streaming services like Netflix and Amazon Prime Video, people *were* turning off their cable.

He was sitting at his desk with the *Baltimore Sun* opened to the full-page ad. Carl was an imposing figure. More round than tall, his barrel chest made him appear almost bear-like—but not teddy bear-like. Although he was furry, with a wad of chest hair always protruding from his too tight, button-down, short-sleeve oxfords, he was definitely not huggable. Carl looked much older than his sixty years, mostly due to the horrible comb-over that he shellacked to his forehead with hairspray. Photos of him with celebrated Baltimore athletes like Cal Ripken, Michael Phelps, and Poe, the Raven's mascot, hung evenly spaced on the walls. On the credenza behind his desk was a framed photo of him and his second wife, Barb, wearing Hawaiian shirts and leis on their wedding day five years earlier. He folded the paper in half, exposing the pube page.

"What's this?" he asked, pointing to the unfortunate typo. When Carl spoke, only the bottom part of his jaw moved, much like a clown puppet Emilie avoided at her grandmother's house when she was a kid. Unfortunately, Carl was as traumatizing as the puppet had been.

"I know. I'm sorry about that, but we have a bigger problem." Emilie told him about the penguins.

Upon hearing the news, Carl's eyes closed, and a vein began to protrude through the thinning strands of hair in his comb-over. "What do you mean, they won't allow them to stay there?" His voice was full of indignation. "Didn't you put it in the contract?"

"No, I guess it wasn't in there." She crossed her legs, trying to cover up the nervous tapping of her foot. "I'm sorry." She swallowed hard.

"What's wrong with you?"

"My husband died," Emilie blurted, holding back tears.

"What?" He looked incredulous. "That was months ago." His eyes narrowed, and he leaned in close. "You better get your act together."

"I'll fix it. Give me some time." Not sure exactly how she was going to fix it, she just needed to get Carl out of the mix and off her back.

Emilie returned to her office. Feeling drained and tired, and since it was already four o'clock, she texted Viv and asked her if she wanted to grab a drink.

• • •

It took thirty minutes for her to drive twelve blocks from her office to Federal Hill, just south of the Inner Harbor. In the summer, tourists flocked to Baltimore's Inner Harbor like the gulls that strolled around its paved brick walkways. The city street crosswalks were filled with meandering people, allowing only a few cars to make it through each light cycle.

When she reached South Baltimore, she found a place to park in front of but across the street from Milo's Watering Hole. She got out of her car, fumbled for her key fob to lock it, and then walked into the restaurant. Viv was already there, sitting at one of only five small square tables with crisp floor-length tablecloths that the restaurant had. Viv was well into a Tanqueray martini.

"Well, hello there, *pubic* relations manager." Viv's eyes twinkled as she talked. She stood up and gave Emilie a hug.

"I had a hard day, and the pube wasn't even the worst part," Emilie said.

"Oh, do tell." Viv took a sip of her drink.

Emilie waved her off. "Can we just change the subject? Where's the waiter? I need a glass of chardonnay."

Once Emilie was seated, Viv said, "You seemed to really hit it off with Colin at the party. Has he asked you out yet?"

"Um, he's gay."

"What?" Viv looked surprised, but then again, thanks to Botox, she always did. "Hmm. Who knew?"

"Obviously not you. He said he told you his partner died."

Emilie gave Viv a wide-eyed look.

"Oh. Yes, he did. I thought he was talking about his law partner, not partner-partner. Too bad." She took another sip of her martini.

"Do me a favor. Don't ever try and set me up again. You're not good at it," Emilie said with a slight laugh.

"So, I've had a few misses. You know, I'm only trying to help." Viv pouted playfully, then pushed the untouched breadbasket toward Emilie. She then raised her hand, trying to get the attention of the bartender, who was wiping off the far end of the bar on the other side of the restaurant. When Viv was sure she had his attention, she pointed to her glass and mouthed, "I'll have another." She was the type who preferred to drink her Weight Watchers points.

Emilie took a roll from the basket and buttered it. "I know. I'm sorry. I'm tired. My job sucks, and I'm the laughingstock of the city. I feel like such a failure. So much for that St. Cecilia's English degree. I can't even proofread a fifteen-word copy. If my dad were alive, he'd ask for all that tuition money back."

Viv frowned. "Aw, it was worth every penny—so what if we skipped a few classes? We had fun, didn't we?"

"Yes, we did have fun, but to clarify, only *you* skipped classes."

Viv mouthed "nerd," and added a wink. Getting no reaction from Emilie, Viv said, "You do look tired."

"I haven't been sleeping well since . . ." Emilie couldn't finish her sentence.

"Everyone needs help getting to sleep every now and then, and honey, after what you've been through, you probably could use an extra dose." Viv bent down and grabbed a brown bottle of pills from her purse and shook them. "Ambien—it's my new drug of choice." With a smile, she took out two pills and handed them to Emilie. "Okay, so only take one. I was kidding about the double dose. They really do work. And don't do anything—I mean any-thing—other than watch TV or read until they take effect.

"Oh, I don't know. I'm not sure I should take something pre-scribed for you."

Viv gave a dismissive wave of her hand. "I give them to Andrew all the time. The first time I did, he kept saying 'it isn't working.' Then, just like a stubborn man, he got in the car and drove to Whole Foods. About twenty minutes later, I got a call from the store manager saying he found him passed out near the frozen foods. Of course, Andrew couldn't drive home, so I had to go get him." Viv rolled her eyes. "I told him they work, just give them a chance, and I'm giving you the same warning. I don't want to have to pick you up from the frozen food section of Whole Foods."

"Okay, thanks." Emilie took the pills from Viv, wrapped them in a paper napkin, and put them in her purse. "Maybe I'll give it a try."

About two hours later, the restaurant filled up, and people were standing outside, waiting to be seated. The hostess walked by them twice, giving them the stink eye. Picking up on the cue, Emilie and Viv requested the check.

After leaving the restaurant, Emilie hugged Viv goodbye and walked across the street to her car. While standing on the curb, the shrill sound of a siren pierced every cell in her body. She looked up as the ambulance passed by. She could see the medics perform CPR in the back as the truck slowed down to dodge traffic. She felt her body become cold and her knees weaken. Her hand shook as she fumbled with her keys. Once inside her car, she reached for a coffee mug in the console and vomited the meal she had just eaten.

• • •

When she got home, it was a little after eight o'clock. She

picked up the morning paper, which had sat all day at the end of her driveway. Then she walked into the garage and plopped the paper in the recycle bin. The bin was overflowing with faded, unwrapped papers. It had long become too heavy to carry to the curb, and for some reason, she lacked the initiative to cancel the delivery. Just another indication of life going on without her.

From the garage entrance, she walked into the house and put her purse on the kitchen counter. The open floor plan gave her a view of Rob's urn, which sat on top of the cabinet they built to house the TV. "Honey, I'm home," she said with a chuckle. The barren halls did not answer.

She removed her phone and the napkin that contained the sleeping pills from her purse. Exhausted and sore, she walked down the hallway to her bedroom. She put her phone and the napkin on her nightstand next to the bed. Undressing, she tossed her clothes on the floor of her walk-in closet. She moved into the master bathroom and to the garden tub. Turning the water on, she added a generous cap of lilac-scented bubble bath and checked the temperature with her hand, making sure the water wasn't getting too hot. When the bubbles were about six inches from the top, she slowly eased her body in. Once her whole body was submerged up to her chin, she closed her eyes and let out a sigh, trying to relax.

As she soaked, she remembered the times when she and Rob would bathe together. Taking turns washing each other's backs, she welcomed his roaming hands as he playfully soaped up her breasts while kissing her neck. Tears began to flow without a sense of if they'd ever stop. She wiped her eyes with her wet hand, squinting from the sting of tears and soap, as she took a deep breath. "Why did this happen . . . to him? To me?"

They were together for ten years, married for eight of them, almost inseparable since meeting at the Rusty Rudder, a Fells Point bar. During a crowded happy hour, Emilie accidentally bumped into him, spilling cold draft beer down his back. "Good thing it's two-for-one," he laughed while he wiped the beer off his neck with a wad of napkins.

"Oh, please let me," she remembered blushing as she grabbed some napkins and began to help to dry off his brown leather bomber jacket. "I'm so sorry. You'll let me pay for the dry cleaning, won't you?"

"Only if that comes with your name and number," Rob said. He extended his hand. "I'm Rob Russell." His blue eyes twinkled as he smiled.

Emilie returned the smile. She put the napkins down on the bar next to them and reached out her hand to shake his. "I'm Emilie Malone. Nice to meet you. Well, I guess it isn't so nice for you." The bar was loud and crowded, and she had to lean in close as they talked. She could feel herself blush and hoped the darkly lit bar wouldn't give her away. She remembered how good he smelled—a memory she hoped would always stay with her.

He told her he worked construction and was born and raised in East Baltimore. They talked about family—he was an only child, she had an older brother, and passions—he had seen every Star Wars movie at least twice, and she dreamed of writing a book someday. His eyes lit up when she told him about her new job at the cable company and how she got to go to most sporting events. It made her smile when he referred to the Orioles as "we," and how he seemed to take it personally that the Colts left town in the middle of the night.

When happy hour ended and the crowd thinned, she somehow got the courage to hand him her business card. "Here, give me a call, and I'll get your jacket cleaned. I really am sorry." He called her the next day, not to have his jacket cleaned but to ask her out.

Two years after meeting, on a beautiful fall day, they were married.

As her mind drifted, the bathwater grew too cold to continue to soak. She got out of the tub and dried off. As the water drained, she put on her blue terry cloth robe. Catching her reflection in the mirror above the sink and she stared at a person she didn't recognize. Her face looked weathered. There were new creases on her brow, and her once vibrant green eyes were now dulled by dark circles underneath. Her thick curly red hair fell well below its normal shoulder-length and was in need of some shaping.

She walked from the bathroom to her bed and sat on the side of it. She looked at the opposite side—his side, which hadn't been touched in five months, not even to pull the comforter up and make the bed. With her feet dangling, she picked up the napkin containing the sleeping pills she had placed on the nightstand earlier. Studying the pills, she doubted their magical, sleep-inducing powers.

"Okay, here goes." She popped one pill in her mouth and swallowed it without water. She got into bed, lying on top of the covers, and curled up in a fetal position, far away from the other side. She waited for any sign the drug was kicking in. With her eyes closed, she prayed for sleep.

• • •

About thirty minutes later, she jolted awake. Her heart was pounding loud and fast, and her skin felt clammy. With her hands trembling, she picked up her phone from the nightstand and texted Colin "Are you free for coffee tomorrow?" and hit send.

3

A little after five the next day, Emilie walked into Purrfect Perks, a cat café and coffee shop on Charles Street, near Colin's office.

When she entered the café, a gray cat lounging on the window-sill stood up, yawned, and then arched its back to stretch before rolling back up into a contented ball. She spied Colin sitting on a couch in the back corner. As she approached him, she noticed he was not alone—a big orange tabby cat sat next to him. The orange cat had its front paws tucked neatly under its large body. Colin stood and gave her a hug and a peck on the cheek. "Emilie, I want you to meet Creamsicle." He motioned to a photo of the cat on the wall behind the couch. Underneath the photo was an index card that read "My Name is Creamsicle. I am 9 years old, and I like to sleep and eat. My hobbies are playing with fake mice and grooming myself. I also love me some good catnip occasionally, but I don't inhale—hey everyone has a vice!"

Colin sat back down, and Emilie sat on the couch next to him. Creamsicle woke from his nap, stood up, walked across Colin's lap, and stuck his nose up to sniff Emilie. She patted him on the head, and he purred. "Are you trying to force me into cat lady status?" she asked Colin.

"What? No. Don't be silly. These cats are rentals. You see, you pay fifteen dollars an hour to enjoy their company. Hooker cats, a true cathouse," he said with a wink. "I've paid for an hour for both of us. So, pet away. He likes it when you do this." Colin rubbed under Creamsicle's chin, and the cat's purr grew louder. "Do you want some coffee?" he asked, motioning for the barista to come over.

When the waitress approached their table, Emilie ordered a skinny mocha and Colin a black coffee. Both drinks were served in big ceramic mugs with pictures of cats on them.

"How are you?" His voice sounded full of sincerity.

"I'm okay. I've screwed some things up at work. I'm sure you saw the pube in the *Sun*."

"Yep." Colin nodded as he took a sip of his coffee. "No big deal. It happens."

"Unless you're the one with the exposed typo."

"True. But still, it happens."

"And I had to call five hotels in the city before I'd find one that would allow penguins. The problem would have been avoided if I were more careful. But it's just been so hard to concentrate."

He nodded. "Penguins? I won't ask, but I'm sure there's a story there. Look, don't be so hard on yourself. I remember some days just getting out of bed was a chore."

"For me, some days getting into bed is a chore." Emilie paused. "Do you ever dream about Howard?" She settled into the couch, stroking Creamsicle, who had made a bed out of her lap.

Colin gave Emilie a knowing smile. He brought his mug to his mouth and gently blew on the steaming liquid. Taking a sip, he nodded slightly. "I used to. I used to all the time. Why? Did you have a Rob dream?"

"Yes. He showed up from a fishing trip, and I was mad at him because he missed his own funeral." Emilie searched for the right words. "You know, how irresponsible of him," she said with a half smile. "But then it hit me—he was alive. I was just happy to see him. It felt so real." Fighting back tears, Emilie looked down.

Colin put his mug down. He grabbed her hand, which was still stroking the cat. He held her hand tightly in both of his. "I know it's hard. I think it takes the brain a long time to catch up with reality. I promise you the sadness dissipates. You will get there. It just takes time." He let go of her hand and leaned back. "In my *Howard* dream, it was our wedding day, and he's sitting on the edge of the bed in his underwear. I would say 'Come on Howard, we're going to be late.' And he'd just sit there, saying nothing, and wouldn't move. Then I'd wake up. I had that dream probably a dozen times. Always the same dream—no changes. The last time I had it, he had been dead a little over a year. The dream was the same, only this time he spoke. He said, 'You're going to have to go without me.'" Colin smiled and paused. "So, you see, the brain catches up." He picked up his coffee from the coffee table and took another sip. "Emilie, have you thought about grief counseling?"

"Yeah. I did, right after Rob died. A room full of a bunch of old ladies. No, thank you."

"It doesn't have to be like that. What I'm saying is to see a therapist. Someone who specializes in grief."

"Naw. I don't know. I just don't think I could open up to a stranger. I think that'd be too weird."

"Look how fast you opened up to me. You can do it. If it's the right person and you feel comfortable, you can do it." He smiled faintly as he nodded.

"Why can't you be my therapist?" Emilie continued to stroke Creamsicle, who yawned, stretched, and then snuggled deeper into her lap.

"Because I can't. I can be your lawyer, but I can't be your therapist. You can always talk to me about anything. I can tell you how I handled things, but I can't ask you the right questions to get you to where you need to be. You know that." He tilted his head to the side and gave her a knowing glance.

Emilie frowned.

"You know I'm right. Let me call my guy up in Philadelphia and see if he can recommend someone down here."

"Okay," she said.

"You'll feel better. I know you will."

4

Two weeks later, Emilie was sitting on the stiff leather sofa of Dr. Alan Jeffries, a grief counselor referred by Colin's therapist.

"So, what brings you here?" Dr. Jeffries asked.

Emilie shifted uncomfortably. She never imagined she'd turn to therapy. It was hard to maintain the perception, deep-rooted in her stoic Irish blood, that she was keeping it all together. Lord knows many of her family members would benefit from therapy, but denial and wishing things away was a family tradition.

Dr. Jeffries's office was sparsely decorated—smart, but sparse. Hues of brown seemed to be the theme. The leather chair he sat in was a deep brown color with a high back and overstuffed winged armrests. A chocolate brown colored shag rug separated his chair and the couch where Emilie sat. To the left of Dr. Jeffries was a small Pottery Barn-style end table stained with a dark brown. Too much brown. Why wouldn't yellow be his color of choice? Yellow was bright and cheerful. Brown was depressing. Maybe the decorating style was deliberate. Emilie knew she was reading too much into the room decor.

She bit her lip and stared at the shag rug, searching for the courage to speak. The sight of Dr. Jeffries's hairy toes poking through bohemian sandals made her smile. Rob would have thought that was funny. When he was alive, Emilie could tell exactly what he was thinking with a single glance his way.

"Um, well . . ." She cleared her throat and diverted her attention up, being careful not to make eye contact with Dr. Jeffries. His long shaggy hair that curled up at his shoulders, his salt-and-pepper goatee, round John Lennon glasses, and dingy white oxford shirt with the sleeves rolled to below his elbows made him appear to be a better candidate for a health food store clerk than a therapist. She fixated on a coffee stain near his shirt pocket—anything to distract her from beginning the conversation.

"We can use this time any way you want," Dr. Jeffries said in a soothing and calm voice, much like a narrator of a meditation app she had once tried soon after Rob died. He had a yellow legal notepad on his lap and a pen in his right hand.

She saw his diploma, the only thing hanging on the walls, centered perfectly on the wall above his head. Alan Grover Jeffries, PhD. The University of Maryland School of Psychology, 2006. *Hmm. We are about the same age,* she thought, prolonging the inevitable discussion. Grover instantly made her think of Cookie Monster—her favorite Sesame Street character. "Cookie," she said in her head in her best Cookie Monster impression. This relieved the tension enough for her to speak and probably betrayed her with a faint smile.

She sighed heavily and clasped her hands together, placing them in her lap. "I want to . . . I want to talk about *it.*" *It* was what changed her life forever. *It* was what was on her mind constantly. *It* was what made her future uncertain. Clearing her throat, she continued. "Um, well, about five months ago, my husband died. He had a heart attack," she said, fighting back tears. "It was all so sudden. It happened so fast, but like in slow motion, you know what I mean?"

Dr. Jeffries nodded, clicked his pen, and began to write on his notepad. "Do you want to talk about what happened?"

"I still can't talk about his death without crying." She took a deep breath and slowly exhaled.

"That's all right. Tell me anything you wish and don't tell me anything you aren't ready to share." He jotted more notes on his pad.

"Funny. I remember that day so vividly. If you ask me 'what's the worst day in your life,' I won't even hesitate to say February the seventh." She smiled slightly. "I wonder how many people have such a definitive answer. The one day I want to forget is etched in my mind, every detail."

Dr. Jeffries clicked his pen again, jotted on his notepad, and nodded.

"I remember being on my way home from work, and I was so happy. Happier than I had been in a long time." She closed her eyes at the memory of that day. "Our lives were finally coming together. We'd struggled with infertility. Hmm, boy was that tough, but nothing like this." She shook her head and pressed her lips together. "So anyway, we had decided to adopt. A foolproof way of having a baby. I was so excited. I was so happy that we were finally going to have the family we always wanted.

"I brought a pizza home for dinner. It was a normal Friday. When Rob came home—Rob, my husband, was my husband—he said he wasn't feeling well. A pulled muscle in his shoulder. No big deal. I gave him Advil and thought everything would be fine. We ate dinner, and while we were watching TV, he started complaining again. Said he felt like he was going to throw up. He got up, sort of staggered from the living room. I followed him to the bathroom in our bedroom, and he started to vomit. He didn't even make it to the toilet. He started vomiting on the bathroom floor, and I'm thinking, great, I'm going to have to clean this up." She took another deep breath.

"I helped him to the sink. And then"—she paused and batted her eyes as tears began to flow from them—"then, he fell forward, and his head hit the mirror. He fell backward onto the floor." Tears started to stream. Dr. Jeffries reached for a tissue from a box on the floor next to his chair and passed it to her. She took a tissue out of the box, dabbed her eyes, and blew her nose before putting the box on the couch next to her. "I'm sorry, but I can still see him lying there." She balled the tissue tightly in her hand.

"Um, he started to gasp for air and his lips started to turn blue. I tried to pick him up. I guess I was thinking I have to get him to the hospital, but I couldn't move him. So, I grabbed the phone and called 9-1-1. I was panicking. I'm not sure what I said. While I was on the phone with the operator, he stopped breathing, and the blue was spreading past his lips. He was lying there, staring at me. He was so scared." Emilie put her head in her hands and began to sob.

She paused to compose herself. With her voice quivering, she said, "I had to give him CPR. I had taken a class years ago, but, honestly, I didn't know what to do. The operator helped me. I'm not sure how long I gave him CPR—maybe five or ten minutes. It seemed like an eternity. I kept screaming in my head and probably out loud 'Where are they? Why isn't anyone here to help me?' Then the paramedics came. When they got there, they took over. Asked me to wait outside. It was cold out, February, you know, and I was standing there freezing in bare feet. I kept saying out loud 'Please make him be okay.'

"It wasn't long before one of them came outside and told me they couldn't get him breathing on his own. Had him hooked up to a machine. I think it was at that point I realized this was bad. Really bad. I never thought it was *that* bad. Isn't that crazy? I never imagined it. I thought they would come in and he'd be okay."

She moved some hair that had fallen over her eyes, grabbed another tissue, and blew her nose again. "They had to take him to the hospital, and as they wheeled him down our driveway on the stretcher, his left arm dangled there. Limp. That should have made something click inside of my head. But it didn't."

"When I got to the hospital, I called my friend, Viv, and asked her to come and be with me. I didn't want to be alone. We sat in the waiting room. It was really crowded. I overheard someone say something like '*That* guy in there had a heart attack.' I knew they were talking about Rob—that's how I found out." She sighed and dabbed her eyes again.

Dr. Jeffries said nothing. Instead, he stared at her, slightly nodding.

She continued. "When the doctor finally told me he was dead, he asked me if I wanted to see him . . . one last time. All I could think of was Rob lying on the floor, turning blue. I was afraid to see him. At first, I said no, but Viv convinced me I should. And I'm glad she did. He looked so peaceful. I guess the oxygen gave him color again. He looked almost like he was resting. It's better for me to remember him that way." Emilie smiled. Her eyes burned and felt puffy from the tears. "So that's it. That's my story."

Dr. Jeffries put his notepad on his lap and leaned forward. "First of all, I'm very sorry for your loss. You've been through a lot. I hope you can see how strong you are. I'm not sure many people would have been able to react as efficiently as you did in an emergency situation. Nor could many people endure the loss of a spouse so young."

Emilie slowly exhaled.

"So, what do you want to get out of therapy? How can I help you?" He leaned back in his chair with his pen and notepad perched, ready to write.

She thought for a minute. "I feel like I'm a mess. I want to feel normal again." It was surprisingly easy to talk to Dr. Jeffries. "This is going to sound pretty bad, but I want the world to stop until I'm ready to live again. I'm afraid of how long that will take."

"What you are experiencing is typical for anyone who has suffered a tragic loss. Grief can be extremely crippling. All the feelings you're having, the fear of never having normalcy, the lack of hope, those are all natural emotions. It's good that you can voice them." Dr. Jeffries wrapped his fingers around his goatee as if he were trying to come up with the right words. "Other than your memories, what brings you the most sadness now? What do you think is keeping you from moving on?"

Emilie thought hard. "I miss him so much. I miss what we had. And I'm afraid I'll never find that again."

"Have you thought about dating?"

"Yes, I know I should want to, but I'm just not there yet." She smiled. "My friend Viv thinks there's something wrong with me. That I should be dating by now."

"There's no time frame for that. You'll do it when you're ready."

"That's what my friend Colin says. He should know, he's widowed too. I guess I'm just surprised at how much it still hurts. Why can't I talk about it without crying?"

"It was a painful event to not only endure, but to witness as well. It may be a while before you can talk about your husband's death without emotion. And don't be surprised if your emotions come back when you think they are gone. Grieving is a cyclical process." He drew a circle in the air with his pen. "You get better, you move on, and then something triggers grief, and you regress, but then you get better again. Therapy can be scary. You are very brave to have come here, and I hope you find talking about things helpful."

Emilie nodded. "Yes. I do feel better. I almost walked out of your waiting room. If you were thirty seconds later, I would have been gone." She laughed, half serious, half joking. She turned her head and fought back more tears. "It was hard to check that box."

"I'm not sure I understand."

"The marital status box on your patient information form. It's still hard to believe and admit I am a widow."

Click, jot, nod. Dr. Jeffries looked at his watch. "Well, I'm afraid we are out of time. How does two weeks from today work for you?" he said, looking at his appointment book.

Emilie checked the date on the calendar on her phone. "That should be okay."

He wrote the date and time on a yellow sticky note and handed it to her. "Of course, you can always call me if you need to meet sooner than that."

"Thank you. I will keep that in mind."

5

"You should be at the bottom of zone four," the spinning instructor yelled through her headset microphone, above the sounds of Rick James's "Super Freak."

"I've always hated this song," Emilie said loud enough for Colin to hear on the bike next to her. "Now, I *really* hate it!"

Colin sang along bobbing his head toward Emilie.

"If you can sing without gasping for air, you're not in zone four!" Emilie said.

They both laughed as the instructor glared at them. Spinning was like a bike ride through hell. The twenty-something instructor had purple hair—on the side that wasn't shaved off—and a nose ring. She frequently shouted above the loud music, "You're not sweating enough," in her hoarse drill sergeant-like voice. The 8 a.m. Saturday morning class usually had a waiting list, and the room had twenty bikes lined up in three chevron-style rows in front of the instructor who rode a bike on a raised pedestal. Laughing definitely was not permitted. It meant you weren't working hard enough. For the past two Saturdays, she and Colin spun with the serious spinners.

Forty-five minutes into a seventy-five-minute class, Emilie had had enough and motioned to Colin that she wanted to leave. There was no easy way to sneak out of the room. They were on the bikes to the instructor's right, furthest from the door, and there was a ritual of cleaning the bike off after finishing. The problem was that the wet naps were on the other side of the instructor. Emilie got off her bike. Walking in front of the instructor, she grabbed a wet nap from the container on the wall. She took the long way back to her bike—weaving in between cycles that were close together was better than putting herself out there for obvious scrutiny microphoned for the whole class to hear. After swabbing down her bike with the wet nap, she took her towel that was draped on the handlebars and wrapped it around her neck. The instructor screamed, "If you're leaving class early, don't forget to stretch." The serious spinners did not hide their judgment as Emilie stretched her tired legs. She took her water bottle from the bike's holder and left the room.

Colin was right behind her. "Where's the fire?" he asked.

"I just wasn't into it today." She continued to walk toward the exit, and he followed her.

"Shame on you for denying a waitlist full of deserving Baltimorons who would love to be spinning right now," Colin said.

"Stop it with the guilt. I stayed for most of the class." Still sweating, Emilie stopped to wipe her face with a corner of the towel.

Colin's eyes shifted down at her hand, and his eyes widened. "You aren't wearing your wedding ring. Oh, my God! I'm so proud of you!" He air-hugged her, doing his best to avoid pressing his sweaty body against hers.

Emilie smiled. It had been tougher than she imagined. She took it off and put it back on probably ten times before she decided she had been widowed for almost seven months now, and it was time to leave it off for good. "Before you get too excited, missy, it's sitting with my engagement ring on my nightstand. I haven't put them away, pawned them, or anything like that."

"My baby is moving on! I am so proud of you. You are such a good student." Colin bowed. As he rose, he wrung his hands and said with a devilish grin, "I know, let's go out tonight—it's time we meet some boys. Since you've been spinning, your ass is looking awesome!"

"Whoa, slow down."

"Okay, I understand. No pressure. I won't ask again. You tell me when you're ready. I'm so proud of you. I know that was a hard thing to do."

Emilie nodded. "Okay, that's a deal."

He smiled as he held the door of the gym open, and the two exited.

• • •

Upon getting home, she noticed she had left the garage door open. For a moment, she worried Rob would scold her, and she got a sinking feeling in her stomach. "Anyone can break in," he'd say. *Oh, right, Rob isn't here.* She pulled her car into the garage, hit the remote, and watched carefully as the door closed. When she got out of her car, she saw a small dog huddled in between the water heater and a tool cabinet. She walked slowly toward the little dog. When she got to it, she crouched down near the dog. She reached her hand out, allowing it to sniff it. The little dog stood up and slowly walked toward her. Its face was full of mats, and it was very thin. It licked her fingers and rubbed its face against them. Emilie felt around for a collar but didn't find one. The poor thing was probably abandoned. Making sure the little dog stayed in the garage, Emilie went inside. She got a bowl of water and a slice of cheese and went back to the garage to feed him. She broke the cheese up into tiny pieces. The dog quickly ate the cheese and looked up as if to ask for more.

Not sure what to do, Emilie dialed her mother, Margaret, who always took care of the family pets when Emilie was growing up.

"Honey, take him to a vet and have him checked out. Do you want me to call Dr. Larsen?" her mother said.

"Can you see if I can get in today?"

"Okay, I'll tell Dr. Larsen it's an emergency. You may need to look around and see if there are any posters. He could be someone's beloved missing pet."

She hung up from her mother and looked down at the dog. It was hard to imagine the poor little dog was someone's beloved pet. Based on its appearance, it must have been on the lam for quite some time.

After her mother called her back to say Dr. Larsen would see her right away, Emilie went into the house and grabbed an old blanket, an empty Xerox paper box, and returned to the garage. When the little dog saw her, it stood up, wagged its tail, and panted. She wrapped it in the blanket, put it in a box, and put the box on the front passenger seat of her car. She pulled the seatbelt around the box, snapping it in place. When she got in the car herself, she looked over at her passenger, who was peeking at her through the two seatbelt straps. It seemed to have a little furry smile on its face.

Once they arrived at Dr. Larsen's office, Lana, the receptionist, sat behind the counter with a Siamese cat in her lap. The office hadn't changed much since the 1980s—when Emilie's family first took their Schnoodle, Auggie, there. There still was the same floor-to-ceiling cat scratching post in the corner of the room, which now was shredded, with strands of rope frayed all over. The sitting area had an overstuffed sofa that appeared to second as a scratching post. Standing at the counter, she held the little dog, still wrapped in the blanket.

"Look at that poor thing," Lana said.

"I know. I just found it this morning."

"So your mother said. Well, we're going to have to get him checked out and cleaned up."

Lana walked Emilie and the dog into the examining room, and a few minutes later, Dr. Larsen entered. He was a little man with bulging biceps that Emilie assumed were due to lifting large dogs. His once auburn hair was now white, but his mustache still had a hint of the red hair she remembered him having. He wore green scrubs and black crocs.

"Hello, Emilie. So good to see you." Dr. Larsen looked her in the eye. "The last time your mom was here, she told me about your husband. I'm so sorry. You're so young."

"Thank you." Emilie put the dog on the examining table. She smiled faintly in an attempt to change the subject. Instead, there was a long, awkward silence. "Well then," she said, "I found this little guy in my garage today."

"So, what do we have here?" Dr. Larsen poked and prodded the little dog, who didn't even let out a whimper. "I think he's okay, but I'd have to do blood work to be sure. I'd say he's a purebred Yorkshire Terrier, and he has been neutered." Dr. Larsen lifted the dog's lips, displaying off-white teeth and pink gums. "By the looks of his teeth, he's about five years old. Looks like some dental neglect. Probably a stray. If so, you gonna keep him?"

"I'm not sure. I haven't had a dog in years," Emilie said. A bone of contention in her marriage, Rob thought pets were a nuisance.

"He's going to have to be groomed and have a flea bath. His fur is pulling from his skin, so he's in pain. I'll see if Molly, our groomer, can do it as an emergency. He'll probably have to be shaved down." Dr. Larsen inspected the dog further. "I don't think he can be combed out. He's a good little fella, aren't ya?" Dr. Larsen playfully tugged at the dog's beard. "Lana," he yelled.

Lana opened the door just a crack and peeked in.

"Can you check with Molly to see if she can bathe and shave this guy right away?" Dr. Larsen said.

"Sure, no problem." Lana closed the door behind her.

"Seems like he needs a good home and some TLC." Dr. Larsen looked squarely at Emilie.

A little unsure of her decision, Emilie thought about it briefly. Could she take care of a dog by herself? Maybe a dog would be a good thing. A dog would distract her and give her company. All the dogs she had while growing up were such good company. But Viv's cat lady words haunted her. Was it semantics that it was a dog and not a cat? Maybe. Probably. Was she considering keeping the dog because she was lonely? Maybe. Definitely. Before she could overthink the decision any further, she said, "I guess I'm adopting a dog."

"Okay then. What do you want to call him?" Dr. Larsen asked as he allowed the dog to lick his face.

"He's a Yorkie, right?" She thought back to her junior year of college when she spent a week at Oxford. "How about Puddin' or Puddie, you know, like Yorkshire Pudding?"

"I like it! Puddie, you're a lucky boy!" Dr. Larsen said. "I suspect you guys are gonna take care of each other."

6

"Ah, come on, Puddie! What do ya think? Your mom's made of money?" Emilie searched her bedroom closet for a pair of shoes that hadn't been used as a dog's chew toy.

She shook the chewed heel of a cherished royal blue stiletto at him. "How could you chew a Choo? Do you know how much these cost?"

Puddie, who was lying on her bed, tilted his head and curled his upper lip in an Elvis-like sneer.

"Stop it with the attitude, mister."

He let out a low bark.

"Okay, you're right. Mommy got them for a steal on eBay, but still, haven't I bought you enough of your own things to chew on? Come on, leave my stuff alone." She clutched the chewed shoe near her heart while she looked for its box. The thought of throwing it in the trash was too painful. When she found the box, she placed the damaged one in it with its mate. Maybe an expert cobbler could repair it.

After selecting an unscathed pair of heeled loafers, she brushed her suit off of any stray dog hair and grabbed her briefcase. Puddie was at the front door, waiting for her.

"Oh, no. Do you have to tee-tee *again*?" The dog had a bladder the size of a walnut. She picked up his leash from the key holder next to the front door and latched it to his harness. "You can't hold it in if you try, can you?" Puddie ignored her comment and sat eagerly waiting for the door to open. Once outside, he sniffed a shrub next to the front door and decided against watering it. He tugged hard on the leash, pulling Emilie into the front yard to, appropriately enough, a pink dogwood. A few weeds sprung through the soil surrounding the slight tree. The once perfectly manicured lawn showed flaws.

After a few sniffs, Puddie seemed pleased with his choice and did his business. Emilie looked at her watch. Eight fifteen. She knew she was going to be late for work again—the fifth time in the short two weeks since Puddie found his way into her garage.

• • •

By the time she got to work, Annette, the department's admin—or "*A Nut*" as Emilie secretly referred to her—barely raised her head when Emilie walked by. There were no sounds of life coming from Carl's office. But, as she turned the corner to enter her office, she found Carl sitting behind her desk, looking more annoyed than usual.

"Hey there. Are you lost? Your office is the big one next door."

"Do you know how long I've been sitting here?" he said.

Good morning to you too! "Hmm, I don't know? A few minutes?"

"Let's just say I expect you to be here by eight thirty, eight thirty-five at the latest, and now it is ten to nine. I would say that makes you late for work." He tapped his sausage-like fingers on her desk.

"I'm sorry. I guess I got a late start today. You know me. I'm good for the time. I'll work through lunch or stay late." Of course, Carl could never acknowledge that Emilie was a good worker who rarely left for lunch and was usually there late in the evening.

"That's not why I'm here. I need to talk with you about

something. Do you want to do it now or later?"

Intrigued, Emilie sat in the guest chair and put her purse down next to her. "Let's do it now."

"Are you sure you don't want to go to the coffee klatch that's forming down the hall first?" His tone was more sarcastic than usual—a very high bar, indeed.

"No, no. I'm ready." Emilie could feel her heartbeat in her neck as she anticipated what her boss would say. He wasn't one to dole out good news or praise, so her brain went to a place of fear. She was sure he was there to fire her. *Stupid pube and penguins. Damn it!* She needed her job now more than ever.

Carl heaved a heavy sigh. "Our staff officers, in their infinite wisdom, have decided each department needs a management transition plan, which means each director has to have a staff member ready to take over, to avoid a loss of business continuity." He paused and rolled his eyes.

Emilie was having a hard time anticipating what Carl was trying to tell her.

"I'm not sure why this is all coming down now, but Mr. Howell himself has asked that you be my director-in-training for the Public Relations Department."

What? The president wants me to be the director of PR? "You mean I'm not getting fired?" Emilie blurted out. Her heart slowly returned to a normal rhythm as the fight-or-flight feeling began to dissipate.

"What? No. What made you think that? Anyway, I tried to tell Howell you couldn't do it."

Emilie's heart sank.

"You know, because of what you've been through this year. And, after the near penguin fiasco last month. I know you managed to pull that one off . . . but barely. We're just lucky I was able to save everything by getting those birds in at the Marriott."

"Actually, I—"

Carl cut her off. The truth was never as important to him as giving himself credit. "Now, I have to do some succession planning. But there really is no one else. I mean . . ." His voice got low as he whispered, "We have no intentions of promoting Annette, nor do I think we'd ever be able to hire an additional manager. So, that leaves you. Apparently, Howell loved the Nature Channel thing. His new Facebook profile picture is of him with those penguins." Carl rolled his eyes again. "So, today's your lucky day. But I don't plan on retiring for a long time, so don't salivate over the corner office." A purple vein became prominent on his balding head as he continued. "Besides, Howell seems high on you. I'm not sure why. Maybe there aren't enough women in management or something like that."

Emilie sat poised, ready to take mental notes. "Okay, what does this mean? What do I have to do?" Her mind was racing. In the twelve years she'd worked there, she really never thought about what would happen when Carl retired. He would probably die in his high leatherback chair.

"They want you to start doing board meetings, effective immediately. This means the board meeting next month at the Ritz in Aspen is yours."

Carl's words were slowly sinking in. Board meetings were a big deal. So big that he'd never trusted anyone to do them before.

The American Communications company board met four times a year—three times near the Baltimore headquarters and one time at a more posh location, like Aspen.

"And just in case you think doing a board meeting at Ritz-Carlton in Aspen is going to turn into a ski vacation, you're wrong. It's tough work. However, I was able to convince them to let me tag along with you, since this will be your first. But you'll have to do all the work from now until then. So, later today I'll give you the file, and you can get working on it."

Carl huffed and heaved his large body out of her chair and left her office. Emilie sat down behind her desk and let the news sink in. This was big. Maybe they wanted Carl out sooner than he wanted to leave. As she turned on her computer and logged in, *A Nut* appeared at her door.

"Hey," *A Nut* said as she walked in and slouched down in the chair next to Emilie's desk. "Do you remember that white jacket you gave me last month?"

"Yes, sure. Michael Kors white jean jacket, right?"

"Yeah, that's the one. Do you remember how much you paid for it?"

"No, not really. I bought it last fall. I'm sure it was on sale. Probably like seventy-five. Why?"

"It had a little stain on one of the sleeves," she said, bending her left arm at the elbow and pointing to a spot midway down her forearm, indicating where the stain would be. "I took it to the cleaners, and they made the stain worse, so now they are going to pay me for the cost of the jacket."

"What? They're going to pay *you* for something *I* gave you?" Emilie squinted to try to comprehend what *A Nut* was saying. For a brief moment, she expected *A Nut* to offer the payment to her, but that thought quickly vanished.

"You don't have a receipt, do you?"

"No, I don't have a receipt. Sorry. Did you tell them you didn't pay for the jacket?"

"What? No." *A Nut* shook her head. "They wanted to know how much the jacket was worth. They don't need to know you gave it to me."

"Sorry. Can't help you."

A Nut paused and then shrugged. "Okay. I'll see what I can do. What do you think it would have cost if it weren't on sale?"

"What? I don't know." Emilie turned toward her computer and started checking emails with her back toward *A Nut*.

A Nut got the point and left Emilie's office. Once Emilie was sure she was alone, she googled things to do in Aspen.

7

When she got off the plane in Aspen, the air hitting her skin felt like the last time she had a facial—cool and invigorating. In the cab from the airport, she pressed her nose against the window, looking like a kid waking up on Christmas. The mountains were magnificent—even in early fall, they had snow caps. And the city was lined with the signature Aspen trees, displaying their amber and sage-colored leaves, ready for autumn. If she could stick her head out of the window and not appear strange, she would have. She didn't want to miss anything.

As the cab pulled up to the Ritz, she smiled. The hotel was situated at the base of a spectacular mountain. A man dressed in a coal-colored uniform with red and gold epaulets opened the cab door and gestured for her to get out. "Welcome to the Ritz, Ms. Russell. It's my pleasure to serve you," said the doorman, who somehow knew who she was. She got out of the cab and followed closely behind as the doorman wheeled her suitcase. As she watched the doorman struggle with her wobbly suitcase, she second guessed the need to pack three pairs of shoes. Entering the Ritz was like walking in Eden. The lobby was full of fresh flowers and was decorated in rich red velvet with gold trim. The smell of lemon and lavender seemed to be piped through the vents. All of Emilie's senses were on overload.

After checking in, a bellman showed her to her room, which

was located on the top floor of the hotel. The room had an inviting balcony with a view of the mountain. On the table were a gift basket of fruit, a box of Godiva milk chocolate truffles, and a split of Moet champagne with a card from the hotel thanking her for the business. She grabbed a chocolate and bit into it. "I think I could get used to this," she said aloud. It was clear to her now why Carl was always so defensive at the thought of letting it go.

Carl was taking a later flight and had insisted they meet as soon as he arrived, so she only had a few hours to herself. She opened the closet and was surprised, but pleased, to find a royal blue velour robe with the gold Ritz-Carlton logo embroidered on the breast. It felt good to drape her body in the plush fabric. Rationalizing it was one o'clock back home, she poured herself a glass of champagne and sat on her balcony to enjoy the view.

The village below was full of activity. Ski season wouldn't officially open for another couple of months, but shopping season seemed to be in full swing. Emilie watched as women wearing Uggs carried shopping bags full of probably overpriced garments from the trendy shops at the base of the mountain. On the peak was a little patch of snow, but the mountain's greenery was lush, with grass the shade of shamrocks, dotted with purple and yellow clovers. Pine trees stood tall, punctuating the landscape. A footpath led from the back of the hotel and seemed to twist all the way up to the peak. And Aspen trees with their turning leaves surrounded the base. "Gosh, Rob would have loved this place," she said out loud.

Rob loved being outside, especially going for hikes and exploring. He used to tell Emilie he wanted to retire to Colorado, even though neither had ever been there, and spend the days hiking and fishing. A lump formed in her throat.

Her cell phone ringing prevented an emotional setback. It was

Colin.

"Hey, girl. Did you get there okay?"

How sweet. "Yes, my flight was fine. I gotta tell you, this place is great. You wouldn't believe how beautiful it is here. And they had chocolate truffles and a bottle of Moet here in my room. How about that? Living like a movie star." She took a sip of champagne. "How's Puddie? Does he miss me?"

"Yeah, I guess. I just checked on him during lunch. He's fine. So, when does your meeting start?"

"Noon, tomorrow. But Carl and I are meeting with the hotel to go over details later today. I'm telling you, Colin, you wouldn't believe this place. It's spectacular."

"Have you seen anyone famous? Have you seen Julia Roberts? George and Amal?"

"No, I haven't even seen a Kardashian or a Real Housewife from anywhere. It's off-season, I think. I'm not sure the movie stars come until ski season starts." She put a strawberry into her champagne glass—something she'd seen "the Countess" from *The Real Housewives of New York City* do and took a sip. She winced, immediately regretting not removing the strawberry stem.

"Get the camera on your phone ready just in case," Colin said.

"Yeah, yeah. Okay. Now you know I'm here for business, not for vacation."

"Whatever. You aren't in Cleveland, are you?"

"Good point. I'll call you later once I've had a chance to walk around. If I see someone famous, I'll text you." She removed the phone from her ear and was about to hit end when a thought crossed her mind. "Um, Colin?" she asked, placing the phone back to her ear.

"Yeah?"

"What did you do with Howard's ashes?"

Colin didn't respond right away. She was about to change the subject assuming she'd asked a question that was too raw and painful for him to answer when he said, "I put them in the Atlantic Ocean off the coast of Massachusetts." His voice had a slight crack in it. "We had talked about it before he died. We used to spend our summers up there. That's where he wanted to go. Why?"

"I'm thinking Rob would have loved it here. I wish I would have brought some of his ashes with me. He never got to see this place, and he always wanted to. The thought just occurred to me that it would have been a nice tribute." Emilie let out a loud sigh. "I would've put them at the base of the mountain. Maybe that would give him a chance to see this incredible view for eternity." She felt the "widow's" lump return in her throat.

"Wow, that's a great idea! Where do you keep him? Do you want me to send you some?"

"Oh, I don't know about that. You mean put some ashes in the mail? What if he gets stuck in customs?"

"Customs? Where do you think you are? Mexico? Besides, I'll put some of him in a cocoa or coffee tin. The package won't be inspected. I'm confident of that."

"I just don't know. I'd be devastated if the package got lost."

"I won't send all of him. Just a little bit. Would you be more devastated if you missed this opportunity?"

Emilie thought about it briefly. "Okay, go ahead. He's in a wooden urn on top of the TV. You promise you'll only send a little bit?"

"Promise. Don't worry. I'll take good care of him. I'll pack it with socks and silk underwear for padding. He'll travel first class."

"Okay," she said. Admittedly, she was a little nervous, but the idea also excited her at the same time. "Oh, and Colin?"

"Yeah?"

"Thanks!"

● ● ●

The FedEx package was delivered to her room early the next day and placed on her bed, propped up by a pillow. At first, she was too scared to open it. Instinctively, she called Colin for support.

"Emilie, it will be okay. This is a nice tribute for Rob. Letting him rest in a place he always wanted to see. Go ahead and open it. I'll stay on the phone."

She tore open the orange and purple package and smiled when she saw how Colin had packed the precious cargo—in a purple Crown Royal bag. "Oh, Colin, Rob loved Crown Royal. How did you know?"

"I found that bag under your sink and thought it would be a way for him to travel in style. Maybe there was a drop or two left in it." He snickered. "Okay, now let's go find a place for your husband to take in the beauty."

Keeping Colin on the phone, she grabbed a jacket with the Crown Royal bag cradled in her arms. She left her room and got into the elevator. Once she was in the lobby, she wondered what people would say if they knew she carried her husband's remains, and with them, a little piece of her heart. She walked out of the hotel and down to a spot at the base of the mountain where an Aspen tree stood. "This is perfect. Rob will always be able to see the mountain, and he will be shaded and peaceful." She emptied the contents onto the ground underneath the tree's shadow. Exhaling slowly, she smiled. It surprised her that the widow's lump was gone and there were no tears welling up. She bent down and, with her free hand, stroked the ground where the ashes lay. "Here you go, baby. Enjoy!"

"Emilie, I am so proud of you," Colin said. "I knew you could do it. Now take a picture for a keepsake."

She fumbled with her phone and took a close-up of the remains underneath the lone tree. Then she backed up, taking another, making sure to get most of the mountain in the background. "Rest in peace, baby, and wake up each day to this beautiful view."

• • •

Two days later, the board meeting ended by 3 p.m. Just before the meeting broke, when the Public Relations Department leadership transition plan was announced, there were several smiles and nods around the table and even a smattering of applause.

Shortly after the meeting, Emilie was in the hotel lobby making sure the board members got into the town cars she had arranged for their trips back to the airport. Carl, who had changed from his suit into a lime green polo shirt and jeans, approached her. "I think things went . . ." His eyes shifted toward a silver tray of the hotel's sinful chocolate chip cookies sitting on the coffee table in front of them. "Things went okay. I would have made sure the linens were seasonal." He grabbed a cookie and took a bite. While chewing, he said, "And I'm sure you didn't notice the large scuff mark on the floorboard of the meeting room. You should have asked them to clean that up. It was an eyesore." Crunch. Crunch. Crunch. "You should meet with the hotel before you leave to give them a critique." He picked up a large crumb that had fallen on his chest and put it in his mouth. When he did, a bit of melted chocolate smeared on his chin.

Emilie bit her upper lip in an attempt to squelch a snicker and remain businesslike.

"You have to be mean to be in this business, and, frankly, Russell, I don't think you have it in you. When you meet with them, tell them the robes are too small. My robe wouldn't fit at all."

Emilie bit her lip harder.

"Okay, I'll let them know when I meet with them before I leave tomorrow morning. Do you want to be there?"

"No, I haven't had any free time at all, so I'm going to go find the wife some souvenirs. I'll see you at eight thirty Monday morning." And he walked out of the hotel.

Her feet were so tired that she plunked herself down in a leather chair by the hotel's main entrance. She kicked off her two-inch navy patent leather heels and immediately realized she made a big mistake. Her feet were swollen, and it was doubtful the pumps would go back on easily. There was one more thing to do before she could rest her weary body. She needed to see Mr. Howell off to the airport. Once the town car arrived to take him, the meeting would be officially over. She was exhausted. Before getting to Aspen, she stressed over every detail, most of them last-minute changes—changes in attendee flight arrangements meant transfers had to be changed, and when one member canceled due to illness, the headcount changed as did the seating chart for dinner. All the worrying over meeting details was a distraction from her personal life, a welcomed displacement. It gave her a sense of confidence and a purpose that had been lacking in recent months.

As the shiny black Lincoln pulled up to the hotel entrance, Emilie fumbled to get her shoes back on. She stood and started limping to the car. Mr. Howell was in the lobby talking with one of the company's vice presidents. He was a tall, thin man who always wore a dark suit and French cuff shirts with the initials KEH embroidered on them. He was also a man of few words, and the ones he did choose were usually thoughtful, which Emilie not only noticed but tried to emulate when interacting with board members. Mr. Howell walked toward Emilie.

"Hello, sir. I have your car just outside."

A bellman held the front door open as Mr. Howell and Emilie walked outside together.

"Thank you, Emilie. You did a great job. I know how hard it is to take care of twenty senior-level executives. Dinner was fantastic, by the way. Great location. Did you choose the menu?"

"Yes, sir, I did." She felt her face redden.

"The salmon was the best I've ever had." He handed the driver his roller bag and sat in the back of the town car. Before closing the door, he said, "I've had my eyes on you for some time. I know you are going to be a fine addition to my management team. When we get back to Baltimore, call Ashley, my assistant, and set up a time for us to talk about your future with the company." She smiled as she helped him into the town car. "Oh, and why don't you take Monday off? Tell Carl I said so."

8

On her day off, Emilie walked into Dr. Jeffries's office. The queasy feeling in her stomach this time was probably due more to the half-pint of butter pecan she'd eaten just before arriving rather than nerves. At least, that's what she told herself. She took a seat on the leather couch.

"Thank you for allowing me to reschedule. I was out of town last week on business," she said, greeting Dr. Jeffries.

"Not a problem." Dr. Jeffries looked emotionless, but then he always did. "So, how are you doing?" He adjusted his body in the high-back leather chair and clicked his pen, ready to write.

"I'm great, um, well, good. I mean better, I guess," Emilie said. "It's been over seven months . . ." She diverted her eyes away from Dr. Jeffries. "It should be getting easier, shouldn't it?"

"Is it?"

"Um, I guess so." She looked away and added, "Maybe."

"This is a process, and there is no timeline. There is no right or wrong answer to any of my questions. Just be honest with yourself."

"If I'm being honest, I have good days and bad days." She crossed her legs, tucking one foot behind the calf of her other leg.

"That's normal. Tell me about some of the bad days."

"A few weeks ago, I ran into someone I went to high school with. No one I was really close to, just an acquaintance. Of course, while we were getting caught up, I had to tell her what happened—to Rob—that he died. And I know what to expect—the dreaded look of pity. I hate it. I really do. Unfortunately, I'm at the age where people count their life's accomplishments by what their husbands do and how perfect their two-point-five wonderful children are. Sometimes I contemplate making up a story—like my husband works for the CIA, so he's always gone, but I can't bring myself to lie." She frowned.

"So, anyway, she gives me the usual, 'I'm so sorry. That's awful. Poor you. It must be hard. You look like you're doing well.' And then she says, 'I don't know what I'd do if my husband died. I don't think I'd be able to live without him.'" Emilie balled both of her fists. "That really pissed me off."

Dr. Jeffries scratched his goatee and looked at her quizzically. "Why would that comment make you mad?"

"It's like she's better than me, in a way. She loves her husband more than I did mine."

The confused look did not ease from his face. "Maybe she was commenting on how strong you are."

Emilie looked off into the distance as she thought about what he said. "Hmm, I never looked at it like that." She should have known he'd have a more positive perspective. He was good at finding different angles—ones she'd never think of on her own. "My immediate reaction is to think about the grief Olympics. I get it a lot. You'd be surprised at how many people compare my loss with them losing a grandparent or even a pet."

"Go on." Dr. Jeffries clicked his pen and jotted something on his yellow notepad.

"One time I was in the ladies' room at work. It was shortly after Rob's death—like literally a few weeks—and a woman I didn't even know came up to me and said, 'You're the girl whose husband died, right?' I was like, 'Yeah,' not really wanting to answer, but I felt like

I had a giant arrow pointing above my head. So, then she goes, 'My friend's husband died of cancer . . . I think that's worse.' I couldn't believe it. I felt like I was punched in the stomach," Emilie said, fighting tears back. "Why do people have to do that? Compare grief?"

"Death is a very terrifying thing for people to deal with, and grief is a very personal emotion," Dr. Jeffries said. "I think when people make comments like those you've heard, they are putting themselves in your shoes. It's natural to try and minimalize something awful. It probably scares them to even think about what you're going through."

"I guess I'm just sensitive to comments that seem judgmental. I mean, trust me, when he died, I didn't know how I was going to cope, but I really didn't think I had a choice. Did I want to kill myself? No. I can honestly say the thought never entered my mind. But if I'm being real here, did I care if I died? No, not really. I have developed a sense of peace about dying. You know, like if I got hit by a car today or diagnosed with some terminal illness, I think I would be okay with it."

Dr. Jeffries tilted his head, nodding slightly, he stared at her intently.

"I'm probably not explaining myself too well. I'm not suicidal or even depressed. It's just that before—before Rob died—I had so much to live for. Now, what I thought was my future is gone. It was a strange feeling to have what you know as your life, what you think is your future, end. It's hard not to miss what you had. Creating a new life is hard."

"That's what we like to call 'a new normal'—finding and settling into a new normal way of life. Things may not seem normal now, but they will. You'll develop new habits, new routines."

"I hope so." She looked at Dr. Jeffries and smiled. "I guess that makes sense." She let his words sink in. It was true. She'd noticed as if there were a new divider in her life—before and after—now, after, everything seemed new and unfamiliar. So much had changed in such a short amount of time. "Did I tell you I got a dog?"

"No, you didn't. What did you get?" Click. Jot.

"Actually, he got me." She felt light inside for the first time in several sessions. "I came home from the gym one day, and there was this little Yorkie in my garage. He was filthy, all knotted and covered in fleas. Poor thing. He didn't have any tags on him, so I couldn't call an owner. I decided to keep him. I grew up with dogs, but when I got married, my husband never wanted to have one."

"How did it feel to make the decision to keep the dog?"

"At first I wasn't sure. A dog is a big responsibility to take care of alone. I have to run home from work to let him out, and I will be traveling a lot for work now. It's added a new level of responsibility. Before, I only had myself to care about and for, and now I have to make sure he's taken care of as well. All in all, I'm glad I kept him. He's been great company. I tell him he's my guy now." Emilie smiled. "Looking back on it, it was kind of freeing."

"In what way?"

"I told myself they're messy, needy, and a big pain. That's what I was used to hearing when I was married. But then I thought, yes, you can get a dog if you want to."

"I'm glad you see it that way. You should do what makes you happy. If getting a dog makes you happy, then that's a good thing."

Emilie nodded. She thought for a moment and then said, "I've done something else lately that makes me happy."

"Tell me." Dr. Jeffries looked very interested—and not in a therapist way. So Emilie told him about her trip to Aspen and what she did with Rob's ashes.

"How did it feel?" Dr. Jeffries asked.

"Honestly, it felt good. It seemed like the right thing to do. A nice tribute. And I think I was ready to say goodbye."

"That's what matters. It sounds like it was a good, cathartic decision on your part."

9

By the end of the week, the late Indian summer had given way to a beautiful fall day. Autumn in Baltimore was the best season, no blooming blossoms to put allergies on high alert, no humidity to make it oppressive to be outside, and no snow to shovel.

The patio of Nick's was on the brim of the harbor's water. It was crowded when Emilie got there just a few minutes past twelve thirty. She approached Viv, who was seated under an umbrella on the edge of the sidewalk.

"Sorry I'm late," she greeted Viv, who stood and gave her a hug. Viv was wearing a long-sleeved white turtleneck that complemented her bleached blond hair and made her tan seem less faded. Viv did not adhere to the never wear white after Labor Day rule because she thought it was her best color, no matter the season.

"So, how ya been? I feel like I haven't seen you in a while," Viv said. It was the first time they'd met for lunch in several months. When they graduated from college, they vowed they'd meet for lunch once a month, no matter what. In nineteen years, they missed only one month five years ago because Viv's sister went into labor, and she had to leave town. Not wanting to break tradition, Emilie went to Nick's as planned and phoned Viv. They spent the hour chatting on the phone as if they were sitting across from each other in the same place. But when Rob died, Emilie canceled their scheduled get-togethers, and they never got rescheduled until now.

"I've been fine. How 'bout you?" Emilie asked.

"I've been good." Viv picked up her martini, raising it in a "cheers" gesture. After taking her first sip, she licked her lips and let out a slight pleasurable moan. She took the tiny sword with three olives out of her drink, and one by one, stabbed them in her mouth. Having completed the food portion of her lunch, she looked at Emilie and said, "How's work? Did that penguin crap get cleaned up?"

"Yeah, it was fine. Actually, it went so well they let me do a board meeting in Aspen last week. Can you believe it?"

"Wow, that's great. I always thought you'd run circles around your jerky boss if you were given the chance." Viv paused and took another sip of her martini. "I miss hanging out with you."

"Yeah, me too." Emilie flagged down the waiter and ordered a glass of chardonnay.

Once the waiter left the table, Viv said, "So, I was thinking of doing a girls' weekend in New York with Heidi and Karen for your birthday." In college, Emilie and Viv lived down the hall from Heidi and Karen. "That is, unless you have other plans. Maybe we can see a show and spend the night. What do you think?"

After thinking about it for a second and weighing her options, Emilie nodded. "I may be able to move some things around." This was, of course, a lie. She didn't want to admit she had no plans other than staying home, watching sappy movies alone, and eating all four corners of a birthday cake she planned to pick up from Wegman's bakery earlier that day.

"Great! I knew you'd be in. I've already talked to Karen. I just need to track down Heidi. Karen thinks we can use her husband's hotel points for a free room. So, we'll just have to pay for the train ride. What show do you want to see?"

Emilie shrugged. "Dunno. What's good?"

"Well, since you like musicals—and I know how much you love ABBA—I hear Mamma Mia is great fun, and we could probably get really good seats because my secretary's son works for one of those Broadway ticket brokers." Viv was talking fast, probably drafting a to-do list in her head. "You used to play that ABBA CD over and over? Remember?" Viv chuckled.

"Yeah, I do," Emilie said. "I loved ABBA Gold."

"I used to say 'enough with the seventies. Leave that decade behind.' Who knew you'd be right? Here we are, more than forty years later, and there's a whole show about that album." Viv began a loud, slightly offkey rendition of Dancing Queen.

Emilie chimed in. She rolled her hands before striking a classic disco pose.

Their performance was interrupted by the waiter, who didn't even acknowledge there was a sing-along. He put her wine on the table and turned abruptly, walking away without taking their food order.

"Must be a music critic," Viv said with a snort. She raised her glass, and so did Emilie. "To bringing back the girls' weekend in New York!" They clinked their glasses.

• • •

Two weeks later, on the 6:20 a.m. train from Baltimore to New York, Viv broke out a thermos of mimosas and poured the mixture into disposable coffee cups so the conductors wouldn't suspect the rowdy middle-aged women were drinking.

"Happy Birthday, Em!" Viv raised her cup and tapped Emilie's and Heidi's. "And here's to twenty-three years of friendship!" She toasted again.

All three women sipped the champagne and let out collective sighs.

"What time does Karen's flight get in?" Emilie asked as she relaxed, letting the champagne take effect.

"I think she's on one of the first flights from Fort Lauderdale that gets her into Newark at around noon. She said not to wait for her if we decide to go to Chinatown. She'll call us when she gets in." Viv had all the details written on a piece of paper she was trying to locate in her messy purse. "Ah, yes, here it is. American Airlines flight number 480. Comes in at ten fifty-five. We can't check in without her because we're using Tim's hotel points."

"Gosh, how great is it that Tim got us the room? Boy, did Karen get a good one when she married him!" Heidi said with what sounded like a hint of jealousy.

"Yeah, see what you could have had? He asked you out first." Viv chimed in.

"Naw, it never would have worked. I'm only attracted to guys that have nothing going for them, cheat on me, or can't hold down a job." Heidi was superb at noticing her faults after it was too late.

The women's loud laughter caused an elderly man across the aisle from them to huff and widely spread open his *New York Times*.

"What does that say about Damien?" Emilie asked. Damien was Heidi's latest and third husband. He seemed like the best so far—an architect, nice-looking, and didn't have a criminal record or a tattoo.

"Damien is all right. He's a workaholic and blames it on the firm. He rarely gets home before nine. When he does come home, he's too tired to do anything but watch TV. I can't remember the last time we had sex. He's probably getting it from his assistant. You could say, after a year now, the honeymoon is officially over." Heidi's sigh had a familiar ring. "I think you said it, Emilie. My picker was broken. I guess I can't pick 'em."

"You aren't throwing in the towel so soon, are you?" Emilie

asked.

Heidi was the stereotypical pretty blond cheerleader. She always had a boyfriend or husband and would jump into a new relationship sometimes before breaking up with a current one. She seemed to be in love with the idea of marriage but had a short attention span once the luster wore off of her diamond ring.

"No, I don't know. I guess we're just going through a rough patch. I think going away this weekend will actually help. You know, absence makes the heart grow fonder stuff," Heidi said.

"So, Emilie, how are you doing? How are things?" Heidi asked. "I haven't seen you since . . . he . . . you . . ."

Viv gave Heidi a noticeable kick to the shin and made a zip it motion with her fingers against her lips.

"It's okay to say it—since Rob died," Emilie said. "I'm okay. It's been tough. I have good days and bad days. I still wish I had a magic wand or a time machine." Viv's frozen raised eyebrows gave the illusion of a faint frown, and Heidi nodded. "I'm trying to make the most out of my new life." Emilie paused and then continued. "I'm really happy about something I've decided to do with his ashes. You know how Rob always wanted to travel and see places. Well, I'm going to disperse his ashes all over the world. I was in Aspen earlier this month when I got the idea. And I hope you don't mind, but I brought some with me on this trip." Emilie reached into her purse and pulled out the purple Crown Royal bag carrying some of her husband's ashes. She cradled the bag in her arms carefully. "I thought we could find a spot in the city to put him."

"What a great idea!" Viv said with a slight slur in her voice. "Andrew and I are going to Italy next month. Do you want me to take some of Rob with us?" Viv poured each of the women another mimosa.

"Yes! Oh, Viv, would you do that for me . . . and him? Thank you, thank you, thank you!" Emilie leaned over and kissed Viv on the cheek.

"I'm going to a conference in Maui in January. Do you want me to take some with me?" Heidi joined in.

"You have no idea how much that would mean to me. I'm so touched that you want to be part of this. I think he'd love the idea. He always wanted to travel, you know."

"So, what do we have to do?" Viv asked. "I don't want to eff anything up."

"Just find the most beautiful, peaceful place—a place you'd want to see every day for the rest of your life—and put the ashes there and take a picture. I think I am going to create an album or a tribute in some way."

"Got it," Viv said. "To Rob!" She raised her glass, and the others followed suit.

The champagne started to work, and they laughed and reminisced about the crazy stuff they did in college. More and more passengers gave disapproving glances their way, which only made them laugh louder.

"Ooh, I almost forgot! Wait till you see what I brought." Viv put down her cup on the floor beside her seat and reached above to the overhead rack. Standing on her tiptoes, she unzipped her suitcase. "Ah, there it is." She grabbed a book, hugged it to her chest, and sat back down. "Okay, are you ready for this? I was cleaning out my closet the other day, and I found this photo album with pictures from college. Wait till you see what you guys looked like." Her voice rose, and she let out a cackle.

Viv opened the first page of the album. On the inside front cover, in her distinctive teenaged bubbly script, with big puffy outlined letters and hearts dotting each *I*, was scrawled *This is the property of Vivianne Marie Parks.*

Viv turned the thick parchment paper to reveal photos taken years earlier. "Oh my God. Emilie, look at you! Your hair. Geez, like out to here." Viv exaggerated with her hands. Underneath the photo was written, *Me and my roommate, Emilie, first day of school, St. Cecilia's College, September 2000.*

Emilie stared down at a timid girl with curly, shoulder-length red hair, cut in an unflattering style that seemed to flare out at the ends into a mane of unruly frizz. "Yeah, I know. Back then, my hair had a mind of its own."

"Good God, girl. Didn't you own a blow dryer?"

Emilie rolled her eyes and shook her head. "Ha Ha. Hilarious. You know my mom told me only whores blow-dried their curly hair straight. Did ya know God gave me curls for a reason." Emilie's eyes grew wide, and she gave Viv a knowing look. "I seem to remember you, on the other hand, spending a lot of time blow-drying your hair!"

Viv laughed. "Yes, and damn proud of it." She turned the page of the album. "Gosh, Heidi, you look the same. You haven't changed." There was blond, perfect, and perky Heidi in one picture after another, each with a different handsome boy. "You still look twenty years old. How is that possible?"

Heidi blushed. "C'mon. You guys look the same too."

"Thank God Emilie doesn't look the same!" Viv said with a laugh loud enough for passengers riding in other cars to hear them. "Aw, you know I love you, Em. But you have to admit, you needed some help back then." She wrapped her arm around Emilie. "I guess your mom never wanted you to get laid. Good thing Heidi and I did." Viv turned the page. "Oh, look. Here you are with that guy you went to the senior formal with. What was his name? Remember? We called him Chip because he was like a geeky computer guy. What was his name?" Viv tapped the photo.

"Morgan. His name was Morgan Whitehead," Emilie said in a low voice, trying not to remember the awful night when she and pimply-faced Morgan, who had the unfortunate last name of Whitehead, went to the senior formal dance.

"Yes! Morgan. Right. I wonder what he's up to. You should look him up on Facebook to see what he's doing. You know, to see if he's single. He *really* liked you," Viv said.

"Naw. That's okay."

"Oh, come on. I'll bet he's probably a dot-com gazillionaire by now." Viv's words were slurring more and more.

"Really, you couldn't pay me enough to go out with him. Ugh! At the end of the night, he actually said, 'Miss Malone, may I have a kiss?' It was so awkward." Emilie made a stink face.

"Did you kiss him?" Heidi asked.

"What? No! Are you kidding? Even though I blow-dried my hair that night, a girl has her standards."

They all laughed.

"Cheers to that!" Viv said as she raised her cup, and Emilie and Heidi followed suit.

Viv turned the page again, and the laughter stopped. A picture of Rob, smiling and wearing a gold 2013 crown, appeared on the scrapbook page. Emilie instantly placed the photograph from memory. It was New Year's Eve, the first year they met. She and Rob double-dated with Viv and Andrew. They had spent too much on an Inner Harbor hotel so they could see the midnight fireworks. It was a magical night. Later that evening, Rob held her and told her he loved her and that he never would leave her. Seeing Rob smiling back at her, Emilie tried to quell the wave of grief that was enveloping her. She ran her finger along the plastic shield, stroking his image, trying to feel his presence. She desperately wanted the last eight months to be just a bad dream. She wanted Rob to be alive again.

Emilie looked up and smiled faintly. As a tear rolled down her right cheek, she said, "God, I miss him."

10

It was midmorning when they arrived in New York City, and it was a beautiful September day. The weather was crisp enough for a light jacket; the sky was blue with puffy clouds that looked almost too much like a painting to be real, and the leaves were just starting to turn hues of red, burnt umber, and yellow.

Today was her first birthday, in ten years, without Rob. Although Emilie was with dear friends, it felt unfamiliar and lonely. Dr. Jeffries said the first firsts would be hard.

After dropping their bags off at the hotel's bell stand, the three women hailed a cab quickly.

"We're going to Canal Street," Viv said as she got in the backseat of the cab. The driver nodded. He had a stack of newspapers and magazines piled in the front passenger seat, which he made no attempt to move. So, Emilie and Heidi both followed Viv into the backseat of the cab.

As they pulled away from the hotel, there was a loud honk coming from the cab next to them. Their cab driver rolled down his window, gestured with his fist, and yelled something inaudible back.

Viv had a determined look in her eyes. She shifted her body so that her hips were no longer touching Emilie's and said, "When we get to there, Karen said to get her a Louis, one with long straps. She sent me a picture." She reached into a pocket in her purse and pulled out a page from a magazine and unfolded it. "Something like this," she said as she pointed to a dark brown hobo-style bag with signature light brown straps and the LV logo all over it.

Purse shopping in Chinatown was something the four had done twice before. Viv had seen an episode of *Sex and the City* where Samantha entered a shop in Chinatown and asked the shop owner to show her "the good stuff." He took her into a back room full of Louis Vuitton, Coach, Prada, and Dolce & Gabbana bags, all at very reduced prices. Emilie, Viv, Karen, and Heidi decided to give it a try on one of their girlfriend weekends in New York, and they were surprised that the lore was true. There was a cloud of suspicion about where the bags actually came from; they preferred to believe the bags were designer rejects because of an off stitch pattern or slightly too long straps made them inauthentic and not able to pass the strict standards. Whatever the sketchy origins were of the potentially illegal items, it made it more exciting.

"What are you looking for this time, Em?" Viv asked.

"I think I'll go with Prada."

"Atta girl!" Viv winked. "The first time we did this, you were too scared. You sat outside the storefront while Heidi and I went in. Remember?" She elbowed Emilie. "You said it was probably best if someone stayed outside to call the police . . . you know, just in case."

"Yeah, I remember. It was pretty scary!" Emilie said. "At least one of us needs to be responsible if for no other reason than to post bail." She was still feeling the champagne.

"You're telling me," Viv said. "They led us into an underground room with a dirt floor and no electricity. Remember that Heidi?"

Heidi nodded. "I thought for sure we were never going to be seen or heard from again." "Me too," Viv snorted. "But then"—she raised her hands in mock adulation—"I saw my best friend 'Louie,' and I was in heaven!"

The cab driver dropped them off at the corner of Canal and Mott Streets, and it wasn't long before a tiny older woman approached them and correctly assumed they were tourists looking for cheap quasi-designer bags. Emilie and her friends resembled bobble dolls when the woman showed them a small cardboard poster with glued-on images of designer bags. The woman then led them down a few streets through a narrow alley strewn with garbage and stray cats until they reached what looked like an abandoned building. The woman unlocked the door and motioned for them to hurry inside. Once they were inside, the woman locked the door and said, "Come, come." They followed her down the hall and into a small room, about the size of a guest bedroom, that smelled like leather, and was covered in handbags hanging on hooks attached to white pegboards. It was overwhelming—nearly a hundred bags in a small space but neatly organized by designer.

Emilie was first drawn to the Prada area, picking a tan-colored python-skin shoulder bag with long straps and a wide zipper. She put it on her left shoulder and grasped the straps with her right hand and tugged. Not bad, she thought, and took a few steps to the full-length mirror to get a better look. She moved her body from side to side, trying to check out every angle of the purse when she saw the reflection of a red leather bag she hadn't noticed before, on the shelf behind her. Turning around, she picked up the deep red Coach purse, unzipped it, and inspected the inside.

"Looks nice," the little old woman encouraged.

"How much?"

"Eighty."

Emilie thought about it. Her budget was sixty to seventy, but she liked it. She reached into her faux Louis Vuitton wallet, or "fluey," as she liked to refer to it—that she had purchased on their last trip to the city—and pulled out four twenties.

Heidi settled on a lime green Dolce & Gabbana satchel. "I think I've seen this in a recent issue of Vogue." She squealed and jumped up and down. "Fifty dollars. Gotta love that!"

Viv got her usual Louis Vuitton, and talked, or rather manipulated, the sweet little lady into throwing in a wallet for free. After getting Karen's purse, they were led to the entrance, where the little lady opened the door a crack and peeked out to see if any police were lurking. "Go! Go! Go!" she said. One by one they ran out onto the streets with their hearts racing, holding tightly to the black shopping bags hiding their new contraband handbags. Once they were a block away, and seemingly out of suspicion, they huddled together and laughed out loud.

"That is never not fun!" Viv said, clutching her chest, trying to catch her breath. "What a crack up! We got some good stuff this time."

"Do you think we could ever get arrested?" Emilie asked, tucking her bag tightly under her arm, trying to conceal it.

"Naw, besides, who cares, it'd be worth it," Viv responded. Viv put her arm around Emilie. "I don't think it's illegal. I think it's like a show for tourists. You know, to lure people here to buy stuff. Why, I think I've seen our salesperson on an episode of Law and Order. She probably works for the Convention and Visitors' Bureau."

It was a little after twelve when they cabbed it to the hotel. After collecting their luggage from the bell stand, they went straight up to the room number that Karen had texted to Heidi.

"I'm glad we're close friends because we are going to be in some close quarters," Karen said as she opened the door, showing off the cramped room with two double beds, a nightstand in between them, and a small armoire that probably housed a modest size television.

"Karen. It's so great to see you. It's been a while." Emilie greeted her friend with a big, long hug.

"Happy birthday, girl!" Karen said, stepping out of the hug, but continuing to hold Emilie by the shoulders. "You look great. It's been too long. How are you doing?"

"I'm doing okay. You know." Emilie shrugged, surprised she was a little choked up. "Thanks for coming all this way to celebrate my birthday. It means a lot."

"I wouldn't miss it for the world." Karen hugged Viv and then Heidi.

"Look at what we got you!" Viv said as she dangled the Louis Vuitton in front of Karen.

"Come to mama, Louis," Karen said as she brought the bag to her bosom.

Emilie wheeled her suitcase to a corner in between the second bed and the window. Surveying the small room, she said, "Guess we're living out of the bag this weekend." She unzipped her suitcase and propped it open. Sorting through her clothing, she pulled out a black palazzo-pant jumpsuit. "I got first dibs on the bathroom," she said, holding up the jumpsuit. "The show starts at two, so no time for showering and forty-five-minute hair and makeup session."

"Got it, Sarge," Viv said with a salute. "Thanks! We need someone to keep us in line."

An hour later, after all the women were properly primped, they decided to go to Pepino's, a place that served large slices of New York pizza within walking distance of the hotel. During the short walk, Emilie told Karen of her plans for Rob's ashes. Karen, like the others, was eager to help.

After lunch, they walked to the theater to pick up the tickets.

"Fourth row orchestra! Looks like Lois's son came through," Viv said, waving the four tickets in the air.

None of them had ever sat so close to the stage. Emilie could see the sweat dripping from the performers, and when the actors encouraged dancing in the aisles, they didn't have to ask the college friends twice. It felt good to let loose, and it was a wonderful distraction for her.

After the show was over, one of the lead actors mentioned they were taking donations for a Broadway charity for actors with AIDS, and anyone giving a twenty-five-dollar donation would get a chance to take a photo with some of the main characters from the show.

"Let's do it!" Viv clapped.

"Yes, we have to," Karen agreed.

"I'm in," Heidi said. "Here's a twenty."

Emilie needed no encouragement. She loved the idea. "Let's take a picture with Rob in it." Emilie pulled the purple Crown Royal bag filled with her husband's ashes out of her purse.

"Love it! Boy, Rob is having a great afterlife," Viv said.

Emilie handed her phone to an assistant who was coordinating the photo op.

The women lined up to have their picture taken with the show's stars. When it was their turn, Viv pushed Emilie in the front. "You know, there's an extra person with us. Someone you can't see," Viv told the actors.

"Really?" the actor who played dad number one said.

"Yep, she's got her late husband in there." Viv pointed to the bag.

"Awesome. Honey, hold the bag high so that it gets in the picture." Dad Number One lifted Emilie's arm, holding the Crown Royal bag until it was at eye level.

Dad Number Two patted her on the shoulder while Dad Number Three put his arm around her.

"Everyone, say 'cheese!' No, wait, what was your husband's name?" Dad Number One asked.

"Rob. His name was Rob," Viv said.

"All right, everyone, say 'Rob.' On the count of three. One, two, three," Dad Number One said.

"Rob!" they all said in unison.

Once the photo was snapped, the men kissed each of the women on the cheek.

"Good luck to you," Dad Number One said directly to Emilie.

"Thank you," Emilie collected her phone from the assistant. Looking at the group photo, Emilie smiled. "What fun! They were so nice. Thank you, guys," she said, giving each one of her girlfriends a big hug.

"Make sure you text it to us," Viv said.

With a quick touch of her phone screen, Emilie did just that.

• • •

It was about six thirty when they left the theater, so they decided to take a cab to Little Italy to grab dinner before the restaurants filled up. Once they found a restaurant that appeared not only to fit their budget but their palates, they continued their fun.

"A bottle of Chianti pronto!" Viv ordered the waiter, who resembled a young Tony Soprano. "It's my friend's birthday, so keep the wine flowing. You know, at our age, we need to be pickled in order to keep our good looks." She touched her face as she laughed.

"So, Emilie, are you dating anyone yet?" Karen asked.

"No one but Colin."

"Colin, who's Colin?" Heidi asked.

"Viv introduced us. He's perfect in every way, but there is only one problem." She definitely had everyone's attention. "He's gay."

"Oh, I see where that would be a problem," Karen laughed. "You know, we have to get you back out there."

Emilie winced. "No, *we* don't. Not just yet."

"Do you think you will be in Florida anytime soon?"

"Why?" Emilie smelled a setup.

"Hmm. My neighbor is recently divorced. He asked me if I had any friends to set him up with. You game?"

"Karen, he's in Florida," Emilie said, stating the obvious and wishing the conversation would end.

"I know, but you don't have to marry the guy. I think dating will be easier once you get your feet wet. C'mon. Why not?"

"C'mon, Em! You should do it!" Viv said.

"Do it! Do it! Do it!" Viv and Heidi pounded their fists on the table and chanted in unison.

"He's really hot! Don't tell Tim, but I've had a crush on him for years. Sometimes, if he's out in his yard, I suddenly start working in my garden or take the dog for a walk. Shameful."

"Who knew you were a 'Desperate Housewife,' Karen?" Heidi said.

"Let's get her done!" Viv slurred, raising her wineglass with the hand that wasn't propping up her head.

"Do him! Do him! Do him!" Viv started, and Heidi chimed in.

"Stop it!" Emilie slapped her fist on the table so hard her wineglass nearly tipped over. She put her head in her hands and cried.

Viv and Heidi stopped their chant. They both stared at Emilie. Their looks softened to acceptance and care. "Oh, Em, don't be mad," Viv said.

"You all treat me like I'm some charity case. Go out with Colin, look Morgan up on Facebook, go out with Karen's neighbor. Look, no one is more afraid than me that I'll be alone forever. I just can't." She wiped her eyes.

Viv put her arm around Emilie. "We love you. I know being alone is scary." She pulled Emilie closer. "You don't have to marry him, just maybe kiss him. Wouldn't that feel good?"

Emilie nodded and buried her face deeper into Viv's side.

"Okay," Viv said. She stroked Emilie's hair. "Think about it some. When, and if, you are ready, let Karen know. Karen will give him your number."

Emilie pulled away. She saw Karen and Heidi nod. "Can we change the subject?" Emilie asked.

Without hesitation, Karen said, "Was it just me, or was the mom in Mamma Mia a whore?"

"I thought the same thing!" Heidi added.

Viv sipped her wine and said, "Three men and one night? Amateur."

The women laughed. And Emilie felt a little better with the attention shifted away from her.

After dinner, they took a cab to Central Park and hired a horse and carriage to take them around the park to find the perfect spot for Rob. The night was cold and clear, and the park looked fantastic, lit by the surrounding streetlights, giving the newly transitioned tree leaves a glow. As the horse trotted slowly around the path, Emilie scoured the perfect spot to put Rob's ashes. On the north side, they came upon a lone tree that overlooked a lake.

"This is it." Emilie tapped the driver on the shoulder, asking him to stop.

They got out and held hands as they walked to the tree. Emilie emptied the contents of the bag on the ground underneath the leafy branches. "Central Park, it doesn't get better than this. Enjoy baby." Overcome with emotion, she began to cry.

Viv grabbed her and held her, saying, "It's okay, it's okay. Rob would love this. This is a great place for him."

After taking a group photo, they got back in the carriage, and Emilie blew a kiss in the direction of her husband's ashes. Viv wrapped her arm around Emilie and whispered, "Happy birthday, girlfriend. You know I love you."

11

In the middle of the next week, Emilie was searching for a parking spot in the lot outside of Dr. Jeffries's office. Spying a driver getting into her car in the next lane, Emilie quickly maneuvered her car until she was two cars away. With her foot on the brake, she turned on her blinker. As she waited for the woman to pull out, a little red Miata convertible pulled slightly in front of Emilie's car. His car was angled in such a way that he blocked her from the spot. The driver put on his blinker as if he was claiming the prized possession. A parking spot at this time of day in this lot was akin to finding buried treasure.

"Oh, no you don't," Emilie said before hitting the horn hard and rolling down her window. "Move, you son of a bitch!" The filter was gone from her once pure mouth. "This is my parking space. I was here first." She nudged the front end of her Honda Accord forward about an inch before stopping—playing a game of chicken with the guy in the sporty red car.

"Stupid bitch," her worthy opponent hurled back.

Emilie proudly displayed her middle finger. "Get your midlife crisis car out of my way!" It had been only three days since her return from New York with the girls. The trip temporarily lifted her mood. Her neck stiffened, and her shoulders became tense. "I'm not moving, and I can sit here all day if you'd like."

The man in the convertible backed up. "You need to get laid," he said while inserting the pointing finger on one hand into the *O* shaped fingers of his other hand. He shifted into gear, and his tires squealed as he drove off.

Emilie pulled into the parking space. Her heart throbbed in a way she could hear nothing else. She took a few deep breaths. She wanted to back out of the spot, track the man down, and pull out a small handgun she secretly had hidden in her purse. Pointing the gun squarely at the man's forehead, she'd say, "You know, you're right. I do need to get laid. But, you see, I can't. Yeah, that's right. I can't because my husband died." Then she'd shoot him in between the eyes, Clint Eastwood-style. But truthfully, there was no small handgun hidden in her purse. Road rage, or any kind of rage, was a new emotion.

She took a few more deep breaths. "Damn it!" She pounded her fists on the steering wheel.

She got out of the car and walked into the building and onto the elevator. After hitting the button for the fourth floor, the doors closed. She glanced at her reflection from the mirrored walls. The fury in her eyes matched the color of her hair, a monster like figure she didn't recognize.

When the elevator reached the fourth floor, she got off and walked into Dr. Jeffries's office. He was sitting in his usual spot, waiting for her. She sat down on the leather couch. "I'm sorry I'm late," she said, folding her dress under her as she sat.

"Not a problem," he said. "Shall we pick up where we did last time?"

Emilie stared blankly at Dr. Jeffries's and then suddenly began to cry.

"How can I help you today?" He handed her a tissue.

"I'm a mess. I'm just a mess. Everything makes me mad these days. Last weekend, I yelled at my friends, and a few minutes ago,

I almost got into a fight with a guy outside over a parking space. A parking space." She wiped her nose with her sleeve.

Dr. Jeffries nodded. "Completely normal."

"Is it completely normal to fantasize about wanting to kill a stranger who tried to take my parking spot? 'Cuz I did. However right I was—I mean, I was there first—the anger was just plain wrong."

Dr. Jeffries jotted something on his notepad and looked up. "Have you ever heard of displaced anger?"

Emilie stared at him. "You mean I'm mad about the death, not the parking space?"

"Yes. It's a perfectly normal reaction. Are you mad at Rob for dying?"

Emilie thought carefully. "Yes, I know I am. I'm mad that he left me. I'm mad that I'm alone and have to start over. But that makes me feel terrible."

"Go on."

"How can I be mad at Rob? I saw the look on his face when he was dying. He was scared. He didn't mean for this to happen to me. I can't be mad at him." She diverted her eyes, feeling a lump develop in her throat and tears well up. Her voice was hoarse, and it was getting hard to swallow. She tried to clear her throat and wiped a tear from her eye.

"It's okay to be mad. What if he would have taken better care of himself? Do you think a doctor could have prevented an early death?"

"I don't know. Maybe." The tears flowed uncontrollably. Dr. Jeffries passed her the tissue box. She wiped her eyes and blew her nose again. "This is very hard for me to say, but I think I resent him for making me go through all this pain." Emilie's lip quivered.

"I feel like I have wasted a part of my life. Years that I will never get back. I know, honestly, this is going to sound mean, but if I knew ten years ago that he was going to die, I never would have married him. I find myself imagining how different my life would be if I would have married the guy I dated before him. He asked me to marry him, but I turned him down."

"There must be a reason why you didn't say yes to your old boyfriend."

Dr. Jeffries always had a way of bringing her back to reality. This somewhat annoyed Emilie. *It's my fantasy,* she thought, *why can't you just join the pity party?* "Yes. I never really loved him," she said.

"You see. Have you thought that if you married your old boyfriend that you'd be in a loveless marriage and probably would be miserable?"

Emilie nodded, even if she found it difficult to admit. "Yes, I know, but he would be alive, and I wouldn't have had to go through the pain of losing someone . . . and enduring the life-changing, suffocating grief." She took a deep breath before she continued. "I wouldn't know what it's like to be a young widow. And I wouldn't be alone."

"Maybe. Maybe not. I think it is only natural to think 'what if,' when you feel that you may have taken the wrong path. But you should accept and understand that you can't undo the choices you made in your life years ago." Dr. Jeffries adjusted his glasses and then rested his chin in his hand. "Yes, you are a young widow, but look on the other side, you are young with lots of life ahead of you. There's no reason to dwell on 'what ifs.' Start thinking about what can be."

After hesitating, Emilie added, "You know what I've had the hardest time dealing with? I think even harder than losing Rob?"

Dr. Jeffries looked up from his notes, his eyes peering over his glasses that had slipped to the end of his nose.

"Right after he died, I was, of course, dealing with losing him, but I was also dealing with not having a family. You know, not being a mother." Tears started to form as if on cue. "It's hard to explain, but for a woman, you think that's what you're meant to do and be—a mother. I dreamed of that day, but it never came.

"I got tired of people who didn't know me, almost complete strangers, telling me that it was a blessing we never had children."

Dr. Jeffries frowned.

She drew in a long breath and let it out slowly. "I know what they were saying—it would be hard to be a single mother, not to mention the pain the child would go through losing a parent—but it was like a knife through my heart to hear. It was so hurtful." She felt her voice start to tremble. With a finger, she wiped a tear from her eye. "And it brought up so many painful memories of my infertility struggles. People really don't know what they are saying when they make comments like that. It was hard, but I guess I've gotten used to it. It has almost become a joke. Whenever I'm introduced to someone, and I tell them my husband died, in my head, I count to three." She ticked off three fingers for effect. "And then they go for the jugular, 'Do you have children?' It's almost automatic."

"Do you want to talk about the infertility? Have you dealt with it?" Dr. Jeffries was adept at having her reach places she tried to avoid.

"Yes, I think I've come to terms with it. I find that time does ease the pain. But five years ago, when we were really struggling to conceive, it hurt so much. I thought I would never recover."

"Tell me what it was like."

"It's like you sit back and watch it happen to people so easily. People that don't even want to become parents. And each month, your body lets you down in a way you can't even imagine. I used to say that baby showers had become a new form of torture." Emilie chuckled sarcastically.

Dr. Jeffries clicked his pen, jotted something on his notepad, and nodded.

"I started to avoid being around my friends that had kids. Not because I didn't like them, but because it hurt so much. I would make up some of the worst excuses. I think I had a lot of migraines back then."

Click. Jot. Nod.

Emilie leaned back on the couch and continued. "When we first decided to try and have a baby, I thought it would be two, maybe three months. But then it was six months and nothing. We saw specialists. One explained it as 'unexplained.'" Emilie made air quotes around the word. She shook her head. "Just relax and keep trying, they would say. So, we did. I kept a meticulous calendar and took my temperature daily. Later, it was determined that I had severe endometriosis, so there was really no way we would conceive . . . not even with medical intervention. I felt like a failed science project."

Click. Jot. Nod.

"Rob was completely fine with not having kids, even if it meant so much to me. It definitely created a rift in our marriage. I didn't know how he could overlook my feelings as he did. It was like he didn't care and ignored the fact that I was miserable.

"After I accepted we'd never have a child of our own, I wanted to adopt. But not Rob. No. You know, 'fruit of the loin,' and all that BS men proclaim. I questioned whether he loved me and even if I loved him. I thought about leaving him during that time." Emilie looked away. "God, there are days I wish I had. Left him then. But I didn't. I stayed and tried to find ways to fill the void and not blame him. It really wasn't fair, I guess.

"Then one day he came to me, said he had thought about it and maybe adoption would be okay." She smiled as she reminisced.

Click. Jot. Nod—with a chin rub.

"I researched domestic and international adoptions and decided on China. At that time, China had an influx of orphaned baby girls because they had a one-child policy. Most families wanting a boy would give up their unwanted daughters to be raised in loving American homes. It felt so right. I remember thinking, 'What can go wrong?' There's a child that needs parents. There's no medical problem to stop you. It seemed like a perfect solution." Emilie sighed.

"So, I found an agency that specialized in Chinese adoptions. That's all they did. We interviewed with them and were accepted. There were lots of hurdles to cross, like a home study with a social worker, a psychological evaluation, and so much paperwork. Mounds of paperwork. But things were progressing. We were told within the year we would be traveling to China to pick up our daughter.

"For the first time, I relaxed. I even allowed myself to get excited . . . buying cute little pink outfits. In retrospect, that was probably not the best thing to do. Maybe it was bad luck. But I thought it was foolproof."

Click. Jot. Nod.

"Everything was going as planned . . . until he died. At first, I was dealing with the death. I was in shock and not sure what the next day would bring, let alone the next year."

She swallowed hard. "And then, three weeks after he died, I was trying to get back to normal when I got a call from the agency. I wasn't sure what I wanted to do, but I didn't want to have to make the decision just yet." Emilie shifted her body, trying to get more comfortable.

"They called me and said they were denying my application because I was no longer married. I remember the conversation verbatim, even though I wish I could forget it. It was this young girl, probably an intern or just out of college. I could tell she was so nervous and had a hard time getting it out. And then she said, and I'll never forget this. She said, 'I begged them not to make me be the one to tell you.'" She started to cry again, this time softly. The tissue in her hand was frayed, so she took another out of the box. "Oh God, this is still so raw." She paused and blew her nose.

Frown. Jot. Nod, nod.

"At that moment, I felt so sorry for her. I couldn't imagine a more difficult conversation. Even as what she was saying was sinking in, I couldn't help but feel sorry for her." She shook her head at the memory, which was still vivid and painful.

"That must have been very difficult." Straying from his monotone, Dr. Jeffries showed a hint of compassion. "How did you handle it?"

"I said I understood, even though I didn't, and she gave me instructions on how to close out my file . . . so that I could get my money back. I still have the letter I wrote. I haven't read it in months. It brings up too much emotion. The end of a dream." She looked at Dr. Jeffries, who looked solemn.

"After I hung the phone up, I ran to the bathroom and threw up. It was a lot to deal with in a short amount of time. First Rob and then the adoption." Emilie wiped her eyes and blew her nose again.

"It does seem a little cruel for them to tell you such devastating news while you are newly grieving." Dr. Jeffries looked at her with his head tilted in a way that reminded her of her father.

"I used to think that, but I don't anymore. The truth is, I had already come to that decision myself. I just couldn't say it out loud.

And hearing it said to me was hard. I've come to realize that telling me then was actually, in a way, kind, especially if no single adoptions is their policy. It would have been far worse to go on thinking everything was okay for months and then have them tell me. It really was considerate, even if it was overwhelming at the time."

"You are a strong person to be able to acknowledge that," Dr. Jeffries said, falling back into his monotone. "You know, there are other ways to become a parent. I think you'd make a great stepmother."

"Thank you. I appreciate that." Emilie stopped to collect her thoughts. "You know earlier when you said if I married my college boyfriend, I would be miserable now?"

Click. Jot. Nod. "Yes, go on."

"I think you're right. I know so many people who are not happy with their lives. I should look at the positive side of things more often. I was married to someone I loved and who loved me, and now I have the opportunity to write chapter two. That seems pretty lucky to me."

"So, does that mean you are ready to date?" Dr. Jeffries asked.

"Maybe," Emilie said and then added, "Yes, I guess so." Maybe.

12

Walking into her house with her arms full of groceries, Emilie heard the phone in the kitchen ring. Shutting the front door with her foot, she unloaded the grocery bags in the foyer and ran to grab the ringing phone from the kitchen wall.

"Emilie?" The voice on the other end was unfamiliar.

"Yes?" she said hesitantly.

"Um, it's Michael Lovell. Karen Radner gave me your number."

What? Karen's hot neighbor? After her appointment with Dr. Jeffries the day before, she emailed Karen, saying it'd be okay if she gave her neighbor Emilie's number—never expecting that he'd actually call. "Yes. Oh, yes . . . Um. Hi." She could feel herself blushing. She removed the phone from her ear, covered the receiver, and mouthed *Oh my God!*—even though there wasn't anyone in the room.

"This is a little awkward, but Karen told me she had this friend she wanted me to meet. I hope you don't think I'm being forward—actually, I guess I am being forward—but I thought, why not give you a call? Um, I hear you're going to be in Miami soon." His voice quivered a bit, making him sound nervous.

"Yeah. I mean, yes, I'm going to be there on Tuesday—for business." *Good! Sound important. Men like that. I think.* Sigh. She wasn't really sure what men like. It had been so long since she had been on a date. She tried to slow her heart rate down by taking a deep breath.

"Great. Do you want to go out for dinner or something?"

He sounds cute. "Yeah, sure." *Or something?* What does that mean? Emilie frowned.

"Okay, where are you staying?"

"I'll be at the Oceanview on South Beach. My meeting doesn't start until nine in the morning on Wednesday, and I am planning to get there around four o'clock on Tuesday. So, if you want to get together for dinner on Tuesday night, that would work. Wednesday would work too, but not as well. I'm not sure what time my meeting will be over." *Shut up, Emilie. You're starting to sound like a jabbering fool.* She felt a rush of adrenaline move up her body, and her face felt flush again. She took another deep breath, covering the phone as she exhaled slowly.

"Sure, Tuesday works for me. I live up in Jupiter Island, which is probably about an hour's drive, so I'll drive down and meet you at your hotel. I know exactly where it is. How about five thirty? We can grab drinks and then dinner. Do you like Cuban food?"

Yes! No! I'm not sure. "Yes. Sure, I'll eat anything." *Great! Now you sound like a gluttonous. Retract, quickly. Fix the damage.* "Um, actually, I've never had it, but I've always wanted to try it." Emilie felt a wave of nausea fill her stomach and move up to her throat. She covered her mouth with her hand and willed herself not to throw up.

Michael laughed. "We don't have to eat Cuban food. I'll think of something else. Is this your cell phone number, or is there a better number for me to contact you while you're in Miami?"

"No, it's my home phone. Let me give you my cell." Emilie hadn't given a man her phone number, or for that matter, been on a date in more than ten years, but somehow it rolled off of her tongue.

"Got it. Great. Here's mine." As he recited the numbers, Emilie jotted them down on a scrap of paper with a reminder note to put it in her cell phone once she hung up. Then she wrote the number on a second piece of paper in case her sweaty palms smeared the first piece of paper.

"Okay. Great! I guess it's a date." As she was about to hang up, she said, "Oh, um, Michael? How will I know what you look like?"

He laughed. "I guess this is a truly blind date. I'm about five foot eight, and I have dark wavy hair. People tell me I look like that doctor that was married to Meredith on *Grey's Anatomy*. What's his name, doctor dreamer?"

Emilie tried to stifle a laugh, but it came out as a snort, which was decidedly worse. "You mean McDreamy?"

"Yeah, that's it. Even my mom says I look like him. I don't know what makes her prouder, the fact that I have a PhD and run the biology department of the University of Miami, or that I look like a doctor on TV. Probably the latter."

Emilie giggled. Yay! He's funny and cute. "Did Karen show you a picture of me?" *Hope so. Hope not. No, definitely hope so.* A week isn't enough time to make major changes.

"Yeah, she showed a picture from your New York trip. Sounds like you guys had a lot of fun."

Oh, dear. Which one? I hope it wasn't the one from the restaurant. I hate that picture. "Yes, we did. Okay, great. I'm looking forward to seeing you next week."

"Me too. If your plans change, just let me know."

"I will. And you do the same. Thanks for calling." When she hung up the phone, she had to sit down and take a minute to realize what she had just done.

She took out her cell phone and meticulously typed in his number in—checking and rechecking she got it right. Then she typed "Professor Dreamy" as the contact name and smiled. She was careful not to hit dial, even though part of her wanted to, to make sure she got the number correct. Instead, she tucked both pieces of paper into a safely zippered pocket in her wallet.

Noticing her hands were trembling, she squeezed them tightly. "It's just a date," she said out loud. "*Just* a date," she repeated. "Holy crap!" She punched in Colin's name on her phone contact list and hit call.

He picked up on the first ring. "Hey there! What's up?"

"Please help me get out of something stupid I just did," she blurted out.

"What?" She heard him adjust the phone. "What's going on?"

"Remember, I told you Karen was going to set me up with her neighbor, the professor? Well, he called. He asked me out . . . and I said yes."

"That's great!" Colin let out a hoot. "Oh . . . this is big."

"No, it's not great. I think I'm gonna throw up. You have to get me out of this."

"You'll be fine. You have to go on your first date. Usually, it ain't pretty. Oh, but you'll be fine. Just calm down." Colin's voice was very soothing. "What's his name? Have you googled him?" Colin asked.

"No, didn't google him. I'm serious. I'm really having second thoughts. Can you come over and talk me off the ledge?"

"On my way."

• • •

Thirty minutes later, Colin arrived. "Yay! My girl's got a date," he said when Emilie opened her front door. "Oh, honey, I'm so proud." He planted a kiss on her cheek. "C'mon, let's see what kind of cyber stuff we can find on him."

"No, that will make me more nervous."

"C'mon, if we find something bad, I'll cancel the date for you."

"Okay," Emilie said. Colin's words comforted her, but only a little.

They went into Emilie's home office, and she sat at the desk while Colin hovered over her head. "I'm an expert at researching a potential date," he said.

She clicked the mouse on the Safari icon and typed Google into the browser.

"Okay, go to Google, and let's see if we can get a picture. Maybe he's been in the press. Nothing bad. Good stuff. Like saving babies in Africa, or something like that. What's his name?" Colin asked.

"Lovell, it's Michael Lovell," she said as she typed.

"Emilie's got a date with Professor of Luuuuuuv!" Colin teased. "What's he teach? I hope it's sex ed."

"Stop it. He's the head of the biology department at the University of Miami."

"Biology, even better. Hopefully, he can teach you about the birds and the bees."

They both laughed, but inside, Emilie's stomach tightened, fearful of what Google would say about her blind date. The first search for Michael Lovell returned more than one million results, with none of the top ten seeming relevant.

"Go ahead and type in Michael Lovell, PhD, and Florida. Maybe that will get you something," Colin coaxed. Adding Florida seemed to do the trick.

"Oh my God, I think this is him." Emilie clicked on a website for the University of Miami that listed Michael Lovell as head of the biology department.

"Go to the About Us section." Colin pointed to the screen. "That's usually where they list the bios."

Emilie clicked on the link, and there he was, staring back at her, Michael Lovell. "Gosh, Colin, look. He's really cute. He said he looked like Dr. McDreamy from Grey's Anatomy, and he does. He really does!"

"Yummy!" Colin said, giving his approval. "Mikey, me likey." He put his arms around her from behind. "You go, girl."

They read the accompanying bio, which mentioned he was from Philadelphia and a graduate of Johns Hopkins University.

"Good, you'll have something you can talk about—Baltimore. He must have lived here during grad school."

Emilie's nerves quieted a tiny bit.

"Okay, now let's go shopping and get you something special to wear. You have to wear a dress, you know. I'm thinking a sexy number that shows off your best parts." He swung her chair around and said, "These things here," pointing to her breasts.

"No!" She put her hands up in protest.

Colin leaned in, hugged her, and whispered, "I know you're scared, but you are awesome. Don't ever forget that. You're gonna be fine."

"I hope so," Emilie whispered back.

13

The flight to Miami seemed to take much longer than the two and a half hours listed on the itinerary. In actuality, the plane taxied to the gate a full twenty minutes early. Emilie took a cab to the hotel, which was located right on the beach.

Once in her room, Emilie put her suitcase on the bed and pulled out the outfit she purchased just for the occasion: a black-and-white polka dot sleeveless dress with a full skirt—perfect for the tropical weather in Miami. She feared underarm sweat stains more than she loathed her untoned upper arms. A black patent leather belt that matched her black patent leather three-inch, high-heeled sandals seemed to fine-tune the outfit. Like most women, the better she thought she looked, the more confidence she had.

Although she showered at home, wanting to be fresh for her date, she showered again. Standing in the bathroom with a towel wrapped around her body, she turned on the hairdryer that was stuck on the bathroom wall, next to the mirror. Even on high heat, the dryer barely emitted puffs of air, so she knew it would take an inordinate amount of time to dry her thick curly hair.

She was grateful she allowed extra time to get ready. With just ten minutes to spare, she put on her dress, belt, and shoes. She looked herself over in the full-length mirror hanging on the closet door. Swaying from side to side made her skirt shimmy. It gave her a flirty feeling, calming her nerves just a bit.

She walked over to the balcony, opened the curtains and the sliding glass door, and stepped outside. The sun was slowly disappearing into the ocean, but it was still hot. The beach was full of sunbathers, hoping to catch the last rays of the day.

While out on the balcony, she heard her cell phone ring. *Oh my God, it's him!* She went back inside and fumbled with her purse, trying to find her phone. Just as she answered, the contents of her purse spilled out on the floor. "Hello. Oh, shoot!"

"Um, hello? Emilie? This is Michael. Michael Lovell."

"Yes. Hi, Michael." She bent over, cradling the phone between her shoulder, and gathered the contents of her purse. Her hand shook as she put the items back in.

"I know I'm a little early. I'm in the hotel lobby."

Emilie had an instant urge to throw up. "Great. I'll be right down." She stood up and took a deep breath. One last look in the mirror gave her the confidence she needed to leave the room.

Walking into the lobby, she saw a man standing near a window in the bar, checking his phone. His glasses were perched at the end of his nose as he stared intently at his screen. As she walked closer, the man looked up from his phone. He smiled and walked toward her. "Emilie?"

"Yes, you must be Michael."

"Yep, guilty as charged," he said. To say he looked like McDreamy would be generous—with thinning salt-and-pepper hair, he could maybe be McDreamy's father. His skin looked like worn leather and showed signs of spending too much time in the hot Florida sun. The photo she saw online was obviously outdated. He was a little shorter and a little rounder than she imagined, but his difference in appearance did not detract from her nerves. He was wearing a Don Johnson-Miami Vice look—white suit and a pastel pink tie-less oxford shirt opened to expose the glimpse of a hairy chest.

"I'm a hugger," he said as he wrapped his arms around her and pulled her in so tight she thought her ribs would crack. She let out an audible groan, which, if possible, made her feel even more nervous.

When they broke the embrace, Emilie said, "It's so nice to meet you. Wow, I can't believe we're actually doing this." Looking down, she moved some hair that had fallen over her eyes.

"You mean you don't fly a thousand miles for a blind date often?" His grayish eyes lit up when he laughed and the wrinkles at the corners of his eyes became more pronounced. "I'll bet you have lots of men wanting to take you out." He grabbed her around her waist and pulled her close to him. "You look like you need a chardonnay," Michael said, turning and walking toward a table in the hotel lobby bar.

Emilie looked up at Michael and smiled. "How did you know that's what I drink?"

"Karen clued me in on a few things." He winked and motioned her to walk with him.

When they reached a small table for two, Michael pulled out the chair for her.

Emilie ran her hand behind her skirt as she eased her body into the chair. The Florida heat and humidity made her skirt cling to her thighs, and unfortunately, her thighs cling to one another.

Michael gestured to the waiter. When the waiter appeared, he ordered himself Dewars on the rocks. He perused the wine list before selecting a twenty-dollar glass of Kendall Jackson for her.

Once the waiter left the table, Emilie asked, "What else did Karen say about me?"

Michael grabbed a handful of wasabi peanuts from the bowl on the table and flicked them into his mouth, one at a time. In between crunching on nuts, he said, "Well, let's see . . . she said you and she went to college together." Crunch, crunch. "And that you are one of the nicest people she knows."

Emilie felt her cheeks redden as he spoke.

"Oh, um . . ." Crunch. "And she also said you are a lot of fun to be around. That's all I needed." The corners of his mouth turned into a warm smile.

"She said some really nice things about you too. I probably shouldn't be saying this, but she mentioned that lots of women in your neighborhood have crushes on you, and I can see why."

Michael blushed. "Karen has always been one of my favorite neighbors. She was very kind to me when my marriage broke up. Most people told me they never liked her, that she was a bitch—referring to my wife, um, my ex-wife—I mean. And that always made me feel worse, you know, like I should have seen it. Karen just said, 'I'm sorry.' Just that. And that was all she needed to say."

"Why did your marriage end, if I may ask?"

"She cheated on me with the gardener." He shrugged his shoulders. "It'd be funny if I weren't being serious. I know it's cliché, but it really happened. I hear they're very happy now." He rolled his eyes. "I guess I should have known, but hindsight is always twenty-twenty. I thought his monthly invoice for pruning the bushes was for pruning the bushes, not for pruning *the* bush." He raised his eyebrows to emphasize the last part of his statement.

When their drinks arrived, they decided to toast Karen. Somewhere mid glass of wine, Emilie realized her nerves were easing a bit. She felt like she was talking to someone she had known for a long time. After the second round of drinks, Michael suggested they go have dinner at a restaurant next to the hotel. He paid the bill, and the two left the hotel bar.

As they walked to the restaurant, he grabbed her hand and

held it. Emilie did not pull away.

During dinner, Emilie barely ate her halibut. That fact and three glasses of wine had lowered her inhibitions and calmed her nerves. He had also become strikingly handsome and charming. She found herself laughing exaggeratedly at Michael's somewhat funny stories, with her hand on her breastbone, grabbing the strand of pearls her grandmother gave her while saying, "Oh, Michael, that's so funny." Yep, in a matter of a few hours, a little food, and several drinks, she became a big flirt.

Michael laughed heartily, and his eyes lit up as Emilie and he chatted.

After declining dessert, he put his hand on her knee and said, "I think I could talk with you forever." Emilie smiled, and in her mind mouthed "thank you" up to the heavens.

Michael paid the check, leaving the waiter a twenty dollar cash tip on a seventy-dollar bill. He pulled her chair out and then gently grasped her shoulders. He leaned in behind her and whispered in a low sexy voice, "Mmm, you smell good."

Emilie felt special. It didn't matter that his affection for her was on display for the entire restaurant to see. Maybe some patrons did not approve of the PDA, but those people didn't know her backstory. What mattered was she didn't feel alone or lonely—those two feelings had been intertwined since Rob died.

They left the restaurant and walked hand in hand slowly back toward the hotel. When they got near the hotel's entrance, Michael pulled her into the shadows, out of plain sight, and kissed her deeply on the mouth. Emilie felt a womanly awakening surge in her body as she kissed him back. Michael moved his lips to her neck, and as he kissed her, he whispered, "Do you want the night to end yet?"

"No, I don't," she said, catching her breath.

"Me neither. Can we go upstairs to your room?"

Emilie couldn't believe it when she heard herself say, "Sure . . . I'd like that."

Michael kissed her again and grabbed her hand, smiling at her as he led her into the hotel.

When they got to her room, Michael sat on the bed and motioned her to sit next to him. He began kissing her neck and slowly pushed his body on hers, forcing her to lie down. With his body firmly pressing on top of hers, she felt his hands all over her as he gave her long, wet kisses, allowing his tongue to explore the depths of her mouth passionately. Emilie became aroused. Viv was right. If she felt it, it would be automatic. However, there was this gnawing feeling inside of her. On the one hand, she was very much enjoying being with Michael, but she was scared. It had been years—more than a decade since—she had been with a man other than Rob, and she never had sex this shortly after meeting someone.

Emilie pulled away. "Will you excuse me?" She got up from the bed and carefully grabbed her cell phone from her purse. When she got in the bathroom, she turned the water on low to drown out the conversation and dialed Colin's number. "Colin?" she whispered. "Colin, it's me."

"Hey, what's wrong? Why are you whispering? How'd the date go?" he asked with rapid-fire precision.

"He's still here. I'm in the bathroom. We're up in my hotel room. Colin, I think I'm going to have sex."

"Of course you are, and you should."

"I don't know. I'm scared."

"You'll be fine. It's like riding a bike, only more fun. You never forget how."

"I'm not worried that I forgot how. I'm terrified. I feel like I'm cheating. It's too soon."

"You're not cheating, and it's not too soon. Do you *like* him?"

"I don't really know him. This is insane. I'm embarrassed to say this, but I'm really turned on."

"Totally understand. Carpe diem. Yep. You don't see a future with him. And the fact that he lives a thousand miles away. That's okay. But why not him? Look, just go for it. Enjoy it," Colin said, his words relaxed her. "I put some condoms in your suitcase, hoping this would happen."

"What?" Emilie was shocked. "You did?"

"Yes, they are in the zippered pocket on the inside. There's about three or four."

"Three or four? Oh my God! Are you optimistic?" Emilie let out a nervous snort.

"Go out there and get him, tigress. And call me tomorrow to give me the details."

Emilie hung up. She decided Colin was right. She composed herself, flushed the toilet, and brushed her hair back into place. When she walked out of the bathroom, Michael was lying on her bed. He had his head propped up on a mound of pillows and patted the empty spot next to him, encouraging her to come join him. She found the condoms in the suitcase and threw them on the bed. "It's better to be safe," she said.

It didn't take Michael long to strip down and expose his excitement. He took a condom from the bed and put it on. After sliding under the covers, he lifted the bedspread and patted the spot next to him. "C'mon. I won't bite. That is, unless you want me to," he said.

"What?" Emilie asked.

"Sorry, bad joke. C'mon. It's okay." His voice was reassuring.

She closed her eyes for a second. Hearing Colin's voice in her head, she took off her dress but left on her bra and panties. She got into bed next to a man she barely knew. She couldn't deny the rush of arousal that enveloped her body as Michael's hands caressed her. He reached down and tugged at black lace panties, for which she had paid full price at Victoria's Secret the day before. "We don't need these, do we?" he asked as she allowed him to remove them.

She returned his kisses and welcomed his tongue on her neck.

"You are so sexy," he said in a low voice. Then he slowly climbed on top of her.

Her mind went to the last time she and Rob made love. It was just two days before he died. She tried to clear her racing mind and give in to the complex feelings that were bubbling inside. She felt Michael's tongue force her mouth open. As he kissed her fully, she kissed him back with as much passion and desire in return. Quickly, his breathing became labored. And then suddenly Michael let out a grunt and a moan and then collapsed on top of her.

Emilie lay still for a moment. It couldn't be over that fast—she still had her bra on. When Michael made no motion other than gasping for air, she realized the deed was indeed done. This definitely was not the way she remembered having sex. With his heaving heavy and sweaty body compressing hers, she patted him on the back and said, "Okay," hoping he'd get the hint. But, of course, he didn't. So she pushed his forearms. "You're going to have to get off of me. I can't breathe."

He unceremoniously rolled off of her and soon began to snore.

Sleep did not come easily to her that night. She stared at the ceiling and tried to identify her feelings. On the one hand, she was lonely and relieved that a man found her sexy and attractive, but on the other, she still missed her husband. What would Dr. Jeffries say? Probably not much. No, he'd make her tell him the pros and cons of sleeping with a stranger. She didn't recognize the new person she was becoming. Maybe loneliness and fear of never being with a man again had overcome her usual good sense.

So, she rationalized, no need to tell Dr. Jeffries.

Before the sun came up, she slipped into the bathroom. She stared at herself in the mirror in disbelief as she noticed her chin was scratched up, apparently from Michael's five o'clock shadow. Her sensitive skin was no match for his rough stubble.

She reached for some cosmetic concealer that the Bobbi Brown lady sold her and rubbed it on her scarred chin. Because the concealer was a few shades lighter than her skin, the patchwork was very noticeable. She then reached for her foundation and rubbed the makeup on top of the concealer. Still not satisfied with the result, she began mixing powder and creams—anything she could find—to cover up her "sex scar." Unfortunately, the more she rubbed, the worse it got. She wiped off the makeup and was shocked to see the little scar had now become a patch of missing skin about the size of a penny. She found the sore impossible not to touch. Deciding a bandage would be a ridiculous choice, she instead selected denial, telling herself maybe no one would notice.

When she walked out of the bathroom, she could see Michael stirring. He sat on the side of the bed and rubbed his eyes. Then he stood up and stumbled as he put on the same clothes he had on the night before, which were piled in a reverse trail leading from the bed. He smiled at her as he buttoned his shirt, but said nothing. Grabbing his jacket, he flung it over his left shoulder and walked toward her.

Putting his free arm around her waist, he pulled her close and kissed her. "Thanks for a wonderful night. I hope we can do it again sometime."

Emilie walked him to the door, where they kissed again.

"If you're ever back in Miami again, give me a call." He followed his statement with a wink.

"Sure, and if you ever get to Baltimore, you do the same." As she closed the door behind him, she wondered if they would ever see each other again—not even sure she wanted to.

When she was sure Michael was gone, she called Colin.

"Hey, there, lover girl. How was professor McDreamy?"

"More like Professor Quickdraw McGraw."

"Ooh. Ouch. I'm sorry. Everyone has to have a first, and usually it ain't pretty."

"Yes, I guess so. It's okay. At least I didn't chicken out. There wasn't time to." She laughed a little at first, but then laughed uncontrollably. The nerves and tension she had kept in for days maybe, even months, were suddenly gone.

She gave Colin enough details to satisfy his curiosity, hung up, and began getting ready for work. While still in a bathrobe, she took a cup of coffee that was finished brewing in the in-room coffeemaker and walked out on the balcony. It was a breezy South Florida morning, and she could see ocean waves for miles rolling in and crashing on the beach, sweeping the sand in a swift motion. The hush sound of the rippling water paired with the occasional caw of some gulls was calming. It gave her an idea.

After getting dressed, she pulled the Crown Royal bag from her suitcase and went to the beach. She walked in the wet sand and let waves tease her feet. She took the purple bag and emptied her husband's remains onto the sand. She snapped a picture with her phone before the waves crept in and took him away. Within seconds, the ashes were gone. Tears came to her eyes. "Sail away, my beloved."

She strolled the beach for a little while before heading back to the hotel. Once in the lobby, she ran into a familiar face.

"Hey, Em!" Carol, from the cable company's marketing

department, waved at Emilie as she approached. "What's that on your face?" Carol asked, squinting to get a better look.

Shoot! That stupid sex scar. What do I say . . . Yes, Carol, I had sex last night with a stranger? Emilie rubbed her chin.

"It looks like you have Ash Wednesday on your forehead," Carol said as she leaned forward to get a closer look and touched Emilie's forehead.

Relieved, Emilie laughed. "Oh, it's just my husband. I put some of his ashes in the ocean. I guess he kissed me goodbye."

Carol hugged Emilie hard. "You are amazing," she said. Then she whispered, "Don't ever change."

14

Once she was back home, things started to return to normal. She rarely thought of her dalliance in Miami. Well, that wasn't necessarily true. During the rest of her trip, while she was in Miami, she obsessed about it—wondering if he'd call her, and then worrying that he would call her, and then feeling insulted that he didn't call her. Happily, though, the sex scar had healed nicely, and she didn't have to explain it to anyone.

On her way to the mailbox at the end of her driveway, Emilie waved to her next-door neighbor. "Hi, Mrs. Rivera."

"How are you?" Mrs. Rivera approached Emilie. The elderly neighbor's bright orange velour jogging suit almost matched the color of her hair.

"I'm fine. Puddie, get down!" Emilie said, tugging harder at the leash. Puddie did not listen and continued to paw at the neighbor's leg.

"He's okay." Mrs. Rivera reached down and petted Puddie on the head while simultaneously pushing him away. "Did you see someone moved into the Miller's house?" Mrs. Rivera pointed toward the house diagonally across the street.

"No, I've been away."

"I think he's in the Navy. Appears to be alone. If I were thirty years younger, I might go after him myself," Mrs. Rivera offered with a wink.

Emilie smiled uncomfortably. "Okay then," she said. "Have a nice day."

"You too." The neighbor turned and walked toward her house.

Emilie got the mail and then she and Puddie walked down the driveway and into the house. Once inside, she unleashed Puddie and placed the mail on the kitchen counter. She methodically put the items into three piles: bills, things that can wait, and junk. She spotted an envelope with the return address of the alumni office of St. Cecilia's, her college alma mater. Since it was almost November, it was likely an invitation to Homecoming Weekend. For the past ten years, she and Rob would join Viv and Heidi and their husbands and make the trip back to campus and back to a time when they were carefree college students. The highlight of the weekend was a lacrosse game between the hometown Seahawks and their archrivals, Salisbury State—a.k.a. "Salisbury Steak." The game was always followed by a fancy sit down dinner in a tent near the college's waterfront where Salisbury steak was served on bone white china and bottles of wine adorned every table. It was a far cry from the dining hall that considered pancakes as a vegetarian option when Emilie, Viv, Heidi, and Karen were students.

Emilie didn't believe she could endure the event without Rob by her side. It had become a tradition she enjoyed, but it was steeped in coupledom. So, she threw the invitation in the trash.

A few minutes later, she dug the invitation out of the trash and read it.

Dear Alumni,

Don't miss this year's Homecoming weekend, Saturday, October 29.

Cheer on your Seahawks as they defeat Salisbury State at 3 p.m. on the athletic field. The game will be followed

*by a dinner and dance at the riverfront
at 6 p.m. This will be a great time to
reconnect with old friends you haven't
seen in years or to make some new
ones. The game is free, but the cost
of the dinner is $55 per person. Please
RSVP by October 20, to the Alumni
Office.*

I hope to see you there!

*Sincerely,
Paul Winters
Director of Alumni Relations*

The back of the card had a cartoon of a giant seahawk eating a piece of meat, dripping in gravy, that read "Salisbury," being served to him on a grand silver platter.

Homecoming was an excellent opportunity to reconnect with people she went to college with. Facebook served that purpose too, but in a different way. Emilie's friends used Facebook to brag about what's going on in their lives—kids' report cards to mood changes—were discussed and liked in great detail, many times with TMI. Emilie had long abandoned the forum, deciding it was for people who had a life to brag about, not for people like her. Her last post was February first. "We got great news today from the adoption agency," it read. "Looks like we'll be headed to China by the end of the year." It was liked by eighty-five, nearly all of her friends, and a few made cheerful comments. She was afraid that many of her classmates wouldn't know the reason for her silence. A few times she attempted to post something heartfelt about her new life, but never got the courage. Fearing if she went, she'd have to tell her story over and over—something she wasn't ready to do—she crumbled the invitation up and threw it in the trash. *Maybe next year. Hopefully.*

She went into the kitchen and opened the freezer and pulled out a Weight Watchers macaroni and cheese. As she read the microwave instructions, the phone rang. She put down the cardboard box on the counter and picked up the receiver hanging on the kitchen wall.

"Hello," she said, cradling the receiver in between her chin and shoulder while picking up the macaroni and cheese box again.

"Hey, girlfriend! How are you?"

"Great. How are you?" Emilie could tell Viv had her on speaker, probably calling from her car.

"Good. Did you get the invitation to Homecoming? We have to RSVP right away. Remember last year we waited, and we had a really shitty table at dinner. So, do it now."

"I don't think I'm going this year."

"What do you mean? We always go. Ah, come on. Hold on, I'm making a left onto Montrose." After a few seconds of muffled sound, Viv said, "Okay, I'm back. What was I saying? Oh, yeah, of course, you're going. It won't be any fun without you."

"It'll be fun without me. Go ahead and go without me. I just don't feel like it this year."

"Is it because of Rob?"

"No." *Yes.* "No, not really, well, sort of. I just don't want to have to tell anyone about Rob dying." Surely Viv would see that it was still too painful to talk about.

"What? Screw those people. You don't have to tell them anything."

"I'll give it some thought."

"Please do. Oh, I almost forgot. Andrew is going to buy a bunch of bottle rockets, so we can shoot them off by the river like we did last year. Remember how much fun that was?" Viv said.

"Oh my God, I have the best idea! Hold on." Emilie heard the horn honk. "Move!" Followed by, "Okay, I'm back. I've got a great idea. You know how you're finding places to put Rob?"

"Yes." Where was Viv going with this? St. Cecilia's? Rob didn't go there. It was a pretty campus but meant nothing to him.

"Maybe we could tape some of Rob's ashes in a little plastic baggies to the rockets. Wouldn't that be fun? Oh my God! He can go to the moon!"

Emilie perked up. "Do you think we can get away with it? Last year, we barely got out of there without being detained by campus security."

"Sure. We'll plan an escape route or maybe use a decoy or something. We'll figure it out. So now are ya in?"

"Yes, I'll come."

"Great. Oh, by the way, how was your date . . . in Miami . . . Karen's friend?"

Emilie frowned as she let out an audible sigh.

"That good?" Viv laughed. "Well, you got to kiss some frogs to find your prince."

"I guess."

"I can't wait to hear all about it on the way to St. Cecilia's. Love you, gotta go." Viv made a kissing sound before she hung up.

• • •

On the day of homecoming, they piled into Andrew's SUV that had three rows of seats and made the two-hour trip to campus, arriving just as the lacrosse match was starting. Andrew and Heidi's husband, Damien, went to get beers while the girls were sent to look for five seats together. As they approached the bleachers, Emilie winced at the site of B.T. Nelson, the senior class president, when they were both students at the college. A grinning B.T.

walked toward them.

"Emilie Malone! Emilie! Over here!" B.T. waved his hand in the air. "How the hell have you been?"

Emilie closed her eyes and braced herself for the bore-fest.

In the eighteen years since graduation, not much about B.T., or Brian Thomas Nelson, III, had changed. Wearing a navy blue striped oxford and a yellow sweater tied just below the collar, B.T. still looked like he could model for an L.L. Bean catalog. His khaki Bermuda shorts were held up with a navy belt that had big white sails on it, and his Docksides had pristine little leather ties looped in perfect bows.

B.T. was from a very well-connected Baltimore family, and he made sure everyone knew it. He was not only class president, but he also edited the campus newspaper, two positions rumored to have been bought by his dad, a Baltimore County Circuit Court judge. When they were classmates, Emilie nicknamed him BS—a not-so-subtle reference to his gift of embellishment. In their junior year, the name made its way around campus and was never attributed to her. During their school years, B.T. was always drawn to Emilie. He treated her like a kid sister—studying with her and occasionally punching her on the shoulder as a show of affection. When they were in college, Emilie surmised he liked her, but because she did not come from Baltimore blue blood, he would not be tempted to ever cross the friendship line.

"Oh, hi, BS, I mean B.T. How are you?" Fearing he would try to hug her, Emilie extended her hand.

After graduating, B.T.'s life and feats were often chronicled in The Voyager, the college's alumni newsletter. He was the youngest person in the state's history to be elected to the Maryland House of Delegates—a position he still held until his recent aspirations to run for the US House of Representatives were documented in a page-long op-ed—the first ever of its kind in the college newspaper.

"Wow, you look great," he said as he grabbed her hand and pulled her close, giving her a wet kiss on her cheek. B.T.'s hair had thinned a little, and there was a tinge of gray in the temple areas. Too much sun, or possible age, had crinkled the skin that framed his eyes. He squinted as he talked, making the creases more pronounced. "How ya been?"

"I've been good. Thanks for asking."

"So, Emilie, where are you living now?" B.T. reached into a back pocket of his shorts and pulled out a small silver case.

"Columbia." *Oh, boy, here we go.* She was sure the conversation was going to turn into a campaign speech. "You remember Viv and Heidi, don't you?" she said, trying to redirect the conversation away from her.

B.T. nodded toward Viv and Heidi and then turned his attention back to Emilie. "Columbia. That's too bad. Did you know I'm running for the US House of Representatives? You're not in my district, so I guess I don't have to bribe you for your vote. Kidding, of course." He took a card from the silver case and handed it to her. "Here's the info on my website if you want to make a contribution to a fellow alum. Hint. Hint." The wink he added was just downright cringeworthy. He laughed before beginning a diatribe about himself. Emilie, Viv, and Heidi stood patiently as he described his perfect wife, perfect children, and how his in-laws could trace their lineage back to the Mayflower. B.T. always liked to talk about himself . . . a lot. At the end of a lengthy soliloquy, B.T. stopped and said, "So, Emilie, what have you been up to?"

Emilie hesitated. She wasn't sure she wanted to tell B.T. about Rob dying. Since college, they had rarely spoken, and discussing Rob's death was such an intimate conversation. And she hadn't written an op-ed for the school's alumni newsletter. Emilie thought for a second. Maybe, just maybe, hearing about what she'd been through would shut him up. "Well," she said, "in February, my husband died, and tonight we're going to shoot his ashes off in a bottle rocket."

B.T.'s mouth fell agape. He placed a hand on the back of neck and shifted his stance.

It worked. Emilie's comments rendered B.T. speechless—albeit momentarily. He stared at her for a second or two before uttering, "Oh, okay. Well, hmm. I didn't know your husband had died. I'm sorry. Bottle rockets. Cool. That's nice, I guess."

For a minute, Emilie thought she had made history with B.T., but the moment was soon lost when he added, "When my father died last year, the Governor proclaimed June fourteenth as Brian Thomas Nelson Senior Day."

Viv grabbed Emilie by the arm and gave it a tug. "Em, I think we need to go find the guys. They probably need help with the drinks." She turned to B.T. and said "It was nice seeing you. Good luck" and took Emilie's hand, forcing her to leave as well. All three women walked as fast as they could in the opposite direction.

"Can you believe that guy? I didn't want him to know I live in his district. He'd be all over me," Viv said. "But, Em, I gotta give it to ya, girlfriend. You found a way to shut him up. Even if it was just for a few minutes. Bravo!"

The three women met up with the guys and settled in to watch the Seahawks demolish Salisbury "Steak" in a very lopsided victory of ten to one. After the game, the girls mingled and walked around campus. As they ran into classmates, it was as if the grief wheels had been greased as Emilie told and retold her story for what seemed like a dozen times. Each time she told it, she was surprised at how easy it got. She also invited several people to the bottle rocket launching that evening. "Viv will give you the sign during dinner," she said.

A little after 6 p.m., they made their way to a tent by the river. At the dinner, Viv was on a mission to collect at least ten empty wine bottles so they could launch as many bottle rockets at one time. Surprisingly, no one asked any questions as she gathered them.

After the main course—the ever-appropriate turkey Salisbury steak and mashed potatoes—and before dessert was served, Dr. Rieken, St. Cecilia's president, stood up from a table near the front of the room and walked to a podium on a riser.

"Go Seahawks!" She raised her wineglass as everyone clapped and a few people whistled. A table of younger alums in the far-left corner of the room began to sing *Hail to the Seahawks*, the unofficial college fight song highly plagiarized from the Washington Football Team. "Birds on the waterfront, fight for ol' SC," the room sang in unison.

Dr. Rieken smiled in a forced way, looking like a cross between she was happy and she was smelling something bad. Her Smith College background never seemed to mesh with the carefree and rowdy vibe of St. Cecilia's. "Thank you," she said, clanking her knife on her wineglass as if she were at a wedding. "Wow, I love that team spirit," she said. "It's what makes St. Cecilia's so unique."

On that note, Viv motioned to the group it was time to escape. Two dozen people got up and walked out. The clinking of empty bottles drew disapproving looks from the seated guests.

Viv led the group to a secluded area not far from the tent. The area, referred to as the "Garden of Remembrance," was a peaceful location on a cliff above the river's edge. It had beautiful roses and a patch of black-eyed Susans, the state flower. "This is perfect," Viv said. With Andrew's help, Viv set up the bottles about two feet apart from each other. Then Andrew removed the prepared bottle rockets from his backpack. Earlier in the day, Emilie and Viv Scotch-taped dime-size baggies of Rob's ashes to each of the dozen firework sticks. Andrew handed the bottle rockets to Viv, who methodically loaded each bottle, and turned the rockets so they were facing the river. "Okay, I think we're ready. Emilie, do you want to say something?"

Emilie looked around at her friends. "I'm touched that all of you think enough of Rob and me and to help celebrate his life and memorialize his death. Rob would have gotten the biggest kick out of this. I know he's probably up there giving the thumbs-up right now. So, with that, honey, I hope you make it to the moon!" Everyone clapped. Viv and Andrew quickly lit each bottle rocket, while the others stood back out of the way. Soon there was a flurry of lights, claps, and pops of noise as each bottle rocket exploded into the heavens. Emilie gave each one of her friends a big hug and thanked them for a wonderful send-off for Rob.

As they were collecting the spent bottles, the familiar sound of the whirr of a golf cart grew closer. "Oh, no! Here come the rent-a-cops!" Viv said loudly, referring to the inept campus security guards. "Quick, let's get out of here!" And the group ran.

With the guards in a golf cart chasing them, Andrew yelled, "Split up. They'll never catch us all. Let's meet by the car." They did just that, running behind buildings where neither the golf cart nor the portly guards could get to.

One by one they reached the parking lot, next to the Athletic Building, on the other side of campus. They were out of breath, but with no security guards in sight. "Quick, get in," Andrew said as he held the back door of the SUV open.

The women got in the back while Damien claimed the front seat.

Once settled in and trying to catch her breath, Viv said, "Hey Em, did that remind you about the time freshman year when we got caught skinny dipping at Church Point?" She managed a hearty laugh. "Remember, we never ran so fast in our lives—that is, until now."

"Yeah, that was fun. And so was this. Thanks. Thanks, girlfriend." Emilie reached over and gave Viv a hug. "I'm glad I came."

15

"Boy, I guess she's planning to eat some turkey *and* a whole pump-kin pie on Thursday," Colin said, referring to the waif of a spin instructor. He steadied himself with one arm on the bike as he bent down and undid the Velcro on one shoe, and then the other, and then took them off. "I've never understood why we have to be pun-ished when the teacher is planning a bad eating day."

"Yeah, whatever." Emilie frowned as she put her shoes in their carrying case.

"Hey, come on now, that was funny. What's wrong with you?"

She softened her expression a little as she shrugged. "You know. The holidays. They're different now," she said.

Thanksgiving was Rob's favorite holiday, and for that reason, Emilie enjoyed it too. They both loved what Thanksgiving stood for—cooking, eating, and football. Typically, she would plan her menu weeks in advance, making sure Rob's favorite sweet potato casserole was on the list. She liked to check the web for creative ideas for other side dishes. Last year she proudly prepared "Pilgrim Corn Pudding," a recipe Foodnetwork.com touted as an original Thanksgiving favorite. But Rob's reaction was anything but thank-ful. As he played with the gooey glop of corn, eggs, and cheese on his plate, he said, "No wonder the first Thanksgiving was such a hit. I'll bet the Indians and Pilgrims used this stuff for an awesome food fight."

This was going to be her first Thanksgiving as a widow. As the holiday approached, she kept telling herself, just make it through these next few weeks, and you'll be fine . . . until Christmas, at least.

"Yeah, I know. I'm sorry. Sometimes I forget that it hasn't been that long for you." Colin draped his arm around her shoulder. "So, what's your mother, the great Margaret Malone, got in store for her family this holiday?"

"Didn't I tell you? She's going on some Silver Fox cruise with her women's group. She leaves Wednesday. She asked me if I wanted to come, said she'd pay, but I was like 'no way.'" Emilie rolled her eyes and grimaced as she imagined her mother and her seventy-year-old friends frolicking in bathing suits.

"What? I didn't know that. Good for her. So, what are you doing? Are you going to Viv's?"

"No, Viv is going to her in-laws. I think I'm just going to get a turkey sandwich from Pete's Deli the day before. No big deal," she said, trying to convince herself, as well as Colin.

"Come to Philly with me. Yes, you must. You'll hate my family as much as I do. It will be fun." Colin said, clapping his hands like a little kid devising a plan. "I need someone on my side." As they walked out of the spinning room, he zipped his fleece jacket.

"No, I couldn't. Your mom probably wouldn't appreciate a last-minute guest."

"Are you kidding? She's always wanted me to bring a girl home. It'll be fine. Bring some of Rob's ashes. We can put some near the Rocky statue."

• • •

The following Thursday, Emilie and Colin drove the two hours from Baltimore to Philadelphia. They pulled into the driveway of Colin's boyhood home—a bright yellow house with a white picket fence that was midway down a tree-lined street. His mother, Ava, opened the front door and hurried down the porch steps.

"You made it," she said. "Did you have any traffic?" She was wearing a brown apron that had an outline of a pilgrim dress on it, with big white lapels draping around her neck, and a fake thick belt around her waist. Looking every bit as Colin described a more uptight version of Betty White, with very blond hair teased in a pseudo-beehive style. She gave Colin a hug and a kiss on the cheek and then extended a hand toward Emilie. "And you must be Emilie," she said with a warm smile. "Please come in."

The inside of the house looked like a set from a fifties sitcom stuck in a simpler time, or maybe denial. Pictures of Colin and his sister, Samantha, in various stages of growing up, flanked a well-polished wooden staircase and crocheted doilies donned every available table surface. The living room, just to the right of the foyer, had a pale blue couch covered in plastic, and an oval coffee table's only function seemed to be to hold a vase of oversized gold and orange silk mums—on top of a doily. A grandfather's clock nestled perfectly in the corner next to a powder blue La-Z-Boy chair that had a large doily draped over the top where someone's head would rest. The clock announced it was eleven with loud gongs when Emilie and Colin walked into the room. Facing the chair on the other side of the wall was an old bulky TV console that was tuned in to the Macy's Thanksgiving Day Parade. "Here comes the MetLife Snoopy Balloon," the three-foot speakers bellowed.

"Greg, turn that down," said a young woman chasing behind a toddler.

A man sitting on the couch, who filled out a Philadelphia Eagles jersey like a linebacker, picked up the remote and put the TV on mute.

"Samantha, this is Emilie. Emilie, this is my sister, Samantha.

And that little guy is Anthony," Colin said, tapping Anthony on the head as he ran by.

"Hi," Samantha said. The young boy took off with his mother in tow. "Anthony, come back here," she said, finally catching up to him and scooping him in her arms. "Greg, you know he's not allowed to eat sugar!"

"He got into your mother's stash—the leftover Halloween stuff she keeps in a bag next to her reading chair," Greg answered, pointing toward a wicker basket of candy next to the blue La-Z-Boy.

"Why weren't you watching him? He's had more than one candy bar. Look!" She grabbed Anthony's hands, which were covered in melted chocolate. She then scooped him up and carried him kicking and screaming to the hall powder room and shut the door.

"No!" shrieked Anthony through the closed door. And then he began to cry.

"Just a normal holiday here at the Meyer house." Colin shrugged his shoulders. "Bet you're wishing you were in front of the TV in the jammies with Ben and Jerry now, aren't ya?"

Emilie laughed. "No, no, really. I welcome the distraction."

"Did I hear my favorite nephew?" Colin's Aunt Dee walked down the hallway from the kitchen toward Colin and grabbed him, giving him a big bear hug. "Hi, baby!" she said.

"Hey, girl. How are you? Any grief counseling lately?" Colin said. Grief counseling was Colin and Dee's code for sex with newly widowed men well into their later years. In the car ride up from Baltimore, Colin told Emilie how Dee had, after burying two husbands of her own, made it a hobby at the ripe old age of seventy-nine of attending funerals in her small Delaware town, offering a shoulder to cry on followed soon after by a bed to sleep in.

"Well, as a matter of fact . . ." Dee looked over her shoulder at her disapproving sister. "I'll tell you later. Oh, I'm so glad you're here. And who is this lovely creature?" she said, pointing to Emilie.

"This is my dear friend, Emilie. Emilie is widowed, too, and this is her first holiday without her husband."

"Come here, precious. Let Aunt Dee give you a big hug."

Aunt Dee's bright purple and red silk kaftan skimmed the floor as she sauntered. Exuding style and confidence, Aunt Dee reminded Emilie of a much rounder version of Dolly Parton, with snow-white hair that curled softly around her neck, black eyeliner highlighting her clear blue eyes, and ruby red lips. Emilie imagined Aunt Dee was responsible for breaking many men's hearts over the last fifty or sixty years.

"Hey Dee, guess what Emilie's doing with her husband's ashes?" Colin said. "She's spreading them all over the place. Where's he been now? Let's see, Aspen, New York City? Didn't your friends take him too?"

"Yes, a friend took some to Italy, and another friend is taking some to Maui after the first of the year. And last month I shot some off in a bottle rocket."

"What? How wonderful! What a great tribute!" Dee smiled.

"We brought some here with us. We're planning to visit the Rocky statue," Colin said.

"He always loved that movie," Emilie added.

"Can I come? What fun! I wanna be a part of this for sure. But let's leave the downers at home." She winked and tilted her head toward Ava.

"Of course, I'd love for you to join us." Emilie smiled.

It wasn't long before dinner was ready. It was obvious Colin's mother was on a schedule and perhaps believed the world would end if the meal weren't on the table by one o'clock, as she had indicated.

After everyone was seated, Ava took Colin's hand. "Colin, would you like to say grace?"

"Wait, before we eat, I almost forgot, I've made everyone something." Colin got up and walked toward the adjacent living room, where he unzipped his suitcase and pulled out a white plastic bag. He smiled as he revealed the bag's contents: turkey hats he made using colorful magic markers to outline his hand—the thumb resembling a turkey's head, equipped with a red gobbler, and the four fingers the feathers—taped to a two-inch brown construction paper headband. "One for you, one for you, here you go, Anthony, Mom, Sam, Greg, one for me and . . . one for Rob!" Colin said as flared out the bands and handed hats to each person. He, Emilie, Dee, and Anthony immediately put theirs on.

"Really, Colin? You don't think we're going to wear these, do you?" Samantha threw her hat down on the table in front of her, and Greg followed suit.

"Yes, I do. Emilie, go get Rob. I made one for him too."

Emilie got up and walked to the living room, grabbed her purse, and pulled out the purple bag containing her husband's ashes. When she returned to the table, she handed it to Colin.

"Who's Rob?" Greg asked.

"Rob is Emilie's dead husband. This bag contains some of his ashes. She takes them with her wherever she goes." Taking a roll of Scotch tape from his plastic bag, Colin taped the homemade turkey hat to the purple bag. "Rob loved Thanksgiving, so we are letting him celebrate with us."

"Colin, please put that away. It doesn't belong at the dinner table," Samantha said.

"No, I won't put the ashes away. Rob is a guest in our house too." Colin held the purple bag in his free hand and dangled it from the straps so that it hovered about an inch above the table, taunting his sister, who sat across the table from him.

Ava folded her hand in prayer. "Oh, come now. It's Thanksgiving," Ava said. She bowed her head. "Colin, let's say grace."

"Fine! Be a jerk and ruin the holiday for us all! Come on Greg, let's leave." Samantha stood up and threw her napkin on the table.

"For God's sake! Samantha, sit down! For once in your life, think of someone other than yourself." Dee's voice was commanding. "Emilie is our guest. Have respect for her loss. Get over yourself and lighten up for a change. You might like it!"

Samantha sat back and tightened her lips. She grabbed her napkin, unfolded it, and threw it in her lap.

The meal was devoured in awkward silence except for the clanging of forks hitting china plates and a few interruptions for requests to pass a dish. No one even tried to mend the rift between brother and sister. Emilie had experienced many family dinners where the conversation was fake, so in a way, she thought, at least Colin's family is genuine.

About forty-five minutes later, Samantha, Greg, and Anthony left before dessert.

Emilie helped Colin's mother clear the table.

"I'm sorry my daughter acted the way she did," Ava said. She took the plates from Emilie and put them in a sink full of soapy water.

"That's okay. I understand. Not everyone is comfortable being around ashes. I should have thought of that. Everyone deals with death differently," Emilie said. Ava handed her a dish towel. "I'm glad you didn't mind that I came today. I didn't want to be alone today."

"Of course. When Colin asked, I didn't even hesitate." Ava used her apron to dry her hands. She lightly touched Emilie's arm.

"You are so young. I can't imagine how hard it is for you."

"No harder than it was for Colin when he lost Howard. He was widowed young too." Emilie said. "Your son has helped me so much. I don't know what I'd do without him. It's like we were supposed to meet each other. He was supposed to guide and teach me, and one day, I'll pay the lesson forward."

Ava nodded. She scrubbed the last plate with a sponge and then gave it to Emilie. "You know, Colin thinks I'm not proud of him. But that couldn't be further from the truth. When Howard died, I saw a strength in Colin that I wouldn't recognize in myself. I have never been prouder of a child in my life."

Emilie reached around and hugged Ava with her free arm and pulled her close. "He knows that. Really, he does."

"I hope so." Ava smiled broadly. "I'm glad you and Colin found each other. And I'm glad you came today."

$$\bullet \ \bullet \ \bullet$$

When Emilie, Colin, Aunt Dee, and Ava got to the Rocky statue, it was close to 6 p.m., and the sun was just beginning to set. A few dozen people walked the granite grounds or sat on the steps leading up to the entrance of the Philadelphia Art Museum. Emilie ran her finger around the bronze piece, looking for the best place to put her husband. Her first reaction was to try to put some in his raised gloves, but the statue was way too tall for that. "Let's put some on the base in between his shoes. That'll give Rob a great view of the steps."

"Perfect!" Colin said. "But first, you have to do it. Take Rob and run up the steps. You know, like Rocky." He raised his hands in the air and sang the familiar Rocky theme.

Emilie needed no encouragement. She walked down the stairs and turned to face Colin, his mother, and his aunt. Clutching the purple bag like a football, she raised the other hand and jogged up all seventy-two steps. When she reached the top, she was out of breath.

"Okay, Rob," she began, while still gasping for air. "Um, I know you always loved this part of the movie, so now you can see it every day. I'm sure you'll laugh at all the tourists as they reenact this scene." She opened the purple bag and put the contents at the base of the statue, in between Rocky's laced shoes.

Colin took the hand she had the bag in and raised it high. "Mom, can you get this?" he asked and handed his phone to his mother.

Emilie had survived her first big holiday, but she knew the real test was coming next month.

16

A few weeks later, Emilie pushed a red shopping cart down the department store's aisle of seasonal decorations. By the limited stock on the shelves, it was obvious her procrastination had repercussions. Five days before Christmas beggars can't be choosers. Other than some gaudy silver and gold garland and boxes of Christmas balls with at least one ball missing, there really wasn't much there. Emilie looked down at her shopping cart—a snowman coffee mug set, with bags of hot cocoa mix for her mother, a knitted turtleneck with a tree with glittery balls on it for Puddie, and a Super Soaker squirt gun for her nephew, not the most practical gift in below-freezing temperatures. Waiting until the last minute to Christmas shop was probably not the wisest thing to do.

The store speakers overhead blared, "Grandma Got Run Over by a Reindeer." Emilie picked up a Santa doll that shimmied in time to the music. Rightfully assuming no one on her list would want it, she placed it back on the shelf. She pushed her cart a little further down the aisle. That song about a heroic, red-nosed reindeer blared on the speakers above. She approached a lone artificial Christmas tree that stood in the corner. She inspected its fiber-optic branches, knowing that Rob would have wanted it. Nothing could trigger him more than trying to find the one burned-out bulb in a strand of several hundred.

"But do you recall . . . the most famous reindeer of all?" the music seemed to get louder.

Letting go of the branch, she realized her hand was shaking. Her heart beat rapidly, and she felt flushed. She covered her mouth in an attempt to stifle the nauseous feeling growing in the pit of her stomach. She turned away from her cart and walked quickly toward the exit while dodging throngs of shoppers. When she got to her car, she pressed every button on the fob until the door unlocked. Once inside the car, she sat behind the steering wheel and sobbed.

• • •

"So, do you have any *holiday* plans?" Emilie could tell Dr. Jeffries was being politically correct by not saying Christmas. His bright red sweater with white snowflakes made him look almost boyish. Definitely someone she'd think twice about taking advice from. She imagined his mother had knitted the sweater for him— yes, he must be a momma's boy.

"I'll go to my mom's on Christmas Eve. That's kind of our family tradition. Me, her, and my brother and his wife and two kids. We go there, and she makes a big dinner, and we open gifts before we all go to midnight mass. I would never tell her this, but I really don't want to go. Not this year, anyway." Emilie had gotten good at recognizing his attempts to trip her up into an emotional turmoil. Sometimes she stepped right on the landmine, while other times she skirted around it, teasing Dr. Jeffries with one or two responses to his loaded questions. Today would probably be a landmine expedition.

"Why don't you want to go?"

"I guess I'm afraid."

"Of what?"

"How I'll feel. I think if I allow the Ghost of Christmas Past in, it will put me in a funk that I can't get out of."

"Do you think your mother will mind if you didn't go?"

"Are you kidding?" Emilie frowned. "My mother would never forgive me. It's a family tradition. Neither snow, sleet, nor grief gets in the way." She forced a smile and a chuckle.

"Surely your mother would understand if you took a pass this year. She's widowed, too, isn't she?"

"My mother?" Emilie asked incredulously. She shook her head. "Yes, she's widowed. My dad died four years ago, but she really doesn't acknowledge my grief. We just don't talk about it. She hasn't mentioned Rob's death since his funeral. It's like it miraculously never happened. I don't know why I expected anything different from her. It's her typical reaction to anything unpleasant. I can remember when I was a child, I would do or say something that would embarrass her—like once one of our nosy neighbors told her I'd had a party while she and my dad were away. Her reaction was to say, 'We must never speak of this again,'" Emilie mocked in her best Southern accent.

She sighed and continued. "That's what it feels like to me, anyway . . . that if we don't talk about it, it didn't happen. And it's so confusing. Whenever my father's birthday comes up or their wedding anniversary, she'll say, 'You know what day it is, don't you?' But Rob's birthday and our anniversary came and went. Not a word. Not a peep."

"Why do you think she doesn't acknowledge your similar situations?"

Emilie tapped a finger on her pursed lips as she thought. "It took me a long time to figure it out, but I think it's too painful for her to accept that I'm having to endure such a difficult loss. I'm sure she knows it's unbearable for me at times—she has to realize that. But I believe for her, it's easier to pretend it never happened—it's easier to pretend that everything is okay. My family is pretty good at denial. Sometimes I wonder if it would be different if my father were still alive. I think he'd mourn with me," she said matter-of-factly.

"It's good that you can recognize that flaw in your mother and not punish her for having it."

There was a distracting and deafening silence in the room that seemed to last forever. Emilie shifted nervously on the couch and heard a small clock on the bookshelf tick loudly—something she hadn't noticed before. She then finally said, "I don't know if this is working for me."

"What isn't working?" Dr. Jeffries peered over his glasses.

"This therapy stuff. I thought I'd be better, but I think I'm getting worse."

"Why do you believe you're getting worse?" Dr. Jeffries asked in his usual emotionless voice.

"I just thought by now I wouldn't feel so sad. It's been almost a year. And I still find myself hoping to get through the day." She told Dr. Jeffries about her Christmas shopping experience the day before.

"It sounds like you had a panic attack. They are usually brought on by fear. Has anything triggered this emotion?"

"I guess it's just kind of tough this time of year."

"In what way?"

Emilie wanted to shriek at him, "What are you, effing stupid? It's the effing 'holidays' you moron!" But instead, she played his game. "I miss having someone to spend the holidays with. I have friends and family, but you know it's not the same. You know, first, you have Thanksgiving, Christmas, and then New Year's all so close together. They're all holidays meant for families. It's a constant reminder that I'm alone. To me, it feels like jab, hook, uppercut. The last one hard and to the gut. Just when I made it through Thanksgiving and think I'm going to be okay, then comes Christmas and pow." Emilie mocked a boxer's punch. "Then comes New Year's." Her hand mimicked a perfect uppercut. "I feel like I'm in the ring with a prizefighter. I'm not sure which will be the knockout punch." She thought her metaphor was clever, and that made her smile a little. "It's just a lot to take in a short amount of time."

Dr. Jeffries nodded. "You mentioned at the beginning of our appointment that you were fearful of a setback. That's probably what triggered your experience while shopping."

Emilie furrowed her brow and thought carefully. "I think I don't want to ever feel the pain I felt when he died. I don't want to feel that way again." Her insides quaked as her mind flashed back to that day and the days soon after.

Dr. Jeffries nodded. "That's why you are working so hard to deal with the grief."

Emilie continued. "I still miss him very much, and I miss the things we used to do, just the two of us. You know, sort of like our traditions. The holidays are just so full of memories."

"Like what?"

"Well, my husband loved Christmas. He really did. I think because he never really wanted to grow up. It's funny. His immaturity is what I loved and hated most about him." Emilie looked down and wiped a tear from her eye. She took a deep gulp, trying to clear the lump in her throat that popped up whenever she had provoked memories.

"Every year he couldn't wait to see those Christmas cartoons—Rudolph the Red-Nosed Reindeer, Frosty the Snowman, and The Grinch. He loved them all. If one of them was on twice, we watched it twice. It was almost like an obsession. Last year, I bought him all three DVDs, but you know, he never opened the boxes. He really just liked watching them on TV for some reason. I think it brought back good memories or something.

"He also loved to decorate, almost to the point of being tacky." She smiled. "And we would go and find the biggest tree and chop it down ourselves. It usually hung too long on our car roof and rarely made it into our house without some major hacksaw modifications. He was always so proud of the tree—he would spend hours cleaning the windows of our living room and moving the furniture until the tree was the focal point. He wanted the neighbors to drive by and say, 'Wow, what a tree.' Now, whenever I see a tree tied to the top of a car, I get sad. I know that tree is going to a happy home and a family eager to celebrate the holidays. I'm not going to decorate this year. No tree, no lights. Why bother?"

"I'm sure this time of year can seem overwhelming. You don't have to do anything you don't want to," Dr. Jeffries said, as if he was giving her his approval. He shifted in his chair. "You've talked a lot about what your husband liked to do to get ready for Christmas. How about you? Was there anything you particularly enjoyed doing this time of year?"

"Me? I guess I liked to bake cookies. Even though it was just the two of us, I would spend days baking, just like my mom did. I would take most into work so that we wouldn't eat them all. This week someone at work said, 'I can't wait for Emilie's cookies this year,' and in my head, I was like, 'Are you kidding? What's wrong with you? Don't you know my husband died? Don't you know I've canceled Christmas?'" She rolled her eyes. "I just wish that people would recognize that I've had a tough year. You know, cut me some slack."

"How can they, when you don't let them know how you're feeling?" Dr. Jeffries said.

Emilie thought about what he said. "Yeah, I know you're right.

I realize people see what I want them to see of me—the smiling, laughing, happy-go-lucky person when in reality, there are times when I couldn't feel more opposite."

"Do you think sad emotions are a sign of weakness? Are you trying to portray this pillar of strength for everyone else's benefit?" Dr. Jeffries clenched his fist and pressed it to his chest to emphasize what he was saying.

"Yes, I guess so. I don't like to ask people for help. I never have. It was hard when Rob first died because I couldn't do everything, but I sure tried. And I don't take it as a compliment when people say, 'You are so strong' because I know on the inside, I'm not. I guess I've just gotten used to portraying that pillar of strength on the outside." Emilie clenched her fist to her chest. "That is made of goo on the inside." She opened her hand as if she were letting all the goo ooze out.

"You know, Emilie, you've been through a major tragedy. I think a little vulnerability wouldn't be perceived as weakness."

Emilie shifted her eyes away from Dr. Jeffries and then looked at her feet. "It's easier to pretend that everything is okay."

"Does that sound familiar to you? It may be easier to pretend everything is okay because that's the way you were raised. But in reality, if it's not okay, it's harder to pretend it is okay. I tell some of my patients who are dealing with loss to start a journal."

Emilie shrugged. "Maybe," she said. "I do like to write."

"It will be helpful to give your feelings a voice. It's okay to be sad and scared this time of year."

"Okay," she said.

Click. Jot. Nod—with just the slightest hint of a smile.

17

It was just past ten when Emilie woke on Christmas morning. She got out of bed and yawned. The sight of a dusting of snow on the ground made her smile. It rarely snowed in December, and snow on Christmas Day was always special. Without hesitation, she looked up to the heavens and said, "Thanks, Rob. Merry Christmas to you too!"

Being with her family the night before turned out not to be so bad. She'd forgotten how much she enjoyed singing Silent Night at mass by candlelight. Seeing her niece and nephew hurry the family to open gifts so they could get home before Santa caught them awake amused her. And at the end of the night, her mother's long and hard hug said all that Emilie wanted to hear even though no words were spoken.

She walked into the kitchen with Puddie in tow and poured herself a cup of day-old coffee. A two-minute zap in the microwave should bring it to life. While she waited for the coffee to heat up, she drummed her fingers on the countertop. With one minute and forty-five seconds left, she walked into her office and picked up the spiral notebook she'd bought two days earlier. She cradled the notebook in her arm and went back into the kitchen just as the microwave signaled the coffee was ready. She opened the microwave door. Steam poured from the black liquid. With a paper towel in hand, she wrapped her fingers around the handle of the mug and slowly brought it out. She carefully walked to the couch and put the mug on the coffee table. She took the notebook from the crook of her arm and removed the pen that was nestled in the spiral. She opened the cover of the book. On the first page, she wrote: Christmas. She thought for a minute or two and then added: Today is the first Christmas without Rob. *How do I feel?* She put the notebook down and picked up her coffee. She searched for the TV remote in the crevice of the couch cushions and turned on the TV. She scrolled through the channel guide: channel two—*It's a Wonderful Life*; channel four—*Love, Actually*; channel five—*The Gift of the Magi*. She turned the TV off. She picked up her notebook again. *How do I feel?* She wrote. *I just want to make it through this day.*

• • •

Two hours later, she gathered Colin's present, kissed Puddie on the forehead, and headed for downtown Baltimore. Colin lived in a renovated row house in South Baltimore, just a few blocks from Viv. By the time she arrived, the snow had melted, and the day had actually become a bit balmy.

She found a spot on the street in front of Colin's house and was proud that it only took her three attempts to parallel park—albeit more perpendicular than parallel in this case—with the back end of her car sticking out a bit too much. She got out of her car and walked the short distance to Colin's house. With his gift in her hand, she knocked on his door.

Colin greeted her wearing a Santa hat. "Merry Christmas!" He raised his hand, revealing a sprig of mistletoe, and planted a big kiss on her cheek.

"Merry Christmas to you too! Yum. It smells good in here. I didn't know you could cook."

"Excuse me! I cook very well, thanks to Honey Baked Ham!" He smiled as helped her off with her coat. "How are you doing today? You holding up?" he asked as he hung her coat in the closet.

"Yeah, not too bad . . . I'm okay . . . well, no, not really," Emilie said. Colin hugged her and stroked her hair. "I know, I know. It's tough. The holidays, they suck."

"It's just so lonely."

"It'll get better. I promise. It will." His voice tapered off to a whisper, and he hugged her harder.

"I'll hold you to that promise," she said with a little laugh and pulled out of his embrace. "You know, I feel so bad for saying this, but I just want these stupid holidays to be over. Enough already with the merriment."

"Hear, hear!" Colin raised his hand in a cheering motion and gave her a knowing smile. They walked into his living room.

He had a white leather couch that was punctuated with two furry black pillows—that Emilie playfully referred to as Colin's pets—and a frilly red throw blanket folded neatly and draped over the arm. The coffee table was a dark-colored wood with a glass top and had wicker baskets tucked in its caverns. It was a table Emilie helped him pick out one day when they were leafing through a Pottery Barn catalog.

In the corner was a white artificial tree decorated only with big red balls. Emilie laughed. "A white tree? Really, Colin?"

"A white tree is very in."

"Said no one ever," she said.

Emilie sat on the couch, which was much more comfortable than it looked. "I feel like I'm in a marshmallow factory," she said.

"Nothing wrong with that," Colin said. He did not sit down. Instead, he said, "Oh! Oh! I can't wait anymore. I want you to open your gift." Colin walked to the tree and pick up a lone gift bag under it.

"Before we eat? That ham smells pretty good." Emilie secretly feared that Colin had out-gifted her, and she didn't want to be embarrassed. "Let's wait," she said.

"Nope." He handed a shiny red bag to her. "Go on," he said, as he sat on the couch next to her.

Emilie took the bag and peeked inside. She was a little puzzled at first to see a folded piece of paper nestled among tissue paper. She pulled the paper out of the bag and unfolded it.

"Go ahead, read it aloud," Colin said.

First, she read the piece of paper to herself. Upon letting the typewritten words sink in, she sighed. She had definitely not been "out-gifted." "What did you do?" she asked.

"Go on. Read it. Read it," he said. And added, "I can't wait."

Emilie stared at her friend in disbelief and not in a good way. She sighed audibly before saying, "This entitles you to a six-month subscription to SecondChance.com."

"It's a dating website for midlife daters. Like you and me." There was glee in his voice.

"Yeah, I know." Emilie felt a little nauseous. "Thanks. Really, thanks." *Thanks really, no thanks, Colin!* She refolded the piece of paper, creasing hard the folds, put it back in the bag, and vowed never to redeem the gift. She was slightly irritated that Colin would think this was something she wanted. "Really, you shouldn't have," she said with a hint of sarcasm. A few weeks earlier Emilie had secretly peeked at a few dating websites, including Secondchances. com, to see what was out there, but she never went as far as to set up a profile. As much as she wanted to meet someone, dating— online or not—was just too scary.

"Okay now, don't get mad, but I already created your profile and . . . guess what?"

Oh, God. "What?" Her heart raced, secretly fearing what was next.

"You already have guys interested in you!" Colin leaped to his feet and clapped.

"What? What do you mean you created a profile for me and that there are guys interested in me?" Her voice shook as she spoke.

"Oh, I knew you needed a nudge, so I gave it to you. Believe me, you'll thank me later, especially after you go out with 'Nevermore' or 'TedEBear.' Come on, let's check them out."

She closed her eyes, not trying to hide her disgust. She wanted to leave but was sure her legs would give way if she stood up. "Colin, this is a lot to take in right now. Give me a few minutes to digest this. Please tell me you didn't pretend you were me and communicate with anyone." Emilie tried to brace herself for what she feared was the answer.

"No, no. That would be too weird. I did blow some kisses from you to some of the guys, though. Okay, admittedly, that sounds weirder than it is."

"What? What do you mean, blow kisses?"

"That's how you let them know you're interested."

"But I'm not interested," she said. The knot in her stomach was by now the size of a watermelon. "Colin, why would you do this to me?"

"Oh, come on now. I only blew kisses to the guys who I know you'd have a connection with, like 'Nevermore' and 'TedEBear.' and looks like they're interested, too, because they sent you emails . . . which I didn't read, I'll have you know."

"Why do I doubt that?"

"Come on, let's check these guys out and then we'll eat." Colin reached out and grabbed her hand, pulling her off the couch.

"C'mon." Colin tugged at her arm and led her downstairs to

his home office.

Once there, he sat in the chair and turned on the computer. He logged onto the website. Emilie's mouth fell open when her profile and picture filled the entire screen. "Hello, Emerald_Eyes," Secondchances.com greeted.

"Oh, God, Colin, why did you use that picture of me from that day we spent on the lake? I look like a beached whale."

"No, you don't! You look beautiful. That bathing suit makes your boobs look awesome. Guys really like that. Plus, they want to see all the goods, you know, no junk in your trunk. Look, here's one of you with a suit from that cocktail party we went to. Grrrr!" He said with a wink. "That way, they'll know you aren't some bimbo."

Emilie began reading the profile Colin had written for her.

EMERALD_EYES

> *STOP! Look no further! I am the girl you've been looking for all your life. I am a laid-back, low-maintenance gal who loves to laugh and have a good time. I enjoy writing and think a perfect date includes a hot dog and a beer from Camden Yards. I love to travel and see new things. The only baggage I have is what I take on my trips. I was widowed much too young and am now ready to write chapter two with a wonderful new guy. Let's see how much fun we can have.*

Satisfied, Emilie nodded. Suddenly her fears subsided and, if she had to admit it, she started to feel a little excited. "Okay, I have to admit, not too bad." She smiled as she shook her head. "I'm still mad at you, but not as mad."

"Look, look at your emails. There are two. Come on, let's read them!"

The first email was from "Nevermore," a forty-nine-year-old divorced computer programmer from Baltimore.

"Hi Emerald, thanks for the kiss. You're real cute. I enjoyed your profile. Email me back if you want to chat. Erik." Attached to an email was a picture of a man in a Ravens jersey with a curly mop of brown hair and a bright smile. Emilie quickly read his profile to see if he was, indeed, someone she'd be interested in.

"So, he's age-appropriate . . . two kids and lives in Baltimore. Says he likes to sail and is a big Ravens fan. His name is in reference to a Poe quote, so he reads. That's good, I guess."

"Yep—let's respond to the Raven. Go ahead," Colin got up from the chair and motioned for Emilie to sit in it.

Once she was seated, she said, "What should I say?"

Placing his hands firmly on her shoulders, he nuzzled close to her neck. "Just say, 'Erik, thanks for your email. I liked your profile too. Tell me a little more about yourself.'"

Emilie typed as Colin dictated. "Do you feel a little like Cyrano?" She laughed.

"Why yes, I do, but only if you let me go on your first date and hide in the bushes."

The email from "TedEBear" was similar. He listed his age as forty-five; he was a never-married insurance agent who lived in Ellicott City. His photo, only a very corporate-looking headshot, showed a very polished professional man with steely blue eyes and hair that was about to thin out. Emilie sent a similar response to him.

As she hit send to TedE, she turned to Colin and said, "There. Okay, now can we eat?"

"Yes, you must be hungry. You worked hard." Colin said, reaching his arm around her and pulling her closer. "You know I only want what's best for you, don't you?"

"Yes, I know. I guess I'm just a little scared. What if these guys are creeps—or serial killers?"

"Then you'll meet someone else . . . if you're still alive." He raised his eyebrows in mock horror. "Just kidding. It's a process. You'll be fine, but it may take time. Remember, Emilie, don't settle. Date around until it feels right. I do know whoever ends up with you will be the luckiest guy in the world."

"Thanks, Colin. I really do mean it. I do miss having someone in my life. Well, you know . . . someone other than you," she said. Getting up she added: "Oh, I almost forgot—you have to open your present. Don't worry, it isn't as bold as what you gave me."

She handed Colin a box wrapped in gold foil paper. He wasted no time tearing the paper from the box. He opened the box and peeled back the tissue paper inside. "Ah! I love it, love it, love it!" he said. He looked at the label and then put the sweater on. "Armani, nothing is better than Armani. Feel how soft it is." He reached his arm toward Emilie, who gave the sweater a stroke. "And black is sooo slimming. Thank you! You are the best!"

"I'm glad you like it. I think it's real cashmere."

"Ah! Cashmere. Yes, that reminds me. There's this guy at work, that's going to Africa next week. I told him about how we put some of Rob's ashes on the Rocky statue last month, and he offered to take some of Rob to the Namib Desert. What do you think of that idea?"

"Will he really do that for me? I don't even know him."

"Yes. I told him about the idea of how you're putting Rob's ashes all over the world, and he loved it. It would be a great way to get Rob to another continent."

"Okay, I'll get you some ashes to give to him. Rob was always fascinated with Africa." Emilie said. She then paused. "Um, Colin?

How did cashmere remind you of the Namib Desert?"

"Isn't cashmere made from camel hair?"

"Maybe. Actually, I'm not sure," she said.

• • •

A week later, on New Year's Eve, Emilie received an email from Colin's coworker.

Dear Emilie,

Greetings from Namibia. Thank you for letting me be a part of your special project. Along with my condolences, I send you pictures of Rob's trip to Africa.

Sincerely,
Ed Williams.

Emilie clicked on the attachment, which was a photomontage of Ed carrying the purple bag to a spot in the desert where he scattered the ashes. Emilie closed her eyes as she touched her hand to the computer monitor. She printed out Ed's email and taped it to a blank page in her journal.

18

Emilie walked into her house and closed the front door behind her. *Why did you let Colin talk you into going on that date?* Keeping one hand on the knob for support, she threw her purse on the floor and removed her brand new, five-inch black stilettos, one foot at a time, and carefully placed them on the floor beside her. Looking down at her newest favorite things, she said, "Definitely not Louboutin worthy." After five emails in ten days, TedEBear finally got the courage to ask her out to dinner, and she had the courage to accept. She slowly slid her body down the door until her bottom touched the floor and her legs sprawled out in front of her. This caused her hot pink pencil skirt to ride up, exposing her thighs and probably her underwear. She rubbed her forehead, trying to erase her feeling of exhaustion—or, more likely, the memory of the evening.

While she was still sitting at the door, Puddie came bounding into the foyer and pounced on her lap, kissing her cheek and ear.

"All right, all right. I'm happy to see you too!" Emilie stroked the dog and turned her face, so her chin got more of the licks than her ear. "Aw, Puddie, you definitely how to make mommy smile when she needs one." She picked him up and kissed him between the eyes before putting him gently back on the floor. Shifting her body to one side, she got up and carried her purse and shoes into the bedroom. The dog dutifully followed.

Before putting them back on the closet shelf, she admired her red-soled shoes--not sure what prompted her to make such a purchase. She used her hands to tap the heels of the shoes together and said, "There's no place like home, there's no place like home, there's no place like home." But unlike Dorothy in the Wizard of Oz, no scarecrow, tin man, or cowardly lion would rescue her.

After she had undressed, she threw her dress on a heaping pile of dry cleaner-bound items in her closet and put on a pair of sweatpants and a T-shirt. Eight o'clock, just a mere ninety minutes after she left the house for her first date in years, and she was all ready for bed. After pulling down the covers, she propped up two pillows against the headboard and sat against them. Grabbing her purse, she fumbled around for her cell phone. Once she found it, she punched in speed dial number one.

"Hey," she said as she squeezed the phone between her shoulder and ear while reaching behind with her hand to make the pillows more supportive.

"Hey, Em, what's up? It's still early. Shouldn't you be on your date with TedEBear?" Colin's voice was playful.

"More like TedEBore. Oh, Colin, it was awful. Just awful. He carries pictures of his cats in his wallet! Who does that?" Emilie shuddered at the flashback. "Like professional posed pictures—you know—like the ones we took at school when we were kids."

"So, what's wrong with that?"

"Oh, nothing, really." She rubbed her temple, which had begun to pound. "Do you remember Newman from Seinfeld? Well, this guy could be his twin, only with less personality. I mean, he just kept staring at me. He never laughed. Never smiled. It was weird." She closed her eyes and let out a deep sigh.

"Sounds like there was no chemistry," Colin stated the obvious.

"No chemistry. There wasn't even a test tube in the room," she said.

"Okay, okay, so he wasn't the one. Give him another chance. He probably was nervous."

"Puleeze! I really couldn't wait for it to be over. I only ordered an appetizer, you know, trying to speed things along."

"Hmm. I was just about to say, 'at least you got a good meal out of it.'"

"Oh, not even. He took me to that steakhouse in Silver Spring. When he told me to meet him there, I thought 'great.' You know I love me some good steak."

"Yep, I know the place. Real good steak."

"But, just a few minutes in and I couldn't wait to leave. He starts staring at me, not saying much. I mean, staring like a serial killer look. After I had eaten my French onion soup, I told him I wasn't very hungry, and he goes, 'Do you want to take in a movie?' I think my mouth must have fallen wide open—I mean, how out of it was this guy? I thought he felt the same way, you know, no real connection."

"Come on, give him a break. Like you, he probably hasn't dated in a while. What guy wouldn't want to spend more time with you? You're beautiful, smart, funny—he probably figured he had some arm candy, and he couldn't wait to show you off!"

"Well, he's going to have to find his candy somewhere else. I told him nicely that I had a good time, but I really didn't think I was ready to date because of Rob's death and all. It was probably too soon for me."

"Nice! And she scores two points for appropriate use of the widow card."

Emilie said, "Yeah, whatever. So, get this." She adjusted her back and got deeper into the covers. "As soon as I get in my car, he's calling me and asking me out again. Said he felt something, and he would be patient with me, given what I had been through. I should have just said, 'Hell no!' but he caught me off guard because I really didn't recognize the number—but I will now. I labeled him 'Newman' in my phone. I said, 'Let me think about it.'" Emilie's sighs grew louder. "What a mess. Colin, why did I let you talk me into this? I could kill you."

"You could, but you won't. Actually, one day, you will thank me for this."

"That's doubtful." There was a pause in the conversation until Emilie added, "Oh, Colin, what am I going to do if he keeps calling me? Or worse yet, what if I run into him? He works downtown. I could see him somewhere." She paused. "You don't think he actually could be a stalker or a serial killer, do you?"

"No, I don't," Colin said.

"He has my number. What if he finds out where I live?"

"Calm down. I don't think that'll happen."

"What do you mean? You showed me how to google him. You said you google all of your dates to find out where they live."

"Yes, but I don't think it's all that accurate," Colin said.

"Really?" Emilie felt her heartbeat in her throat.

"Look, I've been on about a million dates and only had to take out one restraining order."

"Oh, that makes me feel a lot better." One was one too many.

"If the widow card doesn't work, go to Plan B . . . tell him you realized you were gay. That worked on this girl from high school who stalked me."

"But you are gay!"

"Yeah, but no one knew that then. Well, except for me. So, who's next? 'Nevermore?'"

"His name is Erik, but I don't know. I think tonight set me back. I don't think I have the energy to do this again."

"Trust me. I only want what's best for you. Online dating

works. Just give it a chance."

Emilie detected a smile in Colin's voice.

"I know from experience," he said.

She sensed he was holding something back. "Okay, spill it."

"I was going to save this for when I see you, but last night I had a lovely date with this new guy, on Tinder. Tony. I don't know, Em. I have a feeling about this one."

19

After a few days of pestering, and against her better judgment, Emilie let Colin talk her into giving dating another try. Two weeks later was her first date with Erik, a.k.a. "Nevermore," and she had that same nervous feeling she had all the other times she was about to meet a new man. Learning from her failed attempt with "TedEBear," she did things differently. She and Erik didn't just email each other, they also talked on the phone three times, so at least she knew there was some chemistry. There was always a light, fun mood when they talked, and he laughed at appropriate times when Emilie said something funny. In the back of her mind, she kept telling herself, Colin's right, TedE may have been a frog, but Erik could be a prince.

Feeling there *may* be a connection with Erik, she got a manicure and pedicure and spent a little too much on her new mauve, paisley print dress—all things that gave her added confidence.

After showering, she opened a box containing a newly purchased body-shaping undergarment. She'd heard Annette talk about them putting "all the junk in the right places." Hoping the garment would hide the ten pounds she'd gained in the past year, she took them out of the cardboard wrapping and held them up. *Geez, looks like it wouldn't fit a two-year-old. How on Earth is that going to fit me?* She looked at the size chart on the label again and confirmed her selection. She stepped into them. Then she tugged and pulled the constricting garment to mid-thigh, where the body-suit would not budge any further. She began to hop while tugging some more, trying to shimmy it, trying to get her body into the suit. Once she had made it past her hips, she shimmied some more until the underwear was cinching her waist. With one big hoist, she slung the right strap over her shoulder and then the left. Almost out of breath and sweating a little, she stopped to look in the mirror and was wowed at what she saw. Somehow the tight material had enough give so that she could breathe, but enough restriction to give the illusion of a perfect hourglass figure. Annette was right—who would have ever thunk it?

After finishing dressing, styling her hair, and applying makeup, she took a deep breath. *Oh God,* she thought. *What if this doesn't suck? What if you like him, but he doesn't like you? What if you're clueless like TedE was?* The 'what ifs' frightened her enough to hesitate. *No one will blame me if I cancel at the last minute.* She walked to her bed and sat down. *You can do this.* She told herself. *Do you want to be alone for the rest of your life?* She steadied herself as she stood. She walked to the hall closet, removed her coat from a hanger, and put it on.

When she arrived at the restaurant in Baltimore's Harbor East section, Erik was already there. He greeted her with a firm hand-shake. "You must be Emilie. I'd recognize those green eyes any-where." He gave her a quick once over that was obvious, but not in a lecherous way.

Emilie had to admit she liked what she saw. He was about a foot taller than her. He wore jeans and a brown tweed jacket that kind of matched his hair. He looked very much like his picture, except his hair was slicked back. Knowing the unwanted anxiety curly hair can cause, Emilie smiled when she saw curls poking out from behind his ears. *A curly-haired man after my own heart.*

She shook his hand and smiled back. "Have you been here long?"

"Nope, just got here. I made a reservation, so I think they can seat us now." The beer he was drinking was nearly gone, indicating he was being kind and not telling her the full truth.

The restaurant, named Lucky's, was crowded, definitely one of the trendier places in the city. Its floor was covered in pennies, all of them were heads up. It was a small space, seating only about one hundred people with a bar that wrapped around one whole sidewall.

Emilie and Erik followed the hostess as she weaved through the crowd and led them to a nice corner table in the back. The tables were very close together, with only about six inches separating them, and there was a continuous bench that lined the back brick wall. Emilie chose the bench side and instantly regretted it. She imagined how she looked to Erik as she scooted in, her body shifting the tablecloth slightly and the place settings clanged. The hostess caught Emilie's wineglass before it fell over.

"I think we have to fill that pronto," Erik said with a smile. "Can you bring us a bottle of," he pointed as he read the wine list, which doubled as a table tent. "This chardonnay?"

After the hostess left, Erik leaned forward and whispered, "You look much better than your pictures." He winked, then smiled.

"Thanks." Emilie looked away as she felt her face redden.

"I don't know how many of these things you have been on, but let me tell you, most of the girls touch up their photos or something. I think it's fraud." Erik's laugh made Emilie feel at ease.

"Most women lie about their age. Some by a few years, some by a decade. It doesn't really matter to me, other than I find it fascinating."

"I guess I'm new to all of this because everything on my profile was the truth. I figured, why start a potential relationship with a lie?"

Erik nodded.

A server named Paul brought them the wine Erik ordered. As Paul uncorked the bottle, he read from a card describing the day's specials. "We have an ahi steak seared with citrus butter served with broccoli and rice pilaf and a filet mignon, eight ounces, topped with jumbo lump crabmeat and a mornay sauce served with garlic mashed potatoes and asparagus." Paul then poured the wine and stood poised to take their order.

Erik motioned his hand toward Emilie and said, "Ladies first."

"I'll have the filet special, medium," she said.

"Make that two," Erik said. He closed his menu, collected Emilie's, and handed them both back to Paul.

"Cheers," Erik said, raising his glass. "To meeting someone special—and not to mention honest!"

Emilie raised her glass and tapped it against his.

"Your profile says you like to write," he said.

"Yeah, you know, kind of a repressed English major, I guess." She took a sip of the wine. "I always thought I'd write the next great American novel, but instead I write press releases."

"That's cool. Cooler than typing computer code eight hours a day."

"Computer codes seem so intimidating to me. I'm not sure I understand how the inside of a computer works."

"I take it you aren't a repressed video gamer," he said with a chuckle.

Emilie laughed. "You'd be right." She returned the wineglass to the table and realized her hand was not shaking. This was a good sign.

• • •

After dinner, they walked outside the restaurant and stood on the sidewalk. "Thanks for dinner," Emilie said, breaking the awkward moment of silence.

"Emilie, I had such a great time. I don't want the evening to end, but I have to confess, the Ravens are in the playoffs, and I really want to catch the second half. I hope you don't mind."

"Of course not! I'm impressed that you even stayed through the first half. I had a great time too."

"I was wondering. This might seem forward, but please don't take it that way. I just live over there." He pointed to his left. "Just a few blocks away. Would you like to go to my house and watch some of the game?"

Emilie paused. "Hmm. No, I probably shouldn't. I don't really know you that well."

"Don't worry, to quote Popeye, 'I yams, who I yams,'" he added a mock Popeye laugh. "Oh, scratch that. It came out a little creepier than it was supposed to. Even I wouldn't go anywhere alone now with me," he said. "Here, I'll show you my driver's license, or better yet, my Facebook page." He reached under his parka and pulled out his phone from the front pocket of his jeans. Once he had the phone in his hand, he removed the glove on his other hand with his teeth and then pressed the Facebook app. "See, nothing but a normal guy." He handed his phone to Emilie.

His Facebook page had the same profile picture that was featured on the online dating website. Emilie blushed when she read his most recent post: "On my way to meet Emilie. Hope she's as hot as her pix. Wish me luck!"—which had twelve likes and apparently two comments.

Believing no serial killer would list his next victim on Facebook, Emilie handed his phone back to him. "Okay," she said. "But I can only stay for a little while. And first I have to text my friend. That way, if you chop me up, they'll be able to find the body quicker."

Erik smiled at her. "Oh, and by the way, I plan to post later today. Lucky me, she was hotter than her pix!"

Before they started walking to Erik's house, Emilie sent Colin a quick thumbs-up emoji text and received the one with the heart-eyes cat in return. Erik's house was just a few blocks from the restaurant, and even though it was a bitterly cold January night, Emilie didn't want to be anywhere but where she was. For a few hours now, she had been able to forget the rough year she'd had and was excited to be with someone with whom she felt a real connection.

Once in his house, he took her coat and hung it along with his in a closet full of tennis shoes and sports gear. He turned on the TV in the living room and found the game. The Ravens were leading the Steelers seventeen to ten. Erik motioned for her to sit on his couch and quickly grabbed the Baltimore Sun newspaper that was strewn on the floor. "Would you like something to drink? I have a nice bottle of wine I've been saving."

"Sure, that sounds good." She tried to hide the nervousness she was feeling, but was afraid the quiver in her voice gave it away.

Erik returned with two glasses of white wine, which he almost spilled at the sight of a Steeler fumble. From the stains on the carpet, it wouldn't have been the first time something was spilled. The place was definitely a bachelor pad. When Erik sat down, he put the two glasses of wine on the coffee table and smoothly put his arm around her while keeping one eye on the game. "Go! Go! Go!" he cheered as a Raven picked up the loose ball and ran toward the end zone. "You know, if they win, I have tickets to next week's semifinals. Would you like to go?"

She thought about it. "Yeah. I'd really like that. Who will they play?"

"It depends on who wins tomorrow. Probably Indianapolis.

They should be able to beat the Chargers."

By the fourth quarter, it was clear Baltimore was going to win. Erik leaned in and gave Emilie a long, wet kiss. She welcomed his advance, and the two began making out like high school kids. Soon Erik was on top of her, kissing her neck and groping her breast. She began to panic. *Oh, God, he's going to feel the Spanx!* She didn't want Erik to feel the seams of the garment which ran from under her arm to her knees. She removed his hands from her chest and stopped kissing him. "I'm sorry. I can't do this. Not now. But I want to—it isn't that." She was breathless. "It's just . . ."

"It's okay. I understand. It is a little soon." Erik said as he sat up. "I'm very attracted to you. I'm sure you can tell. But I'll be a good boy. Believe me, when I invited you back here, it really was to watch the game, not to jump your bones."

Emilie smiled and got up. "I guess I should go."

"So, do you still want to go to the game next week? I promise I'll keep my hands to myself." Erik winked.

"In that case, forget it!" Emilie said with a laugh.

• • •

When Emilie got home, she picked up her journal that had lain on the coffee table for several weeks. *January 20,* she wrote. *First date with Erik. Relieved that it was actually good. No, actually pretty great. Something to look forward to for a change.*

20

It was Valentine's Day, one month—actually three weeks, four days, and eight hours since Emilie first met Erik—but who was really counting? While she was eagerly anticipating spending the "holiday for couples" as a couple, she couldn't totally escape the fear of being let down. Her relationship with Erik was too new to expect a big deal, but if she was being honest, she wanted the big deal. She secretly hoped that Erik would tell her she was the love of his life, sweep her off her feet, and they would ride into the sunset—to live happily ever after. When she'd catch herself rehearsing "I feel the same way, Erik," she would immediately talk herself back down to reality. After all, it had only been a month—or actually, three weeks, four days, eight hours, and fifteen minutes.

Tonight would be special. They were going to meet Colin and his new "friend," Tony, at Tony's family's restaurant in Little Italy. And then, Emilie imagined, she and Erik would come back to her place, and maybe, just maybe, he'd spend the night.

When she got home from work later that day, she took Puddie on the "express route"—no dogs to engage in a bark fest and no tempting bushes to linger and sniff. Once inside her house, she kicked off her shoes and quickly undressed.

As she showered, she decided to shave . . . all the way up. For a month, she and Erik had been making out like teenagers. Occasionally she'd let him touch her underneath her bra, but the tight-fitting body shaper stayed in place. Taking it off was as difficult as putting it on. She told Colin it was like unleashing the beast . . . or beasts were more like it. Everything that was held firmly in place by the garment seemed to pop out with force, like a slingshot. She knew removing the garment in front of Erik could not, or would not, ever happen. The bodysuit became a chastity belt of sorts.

Opening her lingerie drawer, she picked up the form-cinching garment and held it up, stretching it out with both hands. She folded it up and put it back in the drawer. Without it, she'd be taking a risk and would be letting it all hang out and around. She went to her closet and reached up to retrieve the black jersey knit wraparound dress, which had been hanging above the doorframe for more than a week now. She put it on and smoothed it around her body. Then she gazed at herself in the mirror. Her waist was less defined and her hips a little fuller, but she knew she couldn't hide her body forever. It is what it is.

The doorbell rang just as she was spritzing perfume and stepping into the scent.

When she opened the door, Erik greeted her with a big bouquet of pink roses.

"Happy Valentine's Day!" He leaned in and kissed her on the lips. He handed her the flowers and a heart-shaped box. "Oh, and I brought you some candy too."

Emilie smiled. "Yum! Reese's, my favorite. You remembered. How sweet." She kissed him on the cheek.

"Hey there, Puddie!" Erik leaned down and pet Puddie on the head. "I got you something too." He pulled a heart-shaped rawhide chew from his coat pocket.

Puddie stood on his hind legs to get a better whiff of his gift. Without decorum, he snatched it from Erik's hand and ran into the bedroom.

Emilie went to the kitchen to find a vase for the flowers. Unwrapping them from the red cellophane, she was careful not to let the thorns attack her as she lifted them to her nose to breathe in their fragrance. Underneath the sink, she found a cut glass vase. She drew some water from the sink and dropped the "Flower Feed" into it and then the roses, arranging the blooms until they filled the vase. She gave them one last sniff before she grabbed the white gift bag, adorned with red hearts of various sizes, from the kitchen counter, and went back into the living room. Erik had taken his coat off and was settled on the couch. He looked a little boyish with his dress shirt bunched up a little at the neck, a sure sign it didn't fit and that he probably didn't wear it that often.

"Here, I made you something. I hope you like it," Emilie said, handing the bag to Erik.

Erik took the bag and peeked. After removing the white tissue paper, he pulled out a purple and black striped knitted scarf. "Wow! You *made* this? You're kidding, right?" He stood up and wrapped it around his neck, tossing the left side with a grand gesture, and put his hands on his hips. "There! What do you think? Pretty dapper, eh?"

"Do you like it? It's the Ravens' colors."

"Yes, really, I do like it. And I really do like you!" He kissed her and hugged her tight.

"I really like you too," she whispered. "Come on, I think the reservation is for seven."

He helped her with her coat. And she was happy to see that he kept his scarf tied around his neck as he put on his coat.

• • •

When they got to Mama Rosa's, an older woman with teased,

white-blond hair greeted them. "Happy Valentine's Day, hon. Do you have a reservation?" she said in a thick Baltimore accent.

"We're meeting Tony," Emilie said, struggling to remember Tony's last name. She turned her head and saw Colin's hand waving high in the air from a booth at the far end of the restaurant. "Oh, there they are," she said as she walked toward them.

Black-and-white photos of the same man hugging various celebrities—Baltimore's favorite daughter, Devine—adorned the walls at eye level. The tables were covered in red and white checkered plastic cloths. Each had an old bottle of Chianti, with a white candle in the mouth and with wax dripping down all sides. Colin and Tony were sitting across from each other in a booth. A carafe of red wine on the table was about two-thirds empty. Tony was a nice-looking guy, definitely Italian, with dark hair and eyes and an olive complexion. But Emilie wasn't surprised; Colin usually attracted very attractive men.

When Emilie and Erik approached the table, Colin scooted out of the booth to hug Emilie. Breaking away, he held her hand in his and said, "Emilie, this is Tony. Tony, Emilie." Colin dragged her into the booth, so she was sitting next to him. And Erik complied by sitting next to Tony.

"So nice to meet you." Once Colin released her hand, Emilie extended it out across the table to Tony. "I've heard so much about you."

"Only good things, I hope." Tony smiled widely as he spoke.

"Well, of course only good things." She turned to Colin and smiled. Turning back toward Tony, she said, "Thank you so much for including us for dinner. I'll bet you had to turn people away on a night like tonight."

Tony nodded slightly and took a sip of his wine.

Emilie looked over at Erik and gestured. "And this is Erik."

Erik raised his hand. "I know, I know, you've heard good things about me too!" His eyes twinkled as he chuckled.

Colin grabbed Emilie's hand again, this time under the table, and squeezed it hard. She turned to Colin again, and he gave her the "This guy's okay" look that only best friends could read from each other.

Tony emptied the carafe by pouring Emilie and Erik small glasses of wine and motioned for the waitress to refill it. "To mid-life dating," Tony said, raising his glass of wine.

"Hear, hear," Colin said.

"Cheers," Emilie added.

"You have to look your mate in the eye when you say that or else you'll have seven years of bad sex," Colin said.

"Colin!" Emilie wiped from her lip the little bit of wine she nearly spit out.

"It's true," Colin looked directly at Tony.

Emilie looked everywhere but in Erik's direction.

When the waitress returned with the second carafe, Tony ordered their meal family-style. They started with minestrone soup and then moved on to an abundance of food: veal marsala, chicken piccata, lasagna, and four giant meatballs. All were house specialties, and deservedly so. Being sure to take a bit of each entrée, Emilie couldn't decide which one she liked the best, but did go back for seconds on the chicken. During dinner, Emilie looked at Erik with pride, as he told funny story after funny story about his pre-Emilie, midlife dating experiences. "The bar was here," he said, placing one hand under the table. "And when Emilie told me she never had a restraining order placed against her, I said, 'She's perfect!'"

"I agree. She is perfect." Colin winked at her. Emilie was relieved Erik fit right in with Colin because Colin was a very important part of her life. She couldn't be with someone who did not accept him.

For dessert, Tony ordered two pieces of the cannoli cake, his grandma Rosa's special recipe—one she had brought from Italy when she was a teenager, tucked inside her diary. The waitress put one piece across from Colin and Tony, and the other across from Emilie and Erik.

Feeling a little drunk from the two glasses of wine she had with dinner, Emilie reached her index finger into the cake's frosting and swiped a finger full. Within seconds, Erik grabbed her hand with both of his and stuck the frosting finger in his mouth, flickering his tongue against her finger in a very suggestive way. She removed her finger from Erik's mouth and reached for a fork.

"I love cream cheese icing," he said, as his eyes looked deep into hers. Emilie wanted to yell, "Check, please!" but thought it rude to leave right in the middle of dessert. After all, they were Tony's guests.

She took a fork and dug it into the cake and put the treat in her mouth. Savoring the taste, she slowly withdrew the fork. "Wow, is this good!" She put her fork down. When she looked over at Colin, he gave her a knowing wink and tilted his head toward the door.

"But I am so full. I don't think I can eat another bite. Tony, the meal was wonderful, and it was so nice to meet you. I think Erik and I will be going."

Even though Erik was in mid-bite, he seemed to take her lead. With widening eyes, he smiled like a young boy about to open gifts on Christmas Day.

As she stood up from the table, Colin did too. He hugged her and whispered, "Go get some, girl."

Emilie smiled. "You too," she whispered back.

When she and Erik got to her home, before she could close the door, Erik was hugging her from behind and kissing her neck. She turned around to face him and put her arms around his neck and smiled. He reached around to feel for the door and shut it, all the while keeping his gaze on her. He put his hands on her hips and stared at her, and then without a word leaned in and kissed her with his mouth open and rapidly exploring tongue.

She broke away from his kiss, turned her head, and let out a pleasure-filled moan. He began kissing her below her right ear and then let his kisses trail down her neck while his hands groped her breasts.

"Do you want to go into the bedroom?" she whispered.

He pulled away from her and smiled. "I thought you'd never ask."

Emilie grabbed Erik's hand and led him into her bedroom, where Puddie lay asleep on the bed. "Sorry, fella, you got to go." She lifted the little dog and plopped him firmly in the hallway and closed the bedroom door. Erik was sitting on the edge of the bed. She approached him and draped her arms around his neck.

"Are you sure?" He stared intently into her eyes.

Emilie looked him directly in the eyes. "Cheers," she said with a smile.

Erik pulled her even closer as he slowly lay back until the two were lying on the bed, her body on top of his. With one swift move, he rolled her over and was now on top of her. He began kissing her neck as he slipped off the left shoulder of her dress and then moved to reach the right shoulder until her bra was exposed.

"Hmm. You smell so good." His kisses lingered on her neck as he pushed her dress up and deftly rolled down her pantyhose and underwear. Once he got the hose and panties off, he rolled off of her and unbuttoned his oxford shirt. Emilie pulled her dress off the rest of the way and sat up to unhook her bra.

"No, wait, let me." He first stood up and removed his pants, tripping over the legs because he was staring so intently at her. Once his pants were safely off, he reached into the back pocket, pulled out a condom, and then tossed the pants beside him. He was wearing boxers with little red hearts on them, and he was still wearing his black trouser socks that went halfway up his calves. He held up the wrapped condom. "Presumptuous of me, no?" He winked at her as he put it on the nightstand. He then dove into the covers next to Emilie. He cradled her head with his hand while he kissed her. His other hand slid underneath her bra and gently caressed her breasts.

"You are so beautiful," Erik said as he removed her bra and let his tongue explore. Emilie decided to let go and enjoy. She felt Erik's soft kisses move down to her stomach and stopped. As he rested his head just above her pelvic region, she was suddenly grateful Colin had talked her into getting a bikini wax two days earlier. "No one wants to get their eye poked out by an overgrown bush," he reasoned. Waxing the unruly mess to form a landing strip—however painful—was definitely good advice.

She took in a deep breath and slowly let it out. Feeling his lips so close made her drip with desire. Her heart thumped loudly as her body pulsed with anticipation of his next move. It had been a long time since a man pleasured her. And she was ready.

He moved his mouth to her right inner thigh and then down her leg. And finally, she felt the tip of his tongue gently touch exactly where she wanted it to. She moaned, "Yes," and didn't care if he heard how grateful she was. She stroked his curly hair as his skillful tongue fluttered between her legs. Soon she couldn't contain herself anymore. Her body bucked as she released months of sexual frustration.

He looked up at her and smiled. And she smiled back.

"Come here," she said in a breathy whisper.

He retraced the path his mouth took, moving up her body while planting soft kisses on her stomach and breasts until he lay next to her on the pillow. He smiled widely but said nothing. He didn't need to. His eyes said it all—big brown pools of warmth staring at her in a way that made her feel alive and desired. He kissed her lightly on her forehead before leaning over to the nightstand to grab the condom packet. After tearing it open, he put it on. He stroked her cheek with one hand as his eyes said, "My sweet Emilie."

She kissed the inside of his hand and pulled it down from her cheek while she gently guided his body on top of hers. He pressed his mouth on hers and forced her lips apart. His tongue circled hers. He began to make love to her, thrusting slowly at first, pulling away to check her facial expression. His thrusts sped up, and soon it was obvious he was about to climax. Emilie held onto him tightly as he became satisfied.

He slowed his thrusts down to a stop, kissed her on the lips, and then rolled off of her. "Happy Valentine's Day!" he said, trying to catch his breath.

Emilie smiled. *Happy Valentine's Day, indeed.*

21

"Oh my God, he's perfect for you," Colin said. He tugged on Emilie's sweater sleeve, pulling her down next to him on the bulky beige, coffee-stained loveseat. He had insisted they meet the next day at Purrfect Perks so he could get the debrief.

"Can I be your maid of honor?"

"Of course! Will you wear a pink taffeta dress, that you'll spend too much on—and never wear again?" Emilie said with a laugh.

"Of course, I will." He raised a cup of steaming black coffee to his lips and took a sip.

A young woman with dreadlocked hair piled high in a messy bun that resembled a knotted ball of yellow yarn approached them. "Can I get you anything?"

"Yeah, can I have some water?" Emilie asked.

After the waitress had left, Colin said, "What, no coffee? I figured you'd be tired after being up all night." He winked.

"Hilarious. Yes, I am tired, but I've been too all over the place today. Kind of jittery. The last thing I need is coffee." Emilie crossed her legs at the ankles and played with a piece of hair that sprang back to its curly form when let go.

Colin leaned over to her, placing his hand on her shoulder. "I know what you're going through. You're afraid. It's hard to believe that things can or will be good again. But they can and they will."

She looked away and then glanced back at him. Of course, he

was right. "It's just hard for me to relax. I like Erik. I like him a lot. Do I love him? Probably not . . . yet. Maybe. I don't know. But I guess I forgot how good it feels to have a man in my life."

"Hey, I resent that!"

"You know what I mean. A boyfriend, not a friend, that's a boy. It makes me so happy to hear from him and to be with him. It feels good to know he wants to be with me." She tugged on her hair some more and then finally tucked the lock away behind her ear. "Looking back on it, when Rob died, it felt like I was walking through a beautiful garden, stopping occasionally to smell the roses, and then wham!" She raised her hands and clapped them together. "It was like I took one step and fell off a cliff. It's hard for me to think that it won't happen again. It's hard for me not to think, 'Any day now it will all be over. Any day now, you're going to walk off that cliff.'"

"I know, I know. Been there, done that. Look, sit back and enjoy it. If you waste too much time worrying about what can go wrong, it will go wrong. Nobody has a crystal ball, so there isn't any sense in predicting the future. Live in the here and now. You and I both know life can change at any second—but it can change for the good as well as the bad. If you start thinking that way, maybe it will take away some of the fear. Now listen, I just saved you years of anguish and therapy. You owe me!" He winked.

"Yeah, yeah. I know you're right." She reached her hand down to pet a gray tabby that wandered over. "By the way, Tony is grrrreat!"

"I know, isn't he? So, believe me when I say it can and will happen. Love will find you again."

• • •

As mid-March and the company's annual shareholder's

meeting of more than ten thousand people approached—her busiest week of the year, Emilie welcomed the distraction her new life had taken on. Usually, she would be so stressed out the week before this meeting—but not this time. On her way to work, she made a mental list of things she needed to do for the big meeting, which was just a few days away.

When she got to the office the Wednesday before the weekend meeting, *A Nut* was sitting calmly using the reflection of the computer screen to put on lipstick. *At least her computer is being used,* Emilie chuckled to herself as she walked by. *A Nut* had an uncanny ability to get out of work when there was a lot to do. It truly was the thing she was best at doing, or maybe even the only thing she was good at doing. When Emilie was a child, her mother told her, "If you wash whites with reds, they turn pink. You might need that information someday if you never want to do your husband's laundry again." Emilie was convinced *A Nut* intentionally messed up every task given to her so she would never have to "do laundry" again.

After going into her office and removing her coat, Emilie sat down at her desk and began to handwrite the mental list she'd made in the car.

A Nut appeared at the entrance to Emilie's office. "Hey, got a minute?"

No, not really. "Sure, what's up?" Emilie looked up from her desk, which was strewn with paper.

A Nut walked in and plopped down in a chair. One side of her mouth curled up as she rolled her eyes. "I need to take this Friday off, and I know Carl will be mad."

Are you kidding me? Emilie's mind raced to Friday without *A Nut*. Even though she didn't do much, she did answer the phones, and there was no way she herself could answer the phones and prepare the last details for the shareholder's meeting. "Why do you have to take off? Can't you postpone your plans?" Emilie said, making no attempt to hide her disgust and disbelief.

"Well, no, not really. You see, Owen and I are driving to Charleston to buy a monkey."

"I'm sorry. What did you say? You're going to Charleston to buy a monkey?" Emilie repeated the words as if saying them would make more sense. This was weird, even by *A Nut*'s standards. So many questions entered Emilie's mind, but all she managed to ask was, "Why?"

"You know, monkeys are becoming the third most popular pet, after cats and dogs, of course. So, we're buying a monkey to breed and sell the babies. We saw a spider monkey on eBay. Her name is Parker. You know, like Peter Parker from Spiderman." *A Nut* said it so matter-of-factly as if she were talking about buying a new dress.

What? Emilie furrowed her brow further, trying to understand *A Nut*'s bizarre words.

A Nut and her boyfriend had somewhat of an exotic zoo at their house. Fish tanks with piranhas, an air-conditioned state-of-the-art snake house in the backyard. There was even a four-foot-long lizard that roamed freely inside the house. "Can't you buy the monkey next week?" Emilie managed to ask.

"No. You see, we're trading two snakes ..."

Why did I ask?

"And since it's a barter agreement, the guy won't hold the monkey for us. You know, first come, first served. He might sell it to someone else, which would be awful. They're hard to find. One that can breed. Once Parker starts having babies, I'll be able to quit." *A Nut* always bragged about how much her boyfriend made selling creatures on reptibid.com. And as much as Emilie wanted to believe the monkey-get-rich-quick scheme, somehow, she doubted that neither she nor *A Nut* would be lucky enough for the dream to come true.

Not sure what the appropriate response was, Emilie said, "I know Carl's gonna hit the roof, but do what you have to do," What she really wanted to say was, "Now it's official, you are crazy."

"Well, I checked with HR, and he can't fire me," *A Nut* said with an air of entitlement.

"If that's true, I'm not sure why you're worried," Emilie said, wondering if *A Nut* had mentioned the monkey in her meeting with HR.

"I just don't want him to yell at me. That's why I thought you'd tell him for me."

"Sorry, you're on your own."

"You know, it's just that coming from you, he might not be as mad. You can tell him you agree with me and that I deserve the time off."

But I don't agree with you. You don't deserve the time off. And you're buying a monkey! "Sorry, I really can't help you here. Good luck."

A Nut sulked out of Emilie's office and immediately jumped on the phone to one of her friends to complain loudly. A few hours later, Emilie heard a roar come from Carl's office, and then her phone rang.

"Can you believe it? She wants to take Friday off. I mean, we are going to be so busy," Carl said.

"I know. She told me. Did she tell you where she was going?" Emilie tried to contain her laughter, but Carl cut her off.

"Then she says she knows I can't fire her. She already checked. And I checked too. She has complained before that I'm a bully, and if I force her to come in, I will be reprimanded."

Good! Maybe we can kill two birds with one spider monkey!

"Why don't we just get a temp?

"Who's going to pay for a temp? Can I take it out of your salary?" Carl said, his words dripping with sarcasm.

"Maybe you can borrow someone in the building to answer the phones for the day. I mean, really, that's all we need her to do. It's not hard. Even a monkey could do it."

• • •

On her way home, Emilie couldn't wait to call Erik to tell him about the weird events of the day. He always seemed to enjoy the antics of *A Nut* and Carl and even marveled about how Emilie could stand working there. After leaving a few messages and not hearing back, on her third attempt, he answered his phone.

"Hey, glad I got you. I have to tell you what happened at work today," Emilie said with a giggle.

"Emilie," Erik interrupted abruptly, cutting her off. Odd, he sounded distracted. "I was going to call you." Something was definitely off in the tone of his voice. Usually, she could picture his smile and his eyes lighting up on the other end, but not tonight. Maybe she was overthinking things. It had been a long day.

"Listen, Emilie . . . we need to talk."

22

Later that evening, Emilie answered the door wearing her blue terry cloth robe—the one that made her feel better when she was sick. Her eyes burned and felt puffy from crying.

"I brought the only men we can trust—Ben & Jerry," Colin said, motioning to the grocery bag he held in his hand. He wrapped his arms tightly around her.

Emilie felt the cold ice cream on her back. When he pulled away, he held up the bag of ice cream, his version of chicken soup. "It's a three-alarmer. Coffee Heath Bar Crunch . . . Cherry Garcia . . . ooh, and Karamel Sutra. I know how you like to dig out the caramel center," he said. They walked into the kitchen. Colin took each ice cream container one by one from the bag and placed them on the kitchen counter.

He reached his arms wide and pulled her in close again. He rocked her as he soothed her. "Oh, you poor thing. I know how it feels. It will be okay."

"Thanks for coming." Emilie sniffled. She pulled away from his embrace. "You're the best man I know. The rest of them, they're all jerks!" She searched for an unused place to blow her nose on a crusty tissue, which she then stuffed back into the robe pocket. She then slowly walked to the couch and lay down. She didn't have any energy to be a hostess, and she knew Colin would understand. Colin grabbed two spoons and the pint containing Karamel Sutra.

"So, what did he say exactly?" he asked, while putting the other ice cream in the freezer.

"He said he really likes being with me, but he wanted to see other people. He's not ready to only date one person."

"Foul! I'm throwing down a penalty flag on that one," Colin said. Since the kitchen was open, Emilie could see his arms flailing in the air. "Is he still in high school? What is he having a hard time figuring out—who to ask to the homecoming dance? Either he likes being with you, or he wants to see other people. It can't be both."

"He said he really didn't want to be tied down and was afraid if we continued to see each other, I'd get the wrong impression."

Colin walked over to the couch and handed her the ice cream container and a spoon. He sat down next to her, and the two dug in. "Did he give you the wrong impression when he slept with you?" he said, with a mouthful of ice cream.

"Yeah, I know. I think he's just scared. I guess his divorce hurt him bad."

"If that's the case, he shouldn't be out there dating. He should get some help."

"Ha! That'll never happen. He's way too proud for that." Emilie paused. "I should have known. Colin, why didn't I see it coming? All the signs were there."

Colin shook his head.

"Nevermore! Spare me."

Colin nodded. "Get it all out, girl."

"Why did I let him into my heart?" Tears returned to Emilie's eyes.

"Because it was the right thing to do. Even though Erik isn't ready for a relationship, you are, and you had no way of knowing he was going to freak out like this. It's hard to open back up after a loss, but you have to do it. And one day, you'll find the right person who deserves you." Colin took the ice cream container and spoon from Emilie's hand and put them down on the coffee table. He grabbed a throw pillow and put it in his lap and gave Emilie the "c'mon" gesture with his hand. She slowly lowered her head to the pillow and curled the rest of her body into a tight fetal position.

"You need to see Dr. Jeffries. This is an emergency."

"I'm too busy. The timing can't be worse. I have this stupid shareholders' meeting this weekend. I just want to stay in bed and never get out." She blew her nose and dabbed her eyes.

"Can't you take a few days off?"

"No, I can't. This is my big meeting. Like one of your big cases. No one really can fill in."

"Okay then, promise me you'll call Dr. Jeffries tomorrow and schedule an appointment for immediately following your meeting."

"Yes," she said in a weak voice. She blew her nose. "I hate men!" She rocked her head, so the pillow dried some of the tears from her left eye. "Maybe I should give up on men and start dating women."

"You'd be a great lesbian!" Colin said cheerfully.

"Well, I don't think I could ever kiss a girl."

"Okay, maybe you'd make a terrible lesbian."

"You aren't helping things," Emilie said. "Why can't you and I just be together forever? I've never had a boyfriend as good as you."

"Have you forgotten that I'm gay?"

"No, of course not. You know, you're just my best friend. I know you'd never hurt me."

"Em, I know it's hard to see it now, but you will find love. You'll find someone who makes you happy and wants to be with you forever."

Emilie began to sob. "Why did he leave me?"

"Because he's an asshole."

Emilie paused. "Not Erik. Rob. Why did Rob have to leave me?"

Colin stroked her hair and whispered, "Because sometimes life isn't fair."

23

Emilie shifted in the modern, but uncomfortable, bright orange vinyl chair in Dr. Jeffries's waiting room. It was fifteen minutes past her scheduled appointment time. She picked up the *O Magazine* from the table next to her. *October 2018? Old news.* She ran her hand along the perfect rectangle cutout on the left side of the cover. It amused her to picture Dr. Jeffries reading the magazine first—maybe even taking notes before carefully cutting the address label off and taking it into the office.

She put the magazine down and took her phone out of her purse. Raised voices came from Dr. Jeffries's closed door. Even though she could not make out any distinguishable words, she could tell a man and woman were arguing. Marriage counseling, she thought. The man's voice got louder, and the woman began to cry. Feeling like a voyeur, witnessing a private, intimate moment in a couple's troubled relationship, she found her earbuds in her purse and put her music on shuffle.

After a few minutes of shouting, the door to Dr. Jeffries's office opened, and a tall, thin man with graying hair emerged and brushed past her. Removing one earbud, Emilie made sure to avoid eye contact.

A few seconds later, a short, middle-aged blond woman emerged from Dr. Jeffries's office. Her eyes were red from tears, and she still had a tissue in her hand. Emilie instantly felt sorry for her. She seemed to be in a lot of pain. No matter how mad she was, he should have been more of a gentleman.

Dr. Jeffries patted the woman on the back and handed her a yellow sticky note, undoubtedly with their next appointment written on it.

"If you need to see me sooner, give me a call," Dr. Jeffries told the woman. The woman took the sticky note, said, "Thank you," and wiped her nose with the tissue. It seemed cruel to send her off with such raw feelings. And now it was Emilie's turn to cry. She had to admit she was anxious to see Dr. Jeffries. The breakup with Erik had left her full of emotions.

Dr. Jeffries held the door open and motioned to Emilie. "Hi, Emilie. I'm sorry you had to wait. Come on in."

Like a robot, she made her way to the stiff leather couch and took a seat. She crossed her legs and then nervously tugged at her skirt as if the pull would stretch the woolen fabric to cover her knees.

"So, how are you?" Dr. Jeffries asked, without a hint of distraction.

Emilie was surprised that he could shift from one session to the next without residue. It must be part of the job, she thought.

She looked over at a framed picture of a woman on the end table next to Dr. Jeffries. Probably his wife, she thought. She looked earthy: curly hair, no makeup. A perfect match for him. She wondered if he told his wife all his patients' innermost secrets. She trusted him enough to believe that wasn't the case.

Thinking before she spoke, she searched for the words. "Well, Erik broke up with me." She tried to fight back tears.

Dr. Jeffries frowned and said, "I'm sorry to hear that. Did he give you a reason?"

"Yeah, you know, the usual 'It's not you, it's me.'" She shook her head in disbelief. "He said I'd make someone a wonderful girlfriend. I guess I'm just not good enough for him." She looked down.

"I wouldn't say 'good enough,' maybe just not right for him," Dr. Jeffries said, as if the word choice would change the outcome.

Semantics, Emilie thought.

"How did it make you feel?" Dr. Jeffries asked calmly.

Like shit! "I guess I'm depressed. At first, all I wanted to do was stay in bed, watch sad movies, and cry. I thought about calling in sick to work, but I couldn't. I had a work meeting this past weekend that was my responsibility. Even though I went, I was distracted. I'm still pretty shocked and sad."

Dr. Jeffries nodded.

"It was the same kind of feeling I felt when Rob died. The funk I was in made me think I must have been in love with Erik—because it hurt so much. But now I realize I wasn't in love with him. I think I'm mad at myself. I'm mad for trusting him with my feelings. I should have known better."

"What does that mean? Should have known better?"

"It felt so nice to be with someone—a man. It was good to have someone to spend time with and go on dates with dinner, movies, and stuff. It was nice to have someone to talk about life with. I think I miss that the most about being married." With a finger, she wiped a tear that had formed in the corner of her eye. "And, of course, I enjoyed the intimacy we shared. But I had this gnawing feeling that it was just too good to be true. It would never last. Every day I'd think, 'Enjoy it while it lasts because it will be over soon.' I don't remember being this anxious when I dated Rob. It doesn't feel normal. I hate the feeling."

"I think you're experiencing a fear of abandonment. That seems pretty normal. You were definitely abandoned by your husband when he died. You're probably reliving the trauma of that loss."

"I didn't expect the breakup to bring up grief that I thought was gone. I think my reaction to the relationship ending was because I never expected to be alone at this point in my life."

Click. Jot. Head shake. "Maybe, maybe not. There was no guarantee that your marriage wouldn't end for reasons other than death. You've mentioned some problems the two of you were having. I don't want you to hang your hat on 'if Rob were still alive, I wouldn't be alone.' That thinking will hold you back."

Emilie thought about what Dr. Jeffries had just said. "Okay, maybe. I guess you could be right. But it's okay to still miss him, miss what we had, isn't it?"

"Of course. I don't think the grief will ever be gone. You loved him and may always miss him to some degree. What you should aim for is finding a way to cope when grief comes up, so you don't slide back. And I think you're doing just that. This is a setback, but you shouldn't let grief or fear of abandonment stop you from living your life. You've made great strides in dealing with the grief, and the best way to deal with the fear of abandonment is to find and trust in love again." Dr. Jeffries adjusted his glasses. He looked very scholarly. "Live in the moment and don't worry about the future. Don't let this one relationship scar you from finding love."

"Naw, I think I'm done trying to find love. What if Rob was my one chance and I won't get another one?"

"I doubt that is the case. You'll never know if you don't keep yourself open to finding it. People that are alone are alone because they aren't doing anything to change their situation."

Emilie thought Dr. Jeffries sounded like a SecondChance.com commercial.

"You know, Emilie, you have a lot to offer someone, and I'd

hate to think you'd give it all up because one relationship didn't work out."

"I'm just afraid of getting hurt again. I don't think I can put myself out there and run the risk. It's too scary. And it's not like Erik was my only attempt. I went out first with this crazy cat guy—this guy who emailed me a picture of him sleeping with his cats, Boots and Muffin. When we met for dinner, I didn't feel a connection at all. At least my instincts told me to run away from that. I'm afraid the midlife dating world is full of more crazy cat guys, and I don't have the patience or strength to weed through them."

"Give it time. It's still pretty new. When you're ready, I am sure there will be someone out there for you. You just have to believe it too." He picked up his appointment book. "Two weeks?"

She nodded.

24

On April Fool's Day, after weeks of being pestered and having exhausted all of her excuses, Emilie went to her mother's house for dinner. Pulling into the driveway of her childhood home, she cringed at the sight of her mother's elderly widower neighbor hurrying toward her.

"I'm here for my hug," Mr. Walters said as he reached his arms out and brought her in close to him.

"Oh, Mr. Walters, nice to see you." *Lie.*

"You know what? I had a dream about you, Emilie," he said as he pulled away.

Oh God.

"Yes. I dreamed I took you on a vacation." His smile was nearly sinister.

"Hmm. How about that?" *Don't encourage.*

"Yes. We were on a beach somewhere. Maybe you might want to make an old man's dream come true someday."

What? "Oh, um, hmm. Wow. You sure know how to put a girl on the spot."

"Think about it, honey. The offer will always be there." He winked, and then turned and walked away.

Emilie turned toward her mother's front door and could see Margaret spying from the living room window, curtains drawn in her hand like Mrs. Kravitz, the nosy neighbor on *Bewitched*.

When Emilie walked in the front door, her mother said, "What'd *he* want?"

"Well, hello to you too." She kissed her mother on the cheek.

"Dirty old man! He's a menace to the neighborhood. I don't like him talking to you."

"He's harmless," Emilie said, trying to convince herself as much as her mother.

"I mean, really, someone should report him to the authorities. No eighty-year-old man should be hugging a girl half his age. Pedophile!"

"Mom, he may be creepy, but I don't think he's a pedophile. I'm hardly a child."

"Well, you're my child, and forgive me if I want to protect you."

"Thanks. You don't have anything to worry about. Something smells good." They walked into the kitchen. "Did you actually cook?" Emilie looked around and saw a stove full of pots and a whole roasted chicken resting on a cutting board. "I'm impressed."

"Of course, I cooked for my little girl," Margaret said, picking up the potato masher. She pressed down so hard on the masher that she let out a grunt. "I was going to make cold slaw, but I remembered how you don't like mayonnaise."

Cold slaw. Her mother was a walking malaprop. At least this one made sense. Saying that she thought Emilie's brother's wife was addicted to Zantac didn't.

After they set the table and sat down, Margaret said, "I know just the perfect guy for you," her voice slightly raised.

Emilie choked while trying to chew a piece of dry baked chicken breast. *Oh, God!* "Mom, what?" she said, still coughing. She had been suspicious of her mother's invitation for a good, home-cooked meal, especially since Margaret had declared her kitchen a "cook-free zone" after she remodeled it a year earlier.

"I think it's time you start dating again. You seem so mopey these days. Maybe having a man around will lighten up your mood! Put some pep in your step!" Margaret said with a wink as she struggled to cut her chicken with a butter knife. "I'm not sure why this chicken is so dry. That new oven of mine is supposed to be like cooking on autopilot." She shrugged.

It had only been two weeks since Erik broke up with Emilie, and since she hadn't told her mother she was dating someone, there was no reason to tell her about the breakup. Margaret was on a "need to know basis" about her daughter's love life, or lack of thereof, because Emilie didn't want her interfering. But apparently, she had misjudged the powers of a super mother.

"Why not get your hair done, buy a new dress, and have a fella take you out to a dance?"

"Ma! What am I? Twelve? There's no dances at the junior high gym," Emilie said. *Oh, God!*

Margaret dismissed Emilie's objections and continued. "You know my friend Hilda? Well, her son Tommy, the one that lives with her?" Margaret continued as if her superpowers could change the opinion of a mortified daughter.

"Yeah," Emilie rolled her eyes.

"Well, Hilda and I think you two would really hit it off." Margaret giggled. "She showed him a picture of you, and he thought you were really cute. And, you know . . . she'd be a great mother-in-law."

Oh . . . my . . . God! Emilie could not believe her ears. "What? Tommy? Are you kidding? I thought you said he didn't have a job." She tried to contain her anger, annoyance, and . . . embarrassment.

"Oh, no, that was at least three months ago. He works. He works at Starbucks. Hilda and I go in there, and he makes us grande cups of decaf, but only charges us for a tall."

Emilie covered her plate with her napkin, pushed it away, and put her head in her hands. "Mom, come on. Do you really think I want to date a guy who is fifty, serves coffee for a living, and still lives with his mother?"

"I think they like to be called baristas. Doesn't that sound better?" Margaret smiled.

"I think they call it 'weird,' Mom. C'mon. You and I both know he's not for me." Emilie let out a sigh, pushed herself away from the table, and slumped in her chair like a little girl.

Margaret reached over and grabbed Emilie's hand. "I know. I'm just trying to help. I really think it would be good for you if you start seeing someone. After your dad died, I couldn't imagine being with anyone else. But I know how lonely it still is. You're young. You really should fall in love again." Margaret squeezed Emilie's hand and started to cry lightly.

"Mom, I'm okay. I'm just not ready now." Emilie batted away tears from her eyes.

Margaret smiled and seemed relieved. "Consider yourself lucky. I tried to enter your name to be on Win a Date with My Daughter, that TV show you like to watch." Margaret's laugh made it difficult to tell if she was being serious.

Emilie felt the blood rush from her face, and her eyes opened wide with fear. Win a Date with My Daughter was one of her guilty pleasures. It was a reality show in which twenty-something men compete to date twenty-something girls who let their forty-something mothers pick the winner. Most of the mothers had no morals and would usually proposition the "losers" themselves. Emilie had never before seen so many cougars clad in leopard print on the prowl. A forty-something widowed daughter and her seventy-something mother picking over the men would be a show Emilie would love to watch—just not with her in it. "Oh, Mom, please tell me you didn't."

"I tried. Hilda and I watched the show, so we'd know what to do, but then I kept getting an error message when I tried to submit."

Emilie closed her eyes and breathed a sigh of relief. *Thank God for modern technology!*

25

Emilie spent the next Saturday lying on the couch, eating nothing but ice cream and watching *Sex and the City* season one and half of season two. The following day, the bright sun peeked through the semi-drawn blinds and jarred her awake just past 11 a.m.

Still somewhat in a sugar coma from the day before, she slowly sat up, rubbed her eyes, and caught a glimpse of herself in the bureau mirror. Her hair was frozen in a sort of "Bride of Frankenstein" do, and she had a little bit of chocolate smeared in the creases of her mouth. "You look lovely today, Mrs. Russell," she mocked. She tried to flatten her hair with her hand and twisted her camisole back into place. Standing up, she grabbed a pink sweatshirt she found strewn on the floor next to the bed. Not caring if it clashed with her Tweety Bird pajama pants, she slipped it on. Puddie was waiting for her at the front door, wagging his tail.

"Okay, hold on a second." She picked up his leash from the kitchen counter and put it on him.

Once outside, Puddie sniffed a bush next to the front door. Seemingly unsatisfied, he led Emilie out into the front yard. He stood erect and sniffed toward the street. "No, find something here." Emilie pulled back on the leash. Puddie tugged harder. "Find something here." Emilie gritted her teeth as she spoke. Puddie sniffed the ground and did his business. Emilie took a baggie from the leash and bent over to pick up the poop. Just as she did, the leash fell out of her hands, and Puddie took off.

"No! No! Puddie, come back here!" Emilie stumbled to her feet and chased after the little dog. He dragged his leash as he ran across the street to a neighbor's front yard. Emilie followed. Puddie ran to the neighbor's porch. "Buruff! Buruff!" He barked and wagged his tail.

When Emilie reached the yard, the neighbor's front door opened, and a man stepped out.

"Hey there, fella," the man said. He bent down and picked up the leash. "I take it he's yours."

Out of breath from running, Emilie said, "Yes, he's mine."

Standing up, he handed the leash to Emilie, and his smile faded to a look of horror.

She patted her hair down and then tried to cover the chocolate smear with her hand. "Sorry about that," she said, taking the leash from the man. She then turned and she and Puddie hurried back home.

• • •

"What's new?" Colin asked when he met Emilie later that evening at their favorite burger joint.

"Not a lot. Did I tell you Viv and I are going to Key West for Memorial Day?"

"What? No. That's great. I love Key West."

"Yeah, we used to go every Memorial Day until last year." Emilie grabbed a french fry from Colin's plate and dipped it first in a little salt and then in a glob of ketchup.

"Sounds fun. Maybe you'll meet someone."

"Naw, I'm so pathetic my mom wants to fix me up with her friend's son, a fifty-year-old coffee server that still lives with his mother," Emilie said.

"Ew!" Colin curled his lip in disgust. "When Howard died, my mom tried to fix me up with her friend's daughter. Blech!" He shuddered.

"Why do they do that?"

"They remember when we were kids and fell down and skinned our knees. They want to kiss it and make it better again." He slapped her hand as she reached for another fry. "If you want more fries, cough up some onion rings, girl."

"You know the fry to onion ring ratio isn't fair." She picked up the smallest ring, which was missing some coating, and tossed it on his plate. "There! Ya happy?"

"Thanks. Now we're even," he said, not masking his sarcasm one bit. "Hey, whatever happened to that cute Navy guy that moved into your neighborhood? You know, the one that Mrs. Reynolds told you about."

"Oh, it's over between me and him," Emilie said, trying to seem not to care.

"What do you mean, over? Did I miss something? It never really started, did it?"

"Well, no, not really. It's just this morning I think I might have ruined it."

"Oh God, what'd you do?" Colin said, clutching the arms of his chair as if to brace himself for some awful news.

After hearing her story, Colin said, "My God! What were you thinking? You were like an episode of *What Not to Wear* and *Extreme Makeover* combined."

"I know. I will say it wasn't one of my most stylish moments. It was mortifying." She shook her head at the memory.

"Hmm. I think it's great that Puddie is doing his part to help you meet men, but maybe you need a code word for when he should back off."

After a long pause, Colin's eyes lit up, and he added, "Okay. Wait. I got it! Next time you see him, mention that your ugly, unfashionable twin sister was in town." He smiled with cleverness.

"Is that the best you can do?"

"Well, that, and we have to burn that outfit."

"Seriously, I'm done with dating, anyway. The breakup with Erik still smarts. Besides, I seem to attract attention from the wrong men. The ones I'm interested in want nothing to do with me, and the ones I want nothing to do with seem to stalk me. Did I tell you my mom's eighty-year-old neighbor keeps hitting on me? It is so gross," she said with a snarl. "Every time I go to my mom's, he comes running out of his house and asks for *his* hug." She cringed at the recollection. "He even told me he dreams about me."

"Ew!" Colin's face contorted.

"Yep. It's hard to be flattered by some old man's fantasy. My mom thinks he's a pedophile." Emilie laughed. "You know, because he bothers her forty-one-year-old daughter. Wants to warn the neighbors that he shouldn't be alone with children."

"Now that's funny. Good ol' Margaret. She calls 'em as she sees 'em."

"Yeah, pretty funny, only when it's not happening to you!"

Emilie took a bite of her cheeseburger and then wiped ketchup from the corner of her mouth. After chewing and swallowing most of the contents of her mouth, she said, "You know I keep thinking of this joke." She took a sip of Diet Coke to wash down whatever food bits were left. "Where a guy is alone on a deserted island, and he prays to God to be rescued. The next day, a rusted old fishing boat sails nearby, sees him, and sends him a life raft. But the guy waves off the boat and declines the life raft by saying he's waiting for God to rescue him. Of course, he eventually starves to death. When he gets to heaven, he asks God, 'Why didn't you save me?'

And God says, 'Who do you think sent you the life raft?' That's what I feel like. Maybe I should see it as a message and consider some of these unwanted suitors."

"I doubt Mr. Coffee or Viagra Man are meant to be life rafts," Colin said.

"Yeah, I hope you're right." Emilie licked excess salt from her fingers. "Colin, what if we're like swans and Rob and Howard were our one and only true mates, and now we have to swim around honking on some stupid lake, alone, for the next forty years?" She snuck another fry.

"I don't believe that," he said rather abruptly.

"You don't?" Emilie was confused. He usually supported her "What if we're destined to be alone forever" speeches.

"Nope. Not anymore." He looked sheepish as he sipped some Diet Coke.

"What changed your mind?"

"Tony."

"Really? I didn't realize you two had gotten so serious. Wow! That's great."

"I know you've had it rough recently, so I haven't really been oozing with my own love life details. I know how it feels when you think love sucks and someone else doesn't."

"Gosh. That's so sweet of you." She paused. "And it is pretty awful of me not to even ask how things were going. From here on out, tell me everything. Don't hold back. I want to hear. I want you to be happy!" Emilie was truly happy for her friend.

"Well, Tony and I have been spending a lot of time together. That is when I'm not with you." He winked and smiled. "And now I have a toothbrush at his house and"—his voice rose and became pitchy—"he has one at mine."

"Yay! I love sleepovers!" she said and smiled.

"Em, it really is the first time I've felt this way about someone since Howard died. Tony is a good guy. I'm lucky to have him."

"Well, I think he's pretty lucky too! If I was gay . . . No, wait. I mean, if I was a gay man, I'd be all over you, honey!"

"And honey, if I wasn't gay, they'd have to pry me off of you!" They both laughed.

Colin pushed his plate of fries over toward Emilie and said, "And you, you'll meet your swan. You will. I know it."

26

While towel drying her hair, Emilie paused. It had been nearly two months—six weekends of binge eating and TV watching—since Erik dumped her. She pulled her damp hair back into a ponytail and got dressed. Opting for some clean pressed jeans, a crisp white oxford, and a jean jacket, rather than the dingy, day-old yoga pants that lay crumpled on the floor.

"C'mon, Puddie, let's go to the dog park."

"Buruff!" Puddie gave his stamp of approval. He ran to the door and excitedly danced in a circle. "Buruff! Buruff!"

Once outside, Puddie ran ahead, dragging Emilie behind. "Geez, slow down!" she said, taking hold of the leash with both hands while trying to catch her balance. For a little dog, he was strong and usually strong-willed. He could always tell when they were going to the dog park, his version of Disney World.

They walked the four blocks to the park, stopping for an occasional tree watering and bush sniffing. When they arrived, Puddie stood on his hind legs and eagerly patted Emilie's thigh with his front paws. She juggled the leash to open the gate. After re-latching the gate behind them, she took Puddie's leash off so he could have some freedom. Pent up energy abounding, Puddie ran around the park. He chased a butterfly, gave a butt sniff "hello" to a black-and-white Maltese, and even stood with his front paws against the chain-link fence to get a better view of a bunny that hopped by, in rhythm, to the tune of a chorus of barking.

Satisfied that her furry "son" was okay, Emilie sat down on a bench and pulled her journal out of her tote. She took the bookmark from the center of the journal and opened the book. She read her last entry written three days earlier. *Wednesday, Day 461. It isn't better to have loved and lost than to have never loved at all? Cockamamie crap. Clearly, Tennyson was never widowed. What if this is it? What if I've blown my one shot at love? Should I give up? Should I try online dating again?* She glanced up to check on Puddie. She smiled as she saw him wrestling with a black Cairn Terrier. Puddie, always the passive one, was lying on his back, mouth open, tongue to one side, and his hind legs wiggling with delight. The other dog crouched next to Puddie; his head bobbed up and down in a playful attack. Puddie then rolled over, stood up, and ran off, looking behind to make sure his new friend was following. It was sort of like a game of doggie tag.

Emilie settled into her journal again. *Day 464—decided not to spend another weekend in my pajamas. I still think men suck, but I don't want to be alone forever. Please, God, send me someone decent who wants to be with me and is not afraid of commitment. Is that too much to ask? What is wrong with me?* She wrote. She looked up and out of the corner of her eye, she saw Puddie running full speed with the little black dog chasing behind. They were headed right for her. Tucking her notebook close to her chest, she winced and braced herself for the surge of dogs. Puddie leaped into her lap and began kissing her face, and the little black dog followed suit. Covered in dogs and dog kisses, she put her journal down on the bench and pushed the little black dog off her lap and onto the bench. Puddie continued to lick her face as his tail wagged with excitement.

From a distance, Emilie saw a woman running toward her

yelling, "Rowan! Rowan! Bad boy! Get down! Rowan!" When the woman reached Emilie and the dogs, she picked up the little black one and held him out in front of her, nose-to-nose. "Rowan, bad boy!"

The woman then put Rowan on the ground and sat down on the bench next to Emilie. Rowan plopped himself at her feet, panted laboriously before yawning and letting out a big belch. Still slightly out of breath herself, the woman managed to say, "I'm sorry. He's just so friendly." She extended a hand for Emilie to shake. "I'm Janet Goodman. And I see you've met Rowan."

"Yes, we've met." Emilie smiled as she shook Janet's hand. "I'm Emilie. Emilie Russell. Nice to meet you, Janet. And Rowan's partner in crime is Puddin', or Puddie, as I call him."

"Puddie . . . that's cute. I get it . . . Yorkshire Pudding. Very cute." Janet was a tall, slim, blond woman whose big, Jackie O-style sunglasses acted as a headband to a perfect bob. She was probably in her early fifties, but Emilie couldn't tell if her wrinkles were from the sun or age. She was wearing navy blue capris with white pinstripes and a pale polo shirt with an Easter egg-hued Lilly Pulitzer scarf tied in the same fat knot Emilie herself had tried to replicate several times, but never could. "Your little one, he's quite the charmer," Janet said, reaching over to pet Puddie, who was still perched on Emilie's lap, on the head.

Puddie panted his agreement and then tried to lick the back of her hand.

"Yes. He's really a sweet dog. He loves everyone. The only problem is, he thinks everyone loves him back."

"Everyone does wuv him," Janet said in half dog talk. Puddie looked at Janet adoringly. "He'd be great for Pets-on-Wheels. Have you ever heard of us?"

"No." Emilie shook her head, not sure what Puddie would be

great at other than chewing shoes. Skeptically she asked, "What's that?"

"It's a program I manage of volunteer dogs . . . and their owners. We visit local nursing home residents. He's just the kind we're looking for. The residents love the little ones." Janet lowered her head to Puddie's eye level. "You'd do perfect," she said just to him. Puddie reciprocated the compliment with a kiss on her nose.

"How does it work? Does he have to go to training? Because, if he does, I don't think he'll do so well. He's got looks rather than brains," Emilie said half-seriously, remembering how a few months earlier they were both asked not to attend the obedience school graduation ceremony.

"No, there's nothing like that. I just assess his temperament, tug on the ears, pull the tail," she said, while playfully tugging at his ears. "Stuff like that. You'll need to have your vet certify that he's had all of his shots. After we get that, the four of us—me, you, Puddie, and Rowan—will go together on a first visit. From then on, you two can go anytime you want. Give it a try. I think both of you might like it."

"Okay, tell me where to sign us up."

• • •

Thirty minutes after Puddie's playdate at the dog park, Emilie took him home. He pawed at the front door, eager to have her open it. Once inside, he ran to his empty food dish in the kitchen. Emilie opened the pantry and picked up the bag of dry dog food. It felt empty. When she peered inside, she confirmed it was indeed empty. "Shoot," she said. She picked up her car keys from the kitchen counter and set out for the grocery store.

27

About fifteen minutes later, Emilie pushed her cart to the produce section of the grocery store. She picked up a bag of salad mix and inspected it carefully for brown lettuce. She looked at the sell-by date—May 15, two days from now, before tossing it in the basket. She then moved on to the fruit section. She leaned in to get a closer look at the containers of precut watermelon chunks.

Spotting the reddest of the bunch, she reached for the container. A hand touched hers slightly as the man next to her went for the same tub.

"Sorry, please, take it. I'll grab another one," the man said as he smiled at her.

She felt herself blush a little as she smiled back. She put the container of melon in her cart. "Thank you." She pretended to search for something in her purse. When she looked up, he was still there . . . staring.

"You're Emilie Malone, aren't you?"

"Yes, yes, I am." Her mind tried to place him. He looked vaguely familiar, but nothing was registering.

"Do you remember me? Scott Ziegler. We went to high school together." He made a gesture back and forth with his hand from her to him.

Scott Ziegler was all Emilie could think about in high school. He was *the* guy—quarterback of the state champion football team, and he dated the head cheerleader, Hannah Lawrence. Of course, they were Homecoming King and Queen. He and Hannah used to hold court as they walked through the halls holding hands—she wearing his letterman jacket, and he wearing her high school ring on a chain around his neck. They were considered teenage royalty.

Emilie, and probably every other girl in school, had a secret crush on Scott. She dreamed of the day he'd notice the nerdy bookworm that sat in the front of his English class. But he was too cool to speak with someone that wasn't an athlete or a cheerleader.

"Scott, yes, sure, I remember you. How are you?" Emilie said, trying not to convey how shocked she was that he knew who she was.

"I'm good," he said, flashing the dimpled smile that Emilie had memorized many years ago. "You haven't changed a bit. You still look the same as you did in high school."

"Actually, I hope I look better than I did in high school. I was kind of a late bloomer." She winced, thinking about her lack of style in her teenage years—the days before contact lenses and the braces . . . oh God, the awful braces. "You look the same too," Emilie lied. The years had not been kind to him. His head of once thick wavy blond hair was replaced with a few wisps of baby-fine locks. His muscles had turned soft—the teenager six-pack was now more like a middle-aged keg of beer. But he still had the nicest smile equipped with gleaming white teeth.

"You were always so smart in high school. I'll bet you're a doctor or something like that."

Emilie's cheeks felt like they were on fire. "Thanks, but no, actually, I do PR for American Communications. How about you? What are you doing now?"

"I work for my father's insurance company." He laughed and added, "Don't worry, I won't try and sell you insurance—that is, unless you need it." He shifted his weight from right to left and pushed his hands deep into his jeans pockets. He cleared his throat and said, "So if I can be so forward, I don't see a wedding ring. Are you married?"

Emilie looked down at her ringless left hand and shook her head. "No, no, I'm not married anymore."

"Yeah, me neither. Got divorced two years ago. It sucks, doesn't it?"

"Yeah, it does. Well, actually, I'm sure it does. I'm not divorced." She paused. *Just say it.* "I'm a widow." She looked down at the items in her cart.

"Wow, that's awful. I'm so sorry." Scott reached his hand over and rubbed her shoulder. "Do you mind if I ask what happened?"

"No, I don't mind. I'm used to it. My husband died a little over a year ago. He had a heart attack."

"Gosh, I am so sorry to hear that. I can't imagine what you've been through." Scott removed his hand from her shoulder, frowned, and shook his head as if in disbelief.

"Really, I'm okay. People feel worse for me than I do myself. I can't change what happened. You know what I mean?" Emilie smiled faintly, hoping to ease the tension building inside of her.

"I'm not sure I could deal. You're amazing, but then I remember you always did have a good attitude in high school."

I did? I mean, you knew I did? "Thanks."

Scott paused. "So, this is kind of awkward, but I was going to ask you out. Would that be okay? I mean, do you date?" He seemed almost boyish as the words came out of his mouth.

What? Was Scott Ziegler, the high school quarterback, asking her out? "Yes, sure, I'd like that," she said, trying to contain her excitement.

"Great. Give me your number, and I'll give you a call so we can set something up."

Emilie took out a business card and wrote her cell phone number on the back of it. "Here's my work and cell number. Give me a call," she said with a smile.

After picking up a few more items, Emilie headed home.

• • •

Puddie greeted her at the door when she arrived home. "Buruff! Buruff!" He spun around while he barked. Emilie carried the bags into the house and put them on the kitchen counter.

"Okay, okay," she said. She took the bag of dog food from one of the grocery bags. "Is this what you want?" she said before filling his bowl. "There you go." She placed his bowl on the floor. Puddie wasted no time in devouring his meal.

After putting the rest of the groceries away, she went to the couch and sat down. She picked up her journal from the end table.

Day 444, she wrote. *Ran into a guy I used to fantasize about in high school.* She could feel her heart pound through her neck as she wrote. *He actually remembered me! Can't believe it. I thought in high school I was invisible. At least it sure felt that way.* She paused, still trying to wrap her head around her conversation with Scott. Did he really ask her out? How could she get so lucky? She tapped her pen on the journal before writing: *He asked me out!! It makes sense to lift the moratorium on dating and men. I mean, it's Scott Ziegler. Scott Freaking Ziegler. Could it be there was a reason for all the pain? Could it be the heartache is leading me to my one and only true love? Scott Freaking Ziegler.* She put her pen down and noticed her heart had returned to a normal rate. Writing, or more specifically, journaling, was having a calming effect on her.

• • •

Six days later, Emilie arrived at Clyde's on the Lake in Columbia and saw Scott sitting by the window at a cramped table for two. She took a deep breath and ran her hands down the sides of her "first date dress"—a black DVF wraparound, to make sure it wasn't clinging in the wrong places and that the Spanx was doing its job. Scott stood up as she approached the table. He gave her a hug and whispered, "Wow, you look great." Emilie smiled and allowed him to pull her chair out before sitting down.

They ordered drinks, he a beer and she a glass of chardonnay, of course. There was a long, awkward silence until the server brought them their drinks. After the server took their dinner order, Emilie broke the silence by saying, "So, I guess we have twenty-three years to catch up on. What have you been up to?"

Scott took a swig from his Miller Lite and smiled. "Well, after high school, I went to the University of Maryland, but left after a semester. School was no fun if I wasn't playing football. Maryland already had a quarterback—and it wasn't me." He raised one eyebrow. "You know, I thought I was going to be John Elway. So, I never took classes very seriously. And since no scouts were impressed with a kid from Columbia High, who was maybe a little too impressed with himself"—There was a hint of sadness as he spoke—"I realized school wasn't for me. After dropping out of Maryland, I started working for my dad. I've been there ever since. I got married, divorced, and then married again . . . and divorced again."

Emilie nearly choked on a sip of wine. "Oh," she managed to say. She didn't remember him mentioning the second marriage or divorce.

"No kids in either marriage. That's something I regret. You know, I always hoped I'd have a son that I could toss the ball around with, but it never happened." Scott let out a deep breath.

"So, enough about me. How about you? What has Emilie Malone been up to?"

"Well, I went to St. Cecilia's College. Do you know where that is?"

He nodded.

"After that, I worked for a Baltimore PR agency for a few years, and now the cable company. And, well, you know about my husband."

"Yeah, yeah. Again, I'm sorry about that. How long were you married?"

"We were together for ten years—married for eight," she said.

"I feel like a broken record, but again, I can't imagine how tough that was." He shook his head as he spoke.

"Yes, thanks. It was tough, but I've had a little while to adjust." The conversation came to a dead stop. And her nerves reappeared. Emilie took a piece of bread from the basket. "Okay, um, now can we change the subject?" she said with a slight laugh.

"Sure, let's do that. So, what's your best memory from high school?"

"Wow, that's a tough one. Let me think." The words high school made her cringe. Should she say the time she wrote a poem about Mr. Harvey, her favorite teacher, and read it to the class? No, too nerdy. Maybe the time she was an alternate on the *It's Academic* quiz show. If possible, even more nerdy.

She was about to say, "You tell me," when he said, "Okay, while you're thinking, I'll tell you mine. Remember when we played Laurel for the State Championship?"

Um, no, not really. "Yeah, sure—that was a great game."

"Yeah, it really was. No one thought we'd win. We were the real underdogs. Laurel was known for their defense, and they had a hit out on me." He wiped the corner of his mouth with his napkin and then leaned back. "But my line came through. You know Dewey, Razor, and The Hulk. Great offensive line. One of the best ever." Scott smiled and seemed lost in the memory. "After the game, me, and Blake Pennington, you remember him?"

Emilie nodded.

"We got drunk and spray-painted 'Laurel Losers' on their field." He made an *L* shape with his hand and put it on his forehead. "It was awesome. Big red letters on their blue and gold grass. Ha! I don't think anyone ever found out it was us."

"Wow, that must have been something...I remember—" The words barely left her mouth.

"And then we went over to Tyler Miller's. You remember him, don't you?"

No. But instead, Emilie nodded her head yes.

"After we spray-painted the field, we went over to Tyler's house and had an all-night pool party. Were you there?"

"No."

"Boy, were his parents pissed off. They kept coming out and yelling at us—telling us to keep it down. But we didn't listen. Then the cops came. Howard County's finest. Ha! We told 'em we were celebrating our victory, and they were like yeah, party on dudes." He raised a clenched fist. "That was a great night. High five!" He opened his fist and pumped it toward her.

Thankfully, the server interrupted Scott's recount of his glory days, but Emilie had already checked out. During the rest of dinner, Emilie said little more than "oh, yeah" and an occasional head nod followed by a "hmm." Scott talked animatedly with his mouth full of a burger, his eyes widening with each detailed win he had on record.

When dinner was over, Scott walked her to her car. "Thank you, Scott. I had a great time." Emilie reached her hand out to shake his. Scott ignored her hand and leaned toward her with his mouth wide open. *Oh, God!* Emilie tried to hide her shock and dread. She recoiled and turned her head, so his fish lips met her cheek.

Undeterred, Scott hugged her. When he pulled away, he said, "So, you free next weekend? I know it's Memorial Day." He scratched his head as he talked.

"I'm going to Key West with my friend."

"Okay, then. Let's do it when you get back."

"Yeah, let's."

• • •

When she got home, she picked up her journal and wrote: *Who knew Scott Ziegler, All-State quarterback of Columbia High, has no game? Sometimes things aren't as great as they seem to be.*

28

Stepping out into the South Florida sun Memorial Day weekend, Emilie said, "Wow! Feel that humidity!" as she fanned herself with the rental car agreement, the only piece of paper she could find handy.

"Yeah, and it's only gonna get hotter. Where's this stupid car, anyway?" Viv walked slowly, wheeling her Louis Vuitton luggage behind.

"Aisle C, space 131. Remind me why we decided to come to Florida in May, anyway?" Emilie continued walking at a brisk pace ahead, not caring how far behind Viv lagged.

"Hey, slow down. What's the rush?" Viv stopped to put her flip-flop back on.

"I just want to find the car and get out of here. It's so freakin' hot."

"You seem so uptight," Viv said, hurrying to catch up to Emilie. "We need to get you laid this weekend. That is, unless things went well with the quarterback."

Emilie made a stink face.

"Oh, that good."

Emilie nodded her head. "Yeah, that good."

"Do you think you are projecting something on these dates? Maybe a standoffishness."

"Viv! Really?" Emilie stopped dead in her tracks. "Why would you say that?"

Viv stopped too. "Sorry, that was out of place. I just mean, do you really want to meet someone?"

"Yes. I think I'm ready. I've been working on my feelings in therapy. But I know it's complicated. I am so afraid of getting hurt. The breakup with Erik brought up all of these weird feelings."

Viv nodded. "Makes sense. C'mon. Let me see what I can find for you down here. We'll make sure you aren't lonely down here. I'll bet an island boy would be happy to—"

"Excuse me? What am I, some project?"

"Yes. Just call me Professor Henrietta Higgins, Miss Doolittle." Viv put her hand out and mimicked a bow. "Our theme this weekend is 'Get her done!'" It was just like Viv to latch onto one part of the conversation and miss the more important part, the one that equated to feelings.

The two started walking again.

"Thanks, but I'll pass."

"Aw, come on. It'll be like *How Stella Got Her Groove Back* . . . older woman hooks up with a younger stud who rejuvenates her soul."

Emilie rolled her eyes. "You can't be serious."

"Oh, yes, I am. You see, us marrieds are jealous of you single girls. I mean, with all due respect to Rob. You should be enjoying your freedom. Ya know, forty is the new thirty."

Jealous? Of me? You've got to be kidding. What is she more jealous of—my one-way conversations with Puddie or that I watch about twenty-four hours of TV each weekend? "Freedom isn't all that it's cracked up to be," Emilie said, "Here we go, space 131." They stopped at the back of a red Sebring convertible.

"Ooh! Look at this. Fancy," Viv said. She popped the trunk with the car's key fob, and the two women put their bags in it.

Walking toward the driver's side, Viv said, "I'll drive, you navigate."

Once in the car, Viv let out a noise that sounded somewhat like a tropical bird call. "Wahoo!" she said. "Watch out Key West, here we come!"

As they made it to Duval Street, the main drag, traffic came to a complete stop. Viv took off her floppy pink hat and used it to fan herself. "I guess this convertible thing is useless if we aren't moving. I can't wait to get into that pool. I plan to sit in it all weekend and drink." She put her hat back on and looked at herself in the rear-view mirror. She adjusted her sunglass slightly—probably less out of necessity and more because she thought it was a cool thing to do. "Of course, I don't mind vacating the house when you bring one of your gentlemen callers home," Viv said with an exaggerated Southern drawl, ending with a hearty laugh. "You know, I think I'm onto something. When you meet a guy you like in a bar, just say, 'I have a rental house, and I'm not afraid to use it.'"

"Viv, please let it go."

Viv reached over and patted Emilie's shoulder. "It'll be fun. I'll be your wing-woman all weekend. I think we can find you a man or two . . . or three." She lifted her sunglasses and winked.

Before getting to the beach house, the girls stopped at the grocery store to load up on food and at the liquor store for necessities. When they got to the house, they were pleasantly surprised to see a bungalow that actually looked like the online picture. It was a one-story off-white ranch-style house a few blocks from Duval Street and all of the action. On the wraparound porch, there were two white rocking chairs, and the house had long seafoam green shutters on the sides of the large front window. A slight breeze tickled with wind chimes made of forks that hung near the front door.

"Mmm. Feel that breeze," Emilie said, sticking her head toward the sky. "I can feel my muscles already start to relax."

Once inside, the seafoam color scheme continued on the walls. There was a small living room next to an even smaller kitchen. The house had two bedrooms, each with king-size beds and, more importantly, two full baths.

Beyond the kitchen was a sliding door that led to a patio covered in palm fronds. Tucked away in the corner of the backyard, near the east side, was a tiny in-ground pool, no bigger than the size of a hot tub. "Hmm. It looked bigger online, but doesn't everything?" Viv said. "C'mon, get unpacked, put your suit on, and let's relax in the pool," Viv said as she went back inside, and Emilie followed.

They put the groceries away. Viv found tall glasses in the cabinet. "Let's get on the margarita train," she said. "The sooner, the better. Choo-choo!" Viv poured the premade frozen margaritas into the glasses. "Cheers," she said, handing a glass to Emilie.

Emilie took the drink. With her suitcase in the other hand, she wheeled it into the smaller bedroom, the one that didn't have an attached bathroom because she knew Viv would want the master suite.

After unpacking, Emilie put on her bathing suit and inspected her legs and underarms to make sure there weren't any obvious hairs left after the first shave since Erik broke up with her. With her drink in her hand, she walked out to the patio. Viv was standing on the edge of the pool, rubbing sunscreen on her long legs and arms. She adjusted the little swatches of crocheted white fabric so that it covered the more discreet parts of the boob job she had two years earlier. Then she unceremoniously tugged at the strip of material that disappeared in between her butt cheeks. "I hate wedgies," she said. She sat down next to the pool and dipped her feet into the water. "Not bad," she said.

Emilie went and sat next to Viv. "Gosh, Viv, I hate you. How can you still wear a bikini? I haven't worn one since college. I inherited my mom's old Irish potato-filled fat ass." She put one leg at a time in the water. On this humid summer day, the water felt like a warm bath.

"Yeah, but you also inherited Margaret's big jugs of Irish whiskey. You should wear a bikini to show those girls off." Viv pointed to Emilie's chest. "Where did you get your bathing suit? From the gift shop at Leisure World Retirement Community?"

Emilie looked down at her purple one-piece that had a pink hibiscus flowered skirt. "Ha! Very funny, Tim Gunn. You'll be happy to know I read in *O Magazine* that wearing a wraparound skirt on your bathing suit shaves off inches from your hips, butt, and thighs."

"Are you sure you didn't read that in the AARP newsletter? C'mon! You have a hot body. Show it off. That's my second goal this weekend. First, get you laid, second, get you into a bikini."

"I never thought I'd say this, but you have a better chance of number one happening."

"That a girl! Get her done! Cheers!" Viv raised her glass and clinked it to Emilie's. She took a long sip and slowly moved her legs back and forth in the warm water. "Mmm. Boy, does this hit the spot."

The sound of laughter erupted from the other side of the fence.

"Why Emilie, I think we have neighbors," Viv said.

Emilie and Viv got out of the pool and dragged a lawn chair to stand on so they could peer over the wooden fence. There they saw two young men. Playing around, one was squirting the other with a garden hose. "I'll get you, you motherfucker!" the one getting squirted said as he lunged. He grabbed the hose, taking control of it. "How do you like that?" he said proudly, filling his friend's face with cold water.

"Stop! Stop!" the other one protested. "Okay, I give. Let's call a truce."

"Okay, truce."

"Hey, guys! Yoo-hoo!" Viv said, waving to them. "I guess we're neighbors for the weekend."

The one that appeared to be the instigator was drying off his face with a towel. He then looked over in Viv's direction and smiled.

"I'm Viv, short for Vivianne." She batted her eyes as she spoke. "What are your names?"

"Hi, I'm Daniel," he said as he approached the fence.

"And I'm Steve." His friend followed.

"Daniel, Steve, this is Emilie," she said, looking in Emilie's direction.

Emilie gave a faint wave.

Both men appeared to be in their early twenties. Daniel was tall, had dark hair cropped very close and big brown eyes, and definitely model good looks. His dark blue swimming trunks hung low and long. Steve was much shorter, his pale skin was covered in freckles, and his body had less muscle tone. His curly red hair looked as if it hadn't been combed that day or maybe that week, but he definitely won the smile contest.

"What brings you ladies to Key West?" Daniel asked, crossing his arms on the fence post tops and leaning forward.

"We're here for a girls' weekend." Viv winked. "How about you?"

"Us? We're living here for the summer. We just graduated from Penn State and decided to, you know, take it easy before we head off to law school." He pointed a thumb toward Steve.

"Or in his case, grad school—in the fall. Steve and I got gigs bartending at Cap'n Keys. You ladies should come by sometime.

It's a fun place."

"Of course we will. How about tonight?"

Emilie pinched Viv's waist and said in a near whisper, "Viv, what are you doing?"

"We're not working tonight," Daniel said. "It's our first night off in a week. We were just gonna veg."

"Funny, that's what we plan to do. Veg by the pool with some margaritas," Viv said. "You're welcome to veg with us." Viv's exaggerated eye batting looked like a cow swatting flies.

"Um, no they're not." Keeping her voice low, Emilie pinched Viv's waist a little harder.

Viv swatted Emilie's hand from her.

"Sounds cool, doesn't it, Stevie?" Steve nodded as Daniel continued. "Okay, we'll see ya later." The two young men said goodbye and walked away from the fence. As Emilie and Viv got down from the chair, Emilie grabbed her friend's hair, pulled Viv close, and whispered, "Have you lost your mind? What are you thinking?"

"Ow! Stop, that hurts, let go!"

Emilie let go, but still in a low voice said, "Viv, are you nuts? These guys are kids."

"So, what's the harm?" Viv sat down next to the pool and slid in. Wading in the water, she said, "We'll all have some fun."

"You know, you're taking this Stella thing too literally." Emilie got in the pool until the water was waist high.

"Live a little, girl. I've heard young boys truly don't become a man until they've bedded an older woman. Think about it like a bar mitzvah. If you ride that little one, he'll never forget it."

"Little one? So that's what you think? I couldn't get the guy with the six-pack?" Emilie's mood went from annoyed to insulted.

"No, that's not what I'm saying. I just think the taller one was more into me."

"More into you? What do you mean? I don't get this. It's just like when we were their age, arguing over who gets who. I seem to remember getting the short end of the stick, no pun intended, many times back then. This time, I'm the only one that's single. So, I don't understand why there's even a discussion. Besides, I don't plan on doing anything with either of them."

When they were younger, Viv always had a condescending way about her when it came to the two of them and men. Viv put dibs on who would appear to be the better catch—handsome, brainless guys whose wingmen were usually less gifted in the looks department but more gifted in the personality department. Margaret used to tell Emilie that Viv was just insecure and that Emilie was the real prize. Any man that's worth it would see that. But still, it was hard to take from her best friend. Emilie always accepted Viv and her flaws because her goodness outweighed her need for attention . . . usually.

"Suit yourself," Viv said. She then leaned in close and said, "Whatever you do or say, don't tell them our real age. Let them think we could be in our thirties." She tried to wink, but her Botox forbade her from doing so.

• • •

About an hour later, the doorbell rang, and Viv ran to get it. Daniel and Steve stood at the door wearing just their bathing suits and carrying four six-packs of beer—one in each hand. "Let's get this party started!" Daniel said, raising his beer bottle-filled hands.

"Here, take what you want for now and put the rest in the fridge. We have a pitcher of margaritas, if you'd rather," Viv said, walking into the kitchen and opening the refrigerator door.

"Naw, we're good with beer. Really don't do too much of the hard stuff," Daniel said as he removed two bottles from one of the six-packs and put the rest in the refrigerator.

The four went out to the patio and got into the pool. Just like the laws of physics, the laws of attraction seem to be unchanging—Daniel gravitated toward Viv's side and Steve to Emilie's.

At first, the conversation was broad: where they lived, what they did for fun, life in Baltimore versus life in State College. Every now and then, Viv was sure to shoot Emilie looks that said, "Don't tell them our *real* age." Soon, the margaritas and beers started to take effect, and the group got silly.

"Okay, okay. What's the strangest place you ever did it?" Viv asked.

"One time this girl and I did it on a golf course," Daniel offered.

"I guess you got a hole in one!" Emilie said to shrieks of laughter. She felt pretty loose and had to admit, this was fun.

"You chicks seem really cool," Daniel said, followed by a loud belch. "No boyfriends at home?"

"Nope, just a dead husband." Emilie laughed, but realized she was laughing alone.

Steve spit out the beer he had in his mouth. "What?"

"Oops. Didn't mean to blurt that out. Sorry for the buzzkill. Yeah, my husband died last year."

"Wow, no way. What happened?" Steve seemed concerned.

"He had a heart attack."

"Was he some rich old dude?" Daniel said, opening his sixth beer.

"No, not really. He was only forty-two. Just two years older than me." As the words came out of Emilie's mouth, she wanted to take them back. But it was such a natural flow, a part of her usual story.

Viv shot Emilie a look with daggers.

"That's too bad. Gosh." Steve took her hand under the water

and held it in his. Either the boys were too drunk to realize, or didn't care that Viv and Emilie were probably a few years younger than their mothers.

"How 'bout you? You got any dead husbands at home?" Daniel said, inching closer to Viv.

"Nope. No dead husband."

Emilie started to feel uncomfortable. She wasn't sure why Viv was being vague about being married. She didn't like where the conversation was going. She stood up and wrapped a towel around her waist and said, "I've got to use the bathroom. Excuse me, guys."

She hurried inside to the bathroom. *Okay, I have to get rid of these guys. Maybe I'll tell them I have a headache and they'll leave. That's it! The tequila is getting to me. I'm tired and I have a headache. That's what I'll do.* Seeming satisfied with her plan, she opened the door to leave the bathroom and was startled to see Steve standing in the hallway just outside the door. He put one arm on the doorframe and leaned in to give her a kiss. Emilie turned her head, forcing him to miss her lips and instead kiss her neck.

"Look, you know I'm old enough to be your mother—ish," she said, grabbing his hands and holding them in front of her.

"So? That doesn't matter to me. I think you're hot. You know, like MILF. I really want to sleep with you. I think it'd be awesome." He was leaning in very close to her, and she could smell the beer on his breath.

"I'm truly flattered, but I just can't."

Steve hesitated and then backed away. He stared at her for a few seconds. "Oh, I get it. I'm sorry. It's the dead husband thing. I guess it does take a while to kick it again after your husband dies."

"What?" *Oh yeah, that's it! The widow card, use the widow card!* "Yeah. It's just been hard. Thanks for understanding. You're a great guy." Emilie leaned in and gave him a peck on the cheek, and they walked to the patio.

When they got back outside, Emilie saw Daniel with his body pushed against Viv's, kissing her while groping her breast underneath her bikini top. "Oh my God! Get off of her!" She ran to the pool. Without getting in, she tried to pull Daniel off Viv. "Get off of her! What are you doing?" But she soon realized Viv wasn't resisting. "Viv! What are you doing? You're married. Stop it!"

"What?" Daniel seemed dazed. "Married? You didn't tell me you were married."

"Well, you really didn't ask," Viv said, pulling on her top, making sure her nipples were no longer exposed.

Daniel stood up and grabbed a towel. "Look, my dad cheated on my mom when I was a kid. I swore I'd never do that or be that. It's been real, but I'm outta here." He dried off in a hurry and motioned to his friend. "Come on, Stevie. Let's go." When they got to the front door, Daniel turned around and said, "By the way, the invitation for Cap'n Keys still stands. We'll make you some margaritas when you come." He raised a hand and flashed a peace sign to wave goodbye as they left.

Emilie stood staring at Viv. "I can't believe you. What happened? Why did you let him kiss you?"

"I don't know. I knew it would feel good." Viv slumped her shoulders. "Em, I didn't want to say this because you've got your own stuff to deal with. But it's just that things aren't so great at home. Andrew and I haven't had sex in months. He doesn't seem interested in me anymore." Tears welled in Viv's eyes. "I wanted someone to want me."

"Have you talked to Andrew about it?" Emilie huddled close to her friend.

"No, not really. I guess we're just in a rut."

"Look, you may not want my advice, but throwing your

marriage away by having a fling with a kid is not the way to go." Emilie got serious. "Trust me on this—you don't want your marriage to end. Mine ended, and I had no choice. But you do. Go home and talk to Andrew. Make it work."

A few tears trickled down Viv's cheeks. "I know you're right," she said. "This was stupid. I'm stupid. Andrew is a good guy. Thank you for stopping me from doing something stupid."

Emilie hugged her friend tightly. "So, can you and I just enjoy each other this weekend? Just like in the old days? No more talk about pimping me out?"

"Yep."

29

A few days after returning from Florida, Emilie was in the familiar leather chair in Dr. Jeffries's office.

"How have you been?" Dr. Jeffries asked.

"I've been okay. Been busy," she said. "Last week, I went to Key West with my friend, Viv. We skipped last year because, well, you know."

Dr. Jeffries nodded. "That's good. How was your trip?"

Emilie stared intently at Dr. Jeffries. She was detecting something different about him, the way his tone changed. It had more emotion. "Okay, I guess." She shrugged her shoulders.

"It's good that you are getting back into a routine."

"Some things are different now," she said. Was there a hint of a smile coming from him?

"Like?" Dr. Jeffries started taking notes.

"Everyone keeps trying to set me up. I'm not sure how I'm supposed to feel about that."

He looked directly at her. "How does it feel?"

"Good, I guess."

Click, jot, nod, smile.

Yes, Dr. Jeffries was actually smiling. With a front row of gleaming white teeth, that was definitely a smile. "I'm glad you are not offended by dating anymore."

"Offended seems like too strong of a word. Scared may be

more like it," Emilie said.

"Fair enough. Do you want to actively pursue dating again? I know you tried online dating and the breakup with . . ." He flipped through some pages on his yellow notepad. "Yes, the breakup with Erik was a setback. But I think I'm hearing you say you are ready to date again. Again."

"I don't know. I'm still confused. I went on a date a few weeks ago."

Dr. Jeffries raised one eyebrow. Click, jot. "I see. How was it?" And with that, the monotone was back.

Emilie looked away. "Okay, I guess. I mean, I was actually kind of bored. He was someone I went to high school with. Someone I used to daydream about. But in the end, we really didn't have that much in common."

Dr. Jeffries rubbed his chin. "I see. How did it feel? Tell me about it."

"At first, I was so excited. I couldn't believe that someone actually asked me out—in the produce section of the grocery store, as cliché as that might sound. I had all the nerves getting ready for the date—you know, will he like me, will this be the guy, you know, that kind of stuff. After the date, he called me and asked me out again. I just didn't want to go. I guess I don't want all the hard work involved. Getting to know someone only to have them leave."

"Or die?" Dr. Jeffries asked.

"Yeah or die."

"I wish I could guarantee that would never happen, but I can't," Dr. Jeffries said.

Emilie nodded. "I know. No one can." She paused. "You know, I have been keeping a journal."

Dr. Jeffries looked up. "And . . .?"

"And I realize it has been pretty cathartic. When I'm anxious,

I write. When I'm happy, I write."

"That's great news," he said with a hint of emotion.

"Yeah. I feel better after writing about something."

Click, jot, nod. "Keep it up." He looked at his watch. "I'm afraid we're out of time. How about this time, two weeks from today?"

Emilie pulled up her Outlook calendar on her phone. "Two weeks. Oh, no, sorry, I can't. My dog passed his test to become an assisted living therapy dog. That's our first day."

"Well, that's important. How about three weeks, then?"

30

The parking lot was nearly full when Emilie and Puddie pulled into the Sunnyside Assisted Living complex. Once out of the car, Puddie promptly relieved himself on the patch of grass. Emilie grabbed Puddie's leash and held it tightly while she guided him down the walkway toward the community's main entrance. "I think we're supposed to meet Janet and Rowan in the lobby," she said to him as he sniffed a boxwood bush and relieved himself again. Outside of the automatic doors to the entrance sat an elderly man and woman in wheelchairs. Emilie smiled when she saw that they were holding hands.

"Hello there, fella," said the woman to Puddie.

Puddie wagged his tail and tugged on his leash to get closer to the couple.

"Here for a visit, are you?" The woman said as she reached her hand down toward Puddie. "Such a sweet fella," she said. Puddie licked the woman's outstretched hand.

"Yes, it's our first time. We're with Pets-on-Wheels. I'm Emilie, and this is Puddie," she said, struggling to control him.

The old woman stroked Puddie's head, which made his tail wag.

"I'm Ida Goldenbaum, and this is Paul. We love it when our furry friends come to visit. Don't we, Paul?"

"Huh?" The man's face contorted, showing disagreement.

"Oh, don't pay him no mind. Sometimes he's a stick-in-the-mud. But *I* love dogs and would always welcome a visit. I'm in room 216, in the right wing. Stop by anytime," Ida said.

Puddie perched his front paws on Ida's thigh and stretched to kiss her face.

Ida bent closer so that Puddie could reach her cheek. "Goodbye to you too. Hope to see you soon."

"Sure, Ida, we'll stop by sometime."

When Puddie and Emilie walked into the lobby, Rowan and Janet were at the front desk signing in.

"Emilie! Puddie! You're here. Aw, look at you Puddie, all dressed up with your Fourth of July scarf! How cute. I wish I would've thought of that." Janet waved Emilie over to the front desk. She quickly pinned on a badge that read "Pets-on-Wheels, My Name is Emilie," and the name "Puddie" in parentheses. "I'm so glad you're here. Go ahead and sign in with your name, Puddie's name, and the time you arrive. Um, it's three thirty now," she said with a glance at her watch. "When you're done with your visit, sign out with the time that you leave. It's pretty simple. Okay, so let's just dive in here and get started."

The four of them walked down the hallway toward the units where the residents lived. As they passed common areas, Janet would identify the rooms. "This is the TV room. It's pretty crowded during Judge Judy" and "They even have a hair salon here. Isn't that nice?" Whenever they would encounter a resident, some of whom were confined to wheelchairs while the others used walkers, Janet would always smile and say "Hello," and Emilie followed suit. Janet kept Rowan on a tight leash. Rowan was a very well-behaved and disciplined dog. He walked with confidence—tail straight up, eyes looking forward as if he were prancing at a dog show. While Emilie struggled to hold Puddie back as he tried to get as close as he could to the residents.

"A lot of these people had to give up animals when they came to live here, so they really enjoy the visits. Rowan even has a few people that request him. They're special to us, so we always try and stop by." Pointing to a large room on the right, Janet said, "Here's the dining hall. It's best to avoid coming between eleven and one. That's lunchtime. Either come between ten and eleven or after two. There's also a lot of nap time around here, so you want to make sure you visit at the best times."

They reached their destination, a wing where the residents suffered from dementia and other brain diseases. It appeared more of a hospital and less of an apartment building, reminding Emilie that this wasn't some silver swinging condo unit; these people could not live on their own and needed assistance.

Janet knocked on the first door, which was slightly ajar. "Hello, Pets-on-Wheels. Would you like a visit?" As Janet opened the door, Emilie saw two elderly women, one sitting next to the window and one in bed, watching a rerun of Columbo. The room had a homey feel to it—less sterile and hospital-like than the common corridor. There were crocheted blankets and doilies all over the place. The walls were decorated with framed pictures. Potted plants adorned the windowsill, and a large one sat in the corner of the room.

"Hi, I'm Janet and this is Emilie, and these little guys are Rowan and Puddie," Janet said in her sing-songy voice.

An old woman sitting next to the window smiled. "Aw. Did you come to visit me?"

"Yes, we did," Janet said. Rowan walked right up to the old woman and as if on command, sat at her feet close enough so she could pet him.

"I'm Mila. I used to have a dog. I love dogs." She reached down and pet Rowan, patting him firmly on the side. "That little guy over there," Mila said, pointing to Puddie. "He looks like my Winston. Come here, little one."

Emilie picked Puddie up and carried him over to Mila.

"Can I hold him? Will he mind?" Mila asked.

Emilie put Puddie in Mila's lap and said, "Sure, he's a very sweet dog who loves attention." Emilie stroked him to reassure him that he was safe.

"Aw, what a good boy!" Mila said as her eyes lit up while petting Puddie on the head. He gladly reciprocated the affection with a few licks to the back of her hand. "Is he a Yorkie? My Winston was mostly Yorkie. I think he had some other stuff mixed with him, though, because he was about fifteen pounds. That's too big for a Yorkie. He wasn't little like you." Puddie wagged his tiny tail.

"Yes, he's a Yorkie. He was a stray. Just showed up in my garage one day," Emilie said.

"Boy, if you aren't the lucky one! So sweet too." Mila raised her head, giving Puddie full rein to lick her neck.

Emilie and Puddie were just getting the hang of it when Janet said, "Well, I guess we'll cut this visit short." She turned toward the door and allowed Rowan to lead the way out. Emilie was a little surprised at the abruptness of Janet's decision to end the visit. Puddie seemed to be doing so well. Maybe Janet was a little annoyed that Puddie was getting all the attention. Dog parents can be as defensive as real parents.

"Mila, it was very nice meeting you. Puddie and I'll be back soon." Emilie grabbed Puddie and carried him out of the room.

"Oh, I do hope so." Mila smiled and waved to them both.

Once out of Mila's room, Janet took charge. "Okay, never, never, ever let them hold the dogs in their laps. Under no circumstances. You know, dogs can be unpredictable, and if anything happens, Pets-on-Wheels could be liable. So just remember to keep him in your control at all times." Janet's words were stern.

"Oh, sure. I'm sorry. I didn't think about it. It's just that he's so sweet I don't think he'd ever do anything." Emilie held Puddie tighter to her chest.

"He could scratch them—not maliciously, and you know older people have very tender skin. I only let Rowan sit near them. If you want, you can lift him to get closer to the people, but always hold on."

Noted.

The four of them visited a few more rooms, and Emilie maintained a firm grip on Puddie, even though he stretched, strained, and wiggled to get closer to his new friends. It was nice to see how happy the visits, even short ones, made the residents. Janet gave her pointers throughout, like "Write down the room numbers of the residents that seem to enjoy the visits, that way you can start a relationship with them. You think you'll remember the room numbers, but you won't," and "Don't be offended if someone doesn't want a visit. Some people just aren't pet people, you know?"

After they left the last room on the wing, Janet said, "You both did very well. Do you think this is something you will enjoy doing?"

"Yeah. I do. And Puddie really seemed to like it," Emilie said.

"Great! Glad to have you on board. I think you guys will be fine. You can come next time on your own. Just sign in and visit. We ask that you try to visit at least twice a month, that way the residents can count on it. Of course, you can come more often if you like. Now Rowan and I are going down to the physical therapy room. The therapists love it when he comes. I'm looking into getting him certified in pet therapy. You're welcome to join us, but I don't think they'll let Puddie do anything."

"Thanks. I think we'll call it a day. I think we're both a little tired." Puddie yawned his agreement. "Thanks again, Janet. Bye, Rowan."

Janet and Rowan walked away. Emilie, unsure of where the elevator was, looked from side to side, trying to find a familiar landmark.

A voice called out from one of the rooms. "Hi, guys. Yoo-hoo. Emilie, Puddie, over here. You aren't going to forget to visit me, are you?"

Startled, Emilie peeked into the room where the voice was coming from. Inside, she saw Ida, the lady she met at the front entrance. "Come on in," Ida said.

Hesitantly, Emilie walked into the room. Ida was sitting in her wheelchair next to her bed near the window. The other bed in the room was empty, and there were no signs that she had a roommate.

"Hi, Ida. Where's . . ." Emilie paused as she looked at the empty bed.

"What? Who? Paul?" Ida said with a laugh. "No, we aren't married. I guess you could say he's my boyfriend. Not that having a boyfriend at eighty is the same as having a boyfriend at your age. No hanky-panky. House rules," Ida said in a hushed voice as if she were getting away with something. Her eyes twinkled with a hint of naughtiness.

Emilie walked toward her and sat on Ida's bed, which was close to Ida's wheelchair.

"I used to have a roommate, Rosemarie. Not sure what happened to her. I think she died. They told me it's best I don't know what happened. Sometimes people just . . . poof . . . disappear around here . . . gone. No explanation. I think it might be a black market organ thing."

"Really?" Emilie felt her mouth gape open.

"No, just kidding. I wanted to see how you'd react." Ida had a deadpan delivery like a skilled comic. "Rosemarie got sprung. One of her kids checked her out. Built a room for her at his house with round-the-clock nurses. I guess he thinks he's going to inherit a lot, but the joke's on him. Ha! She told me she's leaving everything to the Humane Society in memory of her dead cat, Jake." Ida started laughing so hard she began to cough.

"Are you okay? How about some water?" Emilie put Puddie down on Ida's bed and grabbed a plastic cup and poured from a bottle of water on the nightstand.

"I'm fine. Thanks." Ida reached for the water and swallowed hard. "You know I love it when that happens. They're only nice to you because they think they're gonna get your money. But little do they know." Ida waved a finger in the air. "There's no better way to stick it to them than in the will. God bless her!"

Emilie smiled. She instantly liked Ida—so charismatic, and she had a full and hearty laugh.

"I think I might get a new roommate, but to be honest with you, I don't care if I do. Kind of like it alone."

Emilie sat back down on the bed, and Puddie curled up next to her. "So, tell me about yourself, Ida. Are you from Maryland?" Emilie asked.

"No, I grew up in New York. Brooklyn, to be exact. My husband, Sol, was in the garment business. I always had the nicest clothes. He would have liked this," she said as she pulled on her navy dress, which was covered in bright yellow pansies. "The Nordstrom's sale rack," she said, cupping her hand to the side of her mouth as if she were telling a secret. The little wink she threw in reminded Emilie of herself—those were two things she'd say and do in just that way.

"My Sol, he took such good care of me, that one. Called me his beautiful princess. You may not believe this, but I used to be a real looker. Could've had anyone I wanted." She gave a wry smile, which showed off a slight gap between her two front teeth.

It wasn't hard to believe. Ida was still a beautiful woman. She had the whitest hair Emilie had ever seen tucked in a stylish French twist and the darkest brown eyes that were animated when she talked. And her makeup was appropriately understated, not big, exaggerated, drawn on lips like her mother and all of Margaret's gadfly friends. Emilie imagined Ida would have been a pretty cool mom.

"I was older when we got married," Ida continued to reminisce. "My mom, she thought I'd be an old maid, but you know, I was waiting for the right one—and boy, did I find him! My Sol, God rest his soul. They broke the mold on him." She looked up lovingly at the ceiling with her hands clasped on her chest. "After he died, I lived alone for a little while until I had a stroke two years ago. Then my son Max talked me into moving here. Closer to him so he can visit and take care of me. Did I tell you he's a doctor? A cardiologist . . . Hopkins." Ida raised her eyebrow, nodded, and smiled with pride. "He's such a good boy. Ah, a mother's joy. You don't have to tell me I've been blessed. That's why I don't mind living here." Ida wheeled closer to the bed and Emilie. "So, bring that little fella to me. Let me hold him."

"No, I'm sorry. They told me it's not allowed," Emilie said.

"Allowed, shmowed." Ida gave a dismissive wave of her hand. "Give him here. If I listened to every rule they gave me, I would have died of boredom."

Emilie blushed.

"Tsk, tsk." Ida shook her finger at Emilie teasingly. "You naughty girl, I know what you're thinking. Paul and I have broken the hanky-panky rules. But you're wrong. And it's not that I haven't tried. Damn stick-in-the-mud, Paul. Now give me that little doggie of yours."

While she nervously looked over her shoulder, Emilie placed Puddie in Ida's lap.

"Don't worry. If we get caught, we'll make up something. They think I'm a little meshuga, anyway. Come on, live a little. Life is too short."

A nurse's aide walked into the room and said, "Okay, Mrs. Goldenbaum, time to get ready for dinner."

"Such an exciting existence here," Ida said with a shoulder shrug. "Will you come back again?"

Emilie picked up Puddie from Ida's lap. "Yes, of course we will."

When they left the room, Emilie heard her cell phone signal a text. She reached into her purse and got her phone.

"R U free for coffee tomorrow?" Colin wrote.

31

Close to 5 p.m. the next day, Emilie rushed into Purrfect Perks, which by this time of day was crawling with people . . . and cats. She was about twenty minutes late and hoped Colin hadn't left. It had been one of *those* days—the kind that had become the norm lately at work. She scanned the room and spotted him nesting in their usual leather couch in the far-right corner. She gave him a quick wave as she maneuvered through the crowd of people buzzing with conversation and clearly too much caffeine, careful not to trip over a cat or two. He tapped the face of his watch with his index finger. She shrugged her shoulders and mouthed, "I'm sorry."

When she reached him, she threw herself down on the couch next to him, slouching as she said, "Mea culpa. I just couldn't leave the office when I wanted to. I know, I know." She put her hands up as if to say, *don't give me a hard time about it.* "I should have called, but I was rushing so much. Honestly, I thought I was going to make it, but traffic didn't cooperate. And you know how I feel about driving and talking on the phone."

"It's okay, don't worry about it." Colin took a sip from his iced coffee drink, which was half gone. "Here, I ordered you an iced mocha—with skim milk, of course." He pointed to a glass on the coffee table in front of them.

"Aw, you're so sweet. Not only do you not mind that a girl is fifteen minutes late, but you buy her a drink too. My kind of guy."

She winked. Trying to get comfortable, she shifted her body, being careful not to let her skirt ride up too much. Reaching for the napkin from underneath her drink, she dabbed the perspiration from her forehead. The humidity seemed to make her bare legs stick to the leather. Carefully, she peeled off one thigh and then the other. "Makes you miss winter, doesn't it? Call me crazy, but I'd take snow any day over the heat."

"Okay, I'll call you 'Crazy,' and I'll be sure to remind you of it when you ask me to shovel your driveway in a few months. It'll only be a matter of time before you say, 'Oh, Colin, I miss summer.' So, enjoy it now." There was a playful tease in his voice.

Emilie rolled her eyes, gave Colin a fake smirk, and mouthed "whatever" in an exaggerated way. She slipped out of her shoes and brought her legs up onto the couch, which was just big enough to tuck them comfortably. She reached forward for her mocha. Taking a sip, she closed her eyes and sighed. "Okay, so what's up? Last night, you said you had something big to tell me."

Colin nodded. "Well . . . I want you to be the first to know . . ." He paused and took a deep breath. "I'm getting married!"

"What? Oh my God, that's great. Yay!" Emilie put her drink down, leaned over, and hugged him. "Wow! Tell me everything. Did he ask you, or did you both just decide 'Let's just do it?' Don't leave anything out."

"Saturday night, we were in bed."

"I didn't mean tell me *everything*," Emilie said with a laugh.

"No, no, nothing like that. You know, we've practically been living together at my house since Memorial Day. Anyway, Tony was reading from his Kindle, and he says, 'Does it bother you if I read a little?' And I was like, 'No,' when I really wanted to say yes, because the light was on, but I didn't want him to know it bothered me. You know what I mean, right?"

"Yep, I do. I miss that part of a relationship when lying is a good thing," Emilie said as she sipped her iced mocha.

"He read for about another minute, if that, then turned off the light, rolled over, kissed me on the forehead, and said good night."

Emilie sighed. "Aw, on the forehead? How sweet."

"Yep. And at that very instant, I knew I wanted to spend the rest of my life with him. So, I just blurted it out—'Tony, let's get married.'"

Colin paused while he drank the last sip of his iced coffee. "Last night, we stayed up all night talking about wedding plans. And let me tell you, I don't even feel sleep-deprived—there's no sleep needed on cloud nine. Am I blushing? Because I feel like a blushing bride." He fanned himself with his hand. "So, I want you to be my maid of honor. And not only that, but I also have a big favor to ask you. Will you help me plan the wedding? You're so good with events and stuff."

"What? Of course, I will. '*I do*' to both," she said, making air quotes. "Wow, I can't believe it. Did you guys set a date?"

"We're thinking of Columbus Day weekend. We want to do it in Vermont, 'cuz that's where we spent our first getaway. That's where we fell in love. And what better place than New England in October? It will be beautiful."

"October? You do realize Columbus Day is only like four months away, right? Kind of soon to plan a wedding." She looked at him coyly. "Is this a shotgun wedding . . . do you *have* to get married?"

"Shame on you." Laughing, he slapped the back of her hand. "Yeah, you're right. That does sound like me, but that's not the reason for the rush. We just don't want to wait. It could be illegal any day. Besides, why wait when you've found the right guy? There's no need for a long engagement. In case you haven't noticed, I'm not a traditional bride."

"Well, that's an understatement," Emilie said.

"We've got a lot to do. There are a couple of places I have in mind. Maybe you and I can make a trip up to Vermont to scope things out."

"Love that idea. You know what's there, don't you? I hear the mother ship calling us home."

"Yes, I know it's the land of Ben and Jerry. We'll make time to go visit *the boys*. I think they need to meet the woman that kept them in business during the recession. Can you take next Friday off? We can drive up and then come back on Sunday. I'll do a little research online first."

"Shoot, I can't next weekend. I have to go to the Eastern Shore for a stupid board meeting. How about the weekend after that?" Emilie said.

"Sure, that will work," Colin said.

"I'll put some ideas together. Just leave that stuff to the professional event planner." Emilie smiled and grabbed Colin's arm. "My best friend is getting married." Just saying the words made her swoon.

"As maid of honor, do I get to plan the bachelor party too?"

"Of course."

"When I planned Viv's party, she didn't care about anything but the stripper. I got this guy who dressed as a fireman. He was a real hottie—pun intended." She winked. "I think his name was Five-Alarm Frank, or something like that. He was wearing these little red bikini underwear that had a fire hose in the right place—if you know what I mean. It was pretty funny."

"He sounds perfect. Do you still have his number?" Colin's eyes twinkled as he laughed.

"Hmm, I think so. If not, I'm sure Viv does." Emilie paused.

"Colin, did you ever think you'd get married again? I mean, be as happy as you are with Tony?"

"Yes, yes, of course. I never gave up hope. Hope is almost as important as luck." Colin picked up his glass mug and clinked it with hers. "Cheers to me for being lucky enough to find love after loss . . . and to knowing that one day I'll help plan your wedding."

32

"Get up, Carl," Emilie said to her boss, who was lying on the hotel banquet room floor of the posh hotel on Maryland's Eastern Shore. The board dinner was starting in a little over an hour, and Emilie was exasperated with him. He insisted on a unique setup for their board dinners—two tables of twenty in the shape of a T with a five-and-a-half-foot break where the tables met perpendicularly, which made no sense to anyone but him.

"I am six feet tall and there are at least six and a half feet in between these two tables." Carl, still lying on the ground, raised his hand above his head to prove his point. "I specifically asked for no more than five feet six inches in between them."

Emilie wasn't sure which amused her more—the fact that Carl thought he was six feet tall or that he was making such a big deal about something so trivial. "Come on, Carl. So, there are a few extra inches in between the tables. That'll make it easier for the servers to get around."

Carl rolled onto his side and struggled to get himself up, reminding her of Humpty Dumpty. "You know, it's the details in this business that will do you in." Kneeling and panting a little, he rubbed his hands together as if he were wiping away dirt. "I put the five feet six inches on our banquet event orders to make sure they read them. If they mess up this detail, there's no telling what else they aren't paying attention to." He let out an enormous sigh as he put out his hand for her to assist him up.

Or maybe they think it's the stupidest detail they've ever seen. She gave Carl one hand as she held tightly to the back of a chair with her other hand, fearing hoisting him up would topple her over—and God forbid she fall backward, and they'd both wind up on the floor with him on top of her.

Once he was up, Carl took a minute to catch his breath. "And just look at these tablecloths. I asked for a black overlay with a white underlay. They have them reversed. They're going to have to reset the whole room." He took a handkerchief from his pants pocket and blotted his forehead, forcing the comb-over piece of hair back in place.

Two banquet staff that had been quietly standing nearby looked at each other. One of them, Jorge, the banquet captain, calmly approached Emilie and Carl.

"Excuse me. I am very sorry you are not happy with the setup. The reason we did the white tablecloths on top of the black ones is because the black ones were longer," Jorge said, lifting the end of the black tablecloth to demonstrate his point.

"I think the white on black looks better. It looks more elegant." Emilie said. "Besides, Carl, they don't have enough time to reset the whole room. The dinner starts in an hour. You know people start coming down about a quarter till seven for a drink, so really, we have only forty-five minutes. It's not enough time to take everything off, change the tablecloths—*move* the tables six inches." Emilie made a swaying gesture with her hands. "Plus, the microphones are taped down already on the tables. That job will take at least half an hour itself." Emilie paused. "Carl, you're being unreasonable."

Carl liked to get his way, even when he was wrong. He did not look amused. "Listen, George."

"You mean *Jorge*, don't you?" Emilie was surprised at the firmness in her voice.

"What? Yes. Listen, Jorge, this is *your* problem. Now fix it. You should've gotten it right to begin with." Carl shook his head and pointed at the space in between the tables. "There's too much space in between the tables. At least a foot, or maybe even more. I want that fixed. I guess the tablecloths I can live with, but I want a credit on my bill."

"Yes, sir," Jorge said.

"And these centerpieces aren't at all what I had in mind. I expected taller arrangements—gladiolas, irises, long-stemmed roses. Not carnations, daisies, and lilies. I said fifty dollars per arrangement, and you give me about fifteen dollars' worth of flowers. I'm not paying for them. Not a one."

"Forgive me, sir, but with the taller flowers like gladiolas and irises, it is difficult for dinner conversations to take place. Our florist thought it best to make the arrangements long and low."

Carl pursed his lips and scratched his balding head. Having made his point, it was obvious to Emilie he could not concede, but that he probably agreed. "I realize that, but nothing about these arrangements is right. I'm not paying for them." He turned to Emilie and said, "I have to go change clothes, and I want you to stay down here, making sure they get it right this time. Didn't I ask you to check this out earlier?"

"Uh, no, you said you had it covered." She did not back down from him, even though his glare was intense. "Carl, I can't stay down here. I have to go get changed too. I can't wear what I have on. Jeans are not business attire. And I have to wrap Mr. Porter's gift."

Malcolm Porter was their board chair who was stepping down after this meeting. His wife told Emilie he collected Native

American art, so she was thrilled when she found a sculpture of a Native American chief carved out of a single piece of balsa. Emilie liked Mr. Porter. He had always been kind to her. The gift she selected would be a home run.

Carl sighed. "Well, I guess you'll have to help them, so it gets done faster," he said, muttering something under his breath as he left the room.

Emilie walked over to Jorge, who was discussing the situation with two hotel staff. "Miss Emilie, we followed the directions of your boss. You see?" He pulled out the paperwork Carl had sent to the hotel, which had typed clearly in big bold letters: PLEASE ENSURE THERE IS NO MORE THAN 5 FEET 16 INCHES IN BETWEEN THE TWO TABLES. "When I questioned him, he said just do what the paperwork says."

Ha! That stupid A Nut. Leave it to her to have a typo like that—five feet sixteen inches. "Jorge, I'm not going to have you and your staff reset the room. I think it's as ridiculous as you do. I know Carl. He's a harmless bully who wants to always be right. We just have to make him think we made some changes. Let's see." Emilie looked carefully at the florals. "Do you think we can add some roses to the arrangements? Red, maybe? Bill it to our account—charge us for rosé wine. He'll never know."

She stepped back and put her index and middle fingers to her mouth, with her thumb resting on her chin. "As for the tables . . . let me think." She walked through the opening slowly, moving her head from side to side. "Let's just move the place settings for these two chairs on the end. Right here, near the gap. It might give the optical illusion that the gap is smaller," Emilie said as she moved one of the chairs. Stepping back, she added, "Yes, yes, I think it might work."

Jorge smiled and seemed very relieved as the two banquet staff began moving the silverware, napkins, and gold charger plate for the two seats Emilie identified. "Thank you, Miss Emilie," Jorge said, and shook her hand. "I promise you everything will go very well tonight."

"I know. I'm not worried."

• • •

By the time she got to her room, Emilie had thirty minutes to freshen up, get dressed, and wrap the gift. She quickly removed her jeans and sweater. Wearing just a bra and panties, she went to the bathroom to wash her face and put on some makeup. She could not seem to get the scene out of her mind. "He is so embarrassing . . . such a jerk," she said while putting on a ruby shade of lipstick. She blotted her lips with a tissue and popped them together to make sure they were evenly coated. She inspected her hasty makeover in the mirror and was pleased to see there was no lipstick on her teeth.

After applying the finishing touches of her amethyst-colored eye shadow around her eyelash base, Emilie looked at her watch. "Shoot! It's already six thirty. I've got to hurry." She plugged in her hot rollers and stumbled out of the bathroom, catching her toe on the doorjamb. She grabbed for the doorframe to prevent herself from falling.

She limped to the dresser and pulled out a pair of black pantyhose from the top drawer. Carefully, she slid them on, making sure her nails did not puncture any holes or create any snags. She hurried to the closet to get her little black sleeveless sheath dress. Removing the dry cleaner's plastic wrap, she took the dress off the hanger, unzipped it, and put it on over her head. Pulling it down into place, she smoothed out any wrinkles. Then she reached behind her and started to zip it up. When the zipper got to the middle of her back, she struggled to get a hold of it. She contorted and twisted in every way possible, but the zipper continued to elude her. Giving up on the fight for now, she went into the bathroom to roll her hair.

Quickly, she combed out sections of her hair and wound them around the very hot rollers. While her hair was curling, she had to multitask. She took the box with the statue off the desk and laid it on the bed next to the white gift bag with gold tissue paper. Opening the box, she removed the sculpture and took off the Bubble Wrap around it. She smiled as she held it up to look at it once again. It stood twelve inches from the base to the top of the chief's feathered headdress and had very intricate detail. The light wood felt delicate in her hand. She admired the headdress, each tiny feather carved with obvious attention to detail. The lines on the chief's face depicted a weathered look of a respected leader. In his left hand, he held a spear that was nearly the length of his body. Emilie looked closely at the craftsmanship of the weapon. The head of the spear was no more than a quarter of an inch, and it had roping details that intertwine the length of the handle. The artist was even able to capture the image of moccasins on his feet, with grooves carved to indicate tiny beads.

She carefully laid the sculpture on top of two sheets of gold tissue paper and slowly wrapped the tissue paper around the piece of art. Then she placed the sculpture in the center of the gift bag. She was pleased it fit perfectly—there was about an inch between the top of the sculpture and where the bag handles began. Fearing the sculpture would shift when she carried the bag, she decided to line the bag with scrunched up tissue paper to pad the prized item. As she was filling the bag with the tissue paper, she heard a snap, the distinctive sound of thin wood breaking.

"Oh, no! Oh, no! Shit! No! No! No!" Emilie took a deep

breath as she removed the sculpture from the bag and began to unwrap the tissue paper around it. She was slow and deliberate, trying not to tear the paper or damage the statue more. "Please, God! Oh, please. Let it be okay," she prayed out loud.

When she got the sculpture unwrapped, her heart sank, and she gasped aloud in horror. The spearhead had broken off at the chief's clenched left hand. "Oh, no! Oh, no! What am I going to do? Think, think, think, think, Emilie!" She paced, wringing her hands—trying hard to think of a solution. Looking in her suitcase, she hoped for a miracle and that there would be something she could use to hold the wood together. Finding nothing to help rectify the situation, a thought came to her. *Call Jorge. Someone in the hotel should have some glue or something that would hold the wood together.*

She grabbed her cell phone from her purse and found Jorge's number on his business card. "Jorge. It's Emilie Russell . . . Um . . ."

"Yes, Emilie. The room is set. Just like you instructed," Jorge said.

"What? No. That's not why I'm calling. I have an emergency. Can you come to my room as soon as possible? Room 329. Oh, and bring something that can glue or fix wood."

Amazingly, Jorge did not ask questions. Emilie was grateful for that, because there was no time to explain.

Within a few minutes, there was a knock at her door. Opening the door and seeing Jorge and the hotel maintenance man made her feel relieved. "Thank God." Emilie let out the air she'd been holding in her lungs, probably since the statue broke. "Thanks for coming so fast."

"No problem, Emilie. Oh, uh, this is Clarence, he's the head engineer. He can fix anything." Jorge patted Clarence on his back. Clarence, an older man with gray hair where he had any, was wearing navy blue coveralls and a leather tool belt that looked like it contained everything a handyman would ever need.

Emilie showed them into the room and over to her bed. "Here. This is a gift for our chairman. When I was wrapping it, the spear broke." Emilie picked up the spearhead and handed it to Jorge. "I'm afraid to touch it anymore. I'm afraid something else will break off. You know, it was cut from one piece of wood . . . that is, until now."

Clarence was not afraid to touch it. He picked the statue up and inspected the break. He looked down at his belt and pulled out a tube of clear glue. He then took a pair of magnifying glasses from his overall pocket. With the precision of a skilled surgeon, he spread a little glue on the chief's fist and stuck the spear in it. At first, the weapon went limp. Undeterred, he propped it up again. "Go get your hairdryer," he instructed.

With her toe still smarting a little, Emilie limped into the bathroom to get the hairdryer. She sighed as she caught a glimpse of herself in the mirror and touched the hot rollers to see if they were cool—ice cold was more like it. *Great.* There was no time to worry about what her hair looked like.

As she made her way to the bed with it, Clarence said, "Find a plug near here." Emilie did as she was told, finding one on the wall next to the bed. She plugged it in and placed it on the bed, within Clarence's reach. He held the statue carefully, applied a little more glue, and held the spear in place with a large pair of tweezers. Then he motioned to Jorge. "Here, hold this steady, but not too close to the glue." Jorge's hand shook a little as he held the tweezers. He held onto his right wrist with his left hand to steady it. Clarence bent down until his eyes were level with the break. He added a little more glue and then turned the hairdryer on low. For about a minute, the only sound in the room was the hum of the dryer. Turning it off, he stepped away. "This should work. Let's give it a minute or two. Keep a good hold on it, you hear? Don't move."

Emilie took the opportunity to go into the bathroom and remove the curlers. Once they were out, her hair resembled the bushy mop of Ronald McDonald. She tried to brush some of the big curls out of her unruly hair. After struggling with it for longer than she wanted to, she decided to just leave it as is. As she lifted her arm to spray on some hairspray, she realized her dress zipper was still not all the way up. She again tried to reach it but could not.

She walked out into the room where the two men had completed their project. "Well, I think it's good as new. You can't even tell there's glue on it. Clarence is da man," Jorge said, handing the sculpture to Emilie. She inspected it and could see just a faint line of glue at the top of the chief's fist. In order to find it, someone would have to know it was there. Afraid to put the statue down just yet, she cradled it like an infant. She reached in her purse and pulled out two twenty-dollar bills. "Thank you, guys. You are a lifesaver. Here, I really can't thank you enough." She handed a twenty to each man. "Oh, um . . . this is our little secret, right?"

Both men nodded.

"Thank you. That's very nice of you," Clarence said as he shoved the money into his top pocket.

"Jorge, um, before you go, um, I need your help with something else."

"Sure. What else do you need?

"Can you finish zipping up my dress?"

• • •

By the time Emilie made it down to the banquet room, cocktails were flowing. Carl ran over to her as soon as she walked into the room.

"Where have you been?" he bellowed.

"I didn't get up to my room until about thirty minutes ago. Remember, I had to stay and help get the room reset."

With a scowl, Carl looked around the room and said, "Yeah, I'm still mad that they didn't get it right to begin with. Now, look at the table placement. Isn't that better?" He pointed to the two tables that hadn't been moved.

"Yes, it is," she said.

"Is that the gift? Here, give it to me, and I'll go give it to Ken to present it to Malcolm." Carl grabbed the bag out of Emilie's hand.

"Um, be careful," Emilie called after him.

He walked toward the company president, Ken Howell, and handed it to him. Emilie felt her heart rise to her throat. She held her breath as she spied on Carl across the room, talking closely to Mr. Howell. She couldn't tell what he was saying, but had a scenario play in her head.

Carl: So, Ken, here's an Indian statue that I personally picked out for Malcolm. I hear he collects Indian artwork. I'm sure this will be perfect.

Ken: Oh, Carl, I thought Emilie picked this out?

Carl: Emilie? I couldn't trust her on this one. She did nothing. This was all me.

Ken: Wonderful Carl (Ken looks in the bag.) Oh, what's this? It looks like a split in the wood.

Carl: What? Oh, that? I'm sure it's nothing. It will buff right out.

Ken: Carl, you're fired.

Emilie's fantasy conversation somehow calmed her down.

Mr. Howell clinked his knife to his wineglass and asked the group to be seated. But Emilie was too nervous to sit down and stood in the back of the room.

"Before we get started, as many of you know, this is Malcolm Porter's last board meeting as chairman. These past four years have been a pleasure with you at the helm..." The group clapped politely.

Emilie's heart nearly drowned out what Mr. Howell was saying. Her palms began to sweat, and she felt queasy. She swallowed hard and nervously watched as Malcolm shook hands with Ken.

"We hear you collect Native American art. So, here's a little something to add to your collection." Ken handed the gift bag to Malcolm.

Emilie covered her mouth with her hand to catch any vomit should it come up. *Maybe I should pretend to faint,* she thought to herself. She removed her hand and used it to steady herself against the wall. Malcolm sat the bag on the table in front of him. He reached in and pulled out the gift wrapped in tissue paper. He slowly unwrapped the statue while Emilie stood on her tippy toes to get a better look. *Please be in one piece, please be in one piece.*

"Wow, this is amazing! How wonderful! Thank you! Someone really did a great job of picking this out. Julie and I will cherish this. Look, honey." Malcolm turned toward his wife.

"It's carved out of one piece of wood," Ken added.

Or not.

"Those are rare, and definitely a keepsake. This is really special. Thanks again." Malcolm handed the sculpture to his wife, who held it up and admired it. "Honey, pass it around so everyone can see it. It is magnificent."

NO! Oh, God! NO! Surely one of the forty guests would notice the hairline fracture and patch up glue job. Emilie stared intently, like a new mother at a family reunion as she watched her baby being passed from guest to guest. When the chief made it back safely to Malcolm and the gift bag, Emilie breathed a sigh of relief. *This job is going to kill me.*

33

The next Saturday, Emilie met Colin at Madame Trousseau's Bridal Shop on Charles Street in the heart of downtown Baltimore. When they arrived, the shop was buzzing with business. The sight of consultants scurrying around trying to please the herd of picky brides and bridal parties was slightly overwhelming for Emilie. The last time she was in the store was to shop for her own wedding dress, eight years earlier.

"Colin, it's so busy in here. Can't we just go to Nordstrom's?"

"No, I've told you, Nordstrom's isn't going to have something pink, frilly, and chiffony. C'mon," he said as he grabbed her hand. "And don't roll your eyes at me. It's my wedding—let me be a bridezilla. You can be a maid of honor-zilla . . . to everyone but me. Now remember, if you meet someone at speed dating, feel free to bring him as a guest."

Emilie felt herself slouch and pout, as if on cue. "Eyeroll, eyeroll, eyeroll!"

That prompted an actual eyeroll from him.

Even though she'd never say it to anyone, planning Colin's wedding was difficult for Emilie. He was her best friend, and she was very happy for him, but there was a part of her that ached inside due to her loss. And, for some reason, weddings were particularly hard to endure.

Approaching the reception desk, Colin proudly announced:

"Hi, I'm Colin, *the bride.*" He arched one eyebrow as he pointed to himself. "And this is my maid of honor, Emilie. We have an appointment with Robin at one." The receptionist, a young girl, looked up from her iPhone and seemed unfazed by the nontraditional appointment. She looked at the appointment book. "Yeah, have a seat over there." She pointed to a white circular couch in the center of the showroom. "I'll tell Robin you're here."

Colin made a beeline for the dresses hanging on a rack behind the receptionist, while Emilie did as she was told and sat on the white couch. Looking around the room, she noticed how white everything was: white shag carpet, white paint on the walls, and even big, fake, white leafy plants in giant white vases for decoration. "How do they keep everything so clean . . . and white?" she mumbled out loud.

About ten minutes later, a woman appeared wearing all black. She smiled broadly and reached her hand out to Emilie. "Hi, I'm Robin. You must be my next appointment," she said.

Emilie shook Robin's hand. "Hi, yes, I'm Emilie. I'm the maid of honor. The bride is around here somewhere." Emilie angled her head as she looked for Colin among the sea of women, lace, silk, and taffeta. Spotting him in the corner of the room, Emilie said, "Oh, no," and shook her head. "There he is." She pointed to him. Colin was admiring at arm's length a long baby pink strapless dress with a skirt made of ruffles. To Emilie, the dress looked like a layered pink Christmas tree. "Please don't let him put me in that," Emilie said to Robin.

As she and Robin walked over to Colin, Emilie began to feel an anxious churning in her stomach. She just wanted the day to be over.

"Look at this! Isn't it great?" Colin said, lifting up the dress high. "Pink, frilly, and chiffony. I think it's perfect."

Emilie stared at the dress and hoped Colin could read her mind. "Um, well. I guess you could say it's special."

Robin put a light hand on Emilie's shoulder and said, "You know, I don't think pink is your color. No, not with your pretty red hair. Pink would wash you out. Actually, I wouldn't go pastel at all. How about something chic in black?"

Thank you, Robin! "I like black. I wear a lot of it. What do you think, Colin? Maybe something like Robin has on?"

"Hmm, I don't know. Maybe. You *do* look good in black, and black is very elegant." Colin looked over the pink dress one more time before replacing it on the rack. "Okay, I'll see what else they have."

Pleased, and somewhat surprised at how easily Colin retreated from his pink position, Emilie quickly encouraged the change of mind. "Black is good. Black, I can wear again. We like black," she said, nodding exaggeratedly to make a point.

"Good. Then we agree, black it is," Robin said. "Bride, I don't think we've met. I'm Robin and I'll be taking care of you guys today."

"So nice to meet you. I'm Colin."

"Congratulations. Now, I've reserved dressing room number one over here. Follow me."

"We're number one! We're number one!" Colin chanted while holding his index finger in the air.

"I love enthusiastic brides," Robin said as she took a key out of her pocket to unlock the door to the dressing room. "Okay, Emilie, you wait in here. Bride, come with me." She motioned for Colin to follow.

After Robin and Colin had left the room, Emilie undressed and put on the white silk robe that hung on the hook on the back of the door. She remembered how excited she was the last time she was there in search of the perfect dress: a beaded, strapless, mermaid-style gown that laced up the back, hugged her figure, and made her feel like a fairy-tale princess.

Her parents had agreed to pay for the wedding but not the dress, making the dreamy gowns she saw in *Brides Magazine* not an option. While the more expensive dresses certainly were tempting, the practical side of her couldn't imagine spending money she didn't have on a dress that she would only wear one day. She and her mother had worked out a flawless plan to find a perfect dress that didn't break the bank. As Emilie modeled the dresses, Margaret would discreetly look at the price, and base her opinion on how much it was. If it were out of the budget range, she would criticize the look, the fit, anything indicating it wasn't the right one, so Emilie wouldn't fall in love with it and spend more than she could afford. Unfortunately, the plan fell apart when Margaret became overwhelmed and emotional at the sight of her daughter in the fourth gown she tried on. With tears in her eyes, Margaret declared, "You look so beautiful. This is it! This is the one." After the hugs, tears, and a symphony of happy applause from Margaret and the wedding coordinator, Emilie looked down at the price tag and realized the dress was double what she had planned to spend.

At first, she wasn't sure what to do. It was truly against her grain to be so extravagant, but when she saw herself in the mirror, she loved what she saw. Rationalizing that she wasn't planning to eat much before the wedding, which would save her money on groceries, Emilie decided to take the plunge and buy the dress. Rob's expression upon seeing her on their wedding day made her realize she had made the right decision.

The memory made tears well up in her eyes. She reached for the tissue box, which was there for emotional brides, dabbed her eyes, and blew her nose. *Get it together, Emilie. This is for Colin.*

When Robin returned, she had three black dresses in her arms. "Look what I've found you!" She held each one up as she hung them on the hooks that flanked the walls. "I don't know which one we should start with," Robin said, turning toward Emilie. Robin's smile faded when she saw Emilie. "Are you okay?"

"Um, yeah, it's just allergies." Emilie took a deep breath to compose herself. As she inspected the dresses, she had to admit she was impressed. Each was different, but something she would have picked for herself. There was a simple, but elegant, sleeveless, long satin dress that had a slit up to about the mid-thigh; a strapless silk dress, with a big white flower on the right hip, and a knee-length skirt; and a sleeveless one with a black lace overlay that had a sweetheart neck and a short but full skirt, with lace extending past the hem and a thick white ribbon for a belt. Emilie picked the last one from the hook. The material felt so soft in her hands. She turned it around and noticed it was backless. "I really like this one, but I don't think it will like me. I could never go braless. Not with these." She cupped her breasts over the silk robe.

"Oh, don't worry about that. It's got an underwire bra sewn in it."

"It does?" Emilie inspected the inside of the bodice and saw the saving graces. "Why yes, it does. Let's try this one on first."

She removed the robe, and Robin helped her on with the dress. "It fits you perfectly—like it was made for you," Robin said with excitement.

Emilie looked in the mirror. "Yes. I like it. I really do," she said, turning from side to side to watch the skirt sway and to get a better look from each angle. "Now we just have to convince him. He's pretty picky."

"That shouldn't be a problem. When he sees you in this, he'll know it's the right one too."

Emilie and Robin left the room and walked out to the waiting area where Colin was sitting. "Wow! You look great!" He studied her from head to toe. "But I don't think it's right," he said, getting up from his seat to get a closer look at the dress.

"You don't?" Even though it wasn't her wedding, Emilie felt deflated.

Colin reached over and kissed her on the cheek. "It's not just right, it's perfect." He hugged her tightly and whispered, "You look beautiful."

Emilie felt a tear moisten her neck as he squeezed her even tighter.

• • •

When she got home, Emilie went to her closet to hang up her new black dress. On the top shelf, she saw the big white box that housed her wedding dress. For eight years it sat there unnoticed, but today she was compelled to get it down and look at it. She struggled with the box that was almost as big as her. She carried it to the bed and opened the lid. Inside, beneath a layer of white tissue paper, was the beautiful dress, just as she remembered it, preserved for the daughter she'd never have. She took the dress out of the box and hugged it close.

Instinctively, she decided to put it on, hoping to get the same magical feeling she felt years earlier. She undressed to her bra and panties and stepped into the dress. This soon became a big mistake. For her wedding, she had dieted down to a size four, something she'd never see again. When the dress wouldn't budge past her now ampler hips, it became very apparent a four could not become an eight, no matter how much she tried to force it. Fearing that tugging too hard would destroy it, Emilie let the bodice hang down at the waist. Even though the dress was tight and uncomfortable, something in her did not want to take it off. With the back unlaced and the dress forcing her legs too close together, she staggered to the kitchen, poured herself a glass of wine, and made her way to the couch. She felt emotionally drained.

She took a sip of wine, closed her eyes, and sighed. Instantly she thought of Miss Havisham, the Dickens spinster who was jilted at the altar and sat around for years in her wedding dress while cobwebs collected in her hair. When Emilie read the book in sixth grade, she laughed at how pathetic the character was. But now she understood how someone could long so hard for the past that they become immobile toward the future.

• • •

"Emilie? Emilie? Where are you?"

The voice was unfamiliar and startled her. Emilie got out of the bathtub and grabbed her blue terry cloth robe, wrapping her body in it. "What? Who's there? How did you get in here?" She peeked around the bathroom doorframe to see who it was. Her body, still dripping from the bathwater, stiffened in fear as her heart beat fast.

"Emilie, it's me, Rob."

Rob stood before her in full fishing gear—floppy hat with lures, plaid shirt, vest with mesh pockets, khaki pants, and mud boots. In his right hand, he held up a large, pink-and-gray striped fish. "I've been fishin'. Isn't it a beauty? Oh, but baby, have I missed you!" He walked closer to her.

"How have you been?" he asked.

"I'm okay," she said.

Emilie hugged him tightly and kissed him on the cheek. "Rob," she whispered softly in his ear. "I miss you so much."

"I know you do, baby, but you have to let me go so that you can live."

She woke up groggy and looked around. Rob was gone. Just like Colin said, the brain catches up. And in a weird way, she felt closure.

34

"You're number eight," the receptionist said. "The tables are numbered. Just sit at table number eight. When I ring the bell, stay put. The men will change tables. You will be referred to as number eight on their responses. If you want to give them your name, feel free, but we won't."

Speed dating sounded like such a good idea when she signed up, but now she was having buyer's remorse. All the preparations for Colin's wedding made her long to be in a relationship. With the wedding six weeks away, she thought that was ample time to meet someone and be exclusive enough to have a date for the wedding.

She hesitantly walked into the bar area of the restaurant. "Eight-Minute Dating for over Forty, every Thursday" read the sign above the bar. She took a seat at the small round table with the number eight perched on a stand. Looking around the room, she sized up the competition. Number four looked well beyond forty, maybe even in her sixties, and number one was age-appropriate, but talked loudly on her cell phone. There was an attractive man standing at the bar. His horn-rimmed glasses made him look like a nerdier version of Barack Obama. He looked her way and winked. Emilie blushed. Maybe this won't be so bad after all, she told herself.

The receptionist rang a bell. "Okay, can I have everyone's attention? Welcome," she said. "For those of you here for the first time, let me quickly explain the rules. When you checked in, I gave everyone a number, right?" Simultaneous head nods swept the room. "Okay, so, women, you stay at your table. Men, you start at the table number I gave you and when I ring the bell, move to your right. Okay." Heads bobbed again. "Oh, I almost forgot. Gentleman number seven."

"Here," came a voice from the crowd.

"Lady number seven is stuck in traffic. She should be here any minute. If you feel shortchanged, we can arrange for more time for the two of you at the end of the evening. Okay?" The receptionist scanned the room and seemed pleased with the lack of response. "All right. When I ring the bell, your time will start."

Ding went the bell.

The cute Obama look-alike approached Emilie's table. "Number eight?"

Emilie started to stand and extended her hand.

He waved her off. "Please, stay seated. I'm Jason," he said with a broad smile. Then his attention drifted to the table to Emilie's right—table number seven. Jason's smile turned to a gaping, open-mouthed expression.

Emilie glanced in that direction. Indeed, lady number seven had arrived. With her bleached blond hair, breasts spilling out of her white halter top dress, and her glistening bright red lips, she looked every bit like a modern-day Marilyn Monroe.

"Nice to meet you. I'm Emilie," Emilie said, hoping to regain Jason's attention.

"Oh, yeah, sorry. Nice to meet you too," Jason said as he sat down. "So, what brings you here?" He again looked over to table number seven.

Emilie looked there too. By now, "Marilyn" was seated, and gentleman number seven was talking to her, leaning in very close.

"Marilyn" twisted a strand of hair as she laughed in an exaggerated manner.

This caused Jason to laugh in a giggly, school boyish way.

Emilie looked down at her watch. Seven more minutes in hell, she thought.

Jason turned back around. "Where was I?"

"You were staring at number seven's chest," Emilie heard herself say.

"Oh, was it that obvious?" He blushed, and his demeanor shifted to that of a young boy being caught with a *Playboy* magazine.

"Yes, it was pretty obvious."

"Oh, I'm sorry. So, what do you do?" Jason asked as he again glanced in the direction of table seven.

"Me? I pilot a daily spaceship to Mars," Emilie said.

"Nice." He nodded while continuing to divert his attention elsewhere.

"Yeah, I left my tinfoil hat at home. In my spare time, I like to stalk old boyfriends and really just anyone who shows an interest in me, but never follows through."

Jason's eyes stayed focused on the table next to them.

"Have you ever seen Fatal Attraction? Do you have a rabbit?" Her comments elicited no reaction from her "date."

The bell rang. Jason reached out his hand. "Nice to meet you, Emma. Have a great evening." He stood up and walked toward table seven, which now had three other men hovering around.

The receptionist said, "Okay, remember the rules. Men, move to the table on your left. All of you guys over here"—she pointed to table number seven—"you need to find your table. Only gentleman number six should be at this table."

No one seemed to listen. Chatter from table seven drowned out the receptionist's words.

"Does anyone need help remembering your number?" The receptionist said, this time with a handheld microphone.

Her question fell on deaf ears, and the crowd of men around table seven grew even larger.

"Can you hear me?" The receptionist tapped on the microphone, which emitted some squeaky feedback.

Convinced no one would notice, Emilie got up, walked out the door, and went home.

• • •

The following weekend, Emilie and Puddie went to visit Ida. Since their July visit, they had been visiting her weekly—something Emilie enjoyed as much as Puddie.

"Knock, knock. Ida? You decent?" Emilie peeked through the crack in Ida's nearly closed door.

"Come on in. And no, I'm never decent. What fun would that be?" Ida giggled her signature laugh. "I was just napping a little. But please, come on in."

Carrying Puddie in her arms, Emilie pushed the door open with her hip and entered the room. Ida was sitting in a chair next to the windowsill in a bathrobe, a blanket covering most of her body. "We can come back later if you're resting."

"Don't be silly. Taking a nap around here is like breathing. You do it whether you want to or not . . . and, for that matter, sometimes they force you to do both." Ida reached her hands out. "Come here, little fella. Come to Grandma."

Emilie unleashed Puddie and put him down. With his little tail wagging, Puddie ran to Ida, put his front paws on her legs, and gently eased himself into her lap. "Such a good boy." Ida stroked his head, and he reciprocated with doggie kisses.

"So, Miss Emilie, how'd it go?"

"How'd what go?" Emilie sat down on Ida's bed next to her.

"That minute dating thing. How'd it go? Did you have fun? Did you meet Mr. Right . . . or at least Mr. Right for now?" Ida winked and flashed a toothy grin.

"Ugh. It was awful. At least I know I'll never do that again."

Puddie yawned and then settled comfortably in Ida's lap.

"So, what was so awful about meeting some men and going on short dates? Sounds perfect. You can weed out the crazies. I wish they had something like that when I was dating."

"Oh, Ida. I hated it." Emilie dangled her legs over the side of the bed and laid her body back. She gave Ida a blow by blow of her speed dating experience. "Can you believe it? Just my luck. I'm seated next to a supermodel with big boobs. Like every man's dream. I'm thinking, what's she doing here? Is she some sort of ringer or something? There's no way she has trouble getting dates."

Propping her head up with her hand, she rolled over on her side and faced Ida. "It was mortifying. All the men were drooling over hot blonde number seven and not interested in lukewarm redhead number eight." She frowned. "I think I'm gonna be single forever." Emilie let out a loud sigh and covered her eyes with her free hand.

Ida reached to the windowsill and grabbed a framed picture of her son. "I'm sure my son, Max, would be interested in dating hot redhead number eight. That's why you need to let me fix you up with my Max." She put the picture on the bed close enough for Emilie to reach. "Look at him. Isn't he adorable? If I do say so myself."

Emilie had to admit that Max was very handsome. Deep brown eyes and thick wavy black hair punctuated with gray, both traits he must have inherited from his mother. "You know Ida, we've been through this. I have a rule—I won't let any of my friends fix me up with family members. What if it doesn't work out?" She stretched to put the photo back where it came from.

"What's not to like? He's adorable. Besides, I hear he has a great mother—not too meddling." Ida batted her eyelashes and smiled as she spoke.

"I wasn't referring to me not liking him. I was referring to him not liking me."

"Again, I repeat myself. Adorable. What's not to like? A mother knows these things. My Maxie would feel like he hit the jackpot with you after that pain in the tuchus ex-wife of his." Ida shook her head. "While they were dating, she was as sweet as pie— butter would melt in her mouth, as my mother would say. It was always, 'Oh, Mrs. Goldenbaum, the dinner was delicious' and 'Oh, Mrs. Goldenbaum, let me help you with the dishes.' But I had a feeling we weren't seeing the real person. A mother knows these things. And when they got married—oy vey! Was I right?" Ida clutched her chest, mocking a heart attack. "Don't you know, *that one*, she quit her job as a marketing something or other and spent her days at the spa or the shopping mall. She said it was her job to take good care of herself, for Max's sake. Please!" Ida rolled her eyes and waved her hand dismissively.

Puddie jumped down off of Ida's lap and found a comfortable spot at her feet to rest.

"The only thing that one was good at was spending money. And, if that wasn't bad enough, she ordered my Max around like a slave. We'd go to their house, and it was, 'Max, get me this' and 'Max, why are you doing that?' Oh, I can still hear that scratchy voice in my head. Like a squawking macaw." Ida closed her eyes. "I told him, 'Life is too short. What's wrong with you? Why are you putting up with this? Get out before you have kids. She'll run you to the poorhouse, that one.' Tsk, tsk.

"But he stayed, hoping for a day when things would work out. Here he was, top cardiologist at Johns Hopkins, living a miserable existence at home. Thank God she was too much of a prima donna to get pregnant. As much as I want grandkids, there is a Gott im Himmel." Ida clasped her hands as if she was saying a prayer and looked up to the ceiling.

"Well, don't you know, one day about two years ago he came to me and said, 'Ma, I'm done. I can't do it anymore.' I was so proud of him." Ida's smile turned serious. "Oh, but little miss attitude wouldn't go down so easy. No! Do you know she told the judge that *she* supported him through med school? *She?* If my Sol heard that . . ." Ida shook her head again. "Really, the nerve.

"But my Maxie, such a good boy. Gave her a nice settlement— or severance package, from her job of being a doctor's wife." Ida emphasized with air quotes. "I hear she moved back to New York and is working in the makeup department of Saks. Seems she had plenty of experience in that area. Lord knows she certainly bought up everything they had. I tell him, 'Your next wife, let me pick her. A mother knows.'" She held up her index finger and pointed it at Emilie. "He's very good at fixing broken hearts, an expert at it." She winked.

"I know, I know. Believe me, I'm flattered. Max sounds like a great guy, and who wouldn't want you as a mother-in-law? I just don't think I want to date anyone now. I'm so stressed out at work. It's not a good idea to start a relationship."

"What's going on at work? Besides that meshuggener, Carl?"

"Nothing new. The same stuff. I just hate my job. I dread getting up every day and going in. Maybe I'm burned-out."

"So, quit."

"I can't do that." Emilie frowned and studied Ida to see if she was kidding.

"I don't see why not," Ida said very matter-of-factly.

"I can't just quit. What would I do for a living?"

"What do you want to do? If you could do anything, what would make you the happiest?"

"Hmm." Emilie hesitated. "Don't laugh. I've never told anyone this. I've always wanted to write a book." Emilie felt herself blushing. "But I'm no Nora Roberts. No one is going to pay me to write a book."

"Even Nora Roberts didn't know she was Nora Roberts before her first book. You've got to start somewhere. Take a risk. You'll never know if it's worth it until you try."

"No, I'm not the jump without a net kind of girl. I like to have things planned out in advance. I need to know I'll be okay."

"Excuse me, but I believe when your husband died, you jumped—or rather were pushed—off a skyscraper with no net, and you landed fine. Even soared." Ida patted the bed for Emilie to move closer to her. Once Emilie was near, she grabbed Emilie's hand with both of her hands and squeezed. "You have strength and courage that is enviable, but you don't appreciate or recognize it."

Emilie felt her throat tighten and her eyes well with tears. "That was different. When Rob died, I had to be strong. I didn't have a choice back then."

"Oh, you had a choice. You could've stayed in bed with the covers over your head, but you didn't. You lived life. You thrived. You're still thriving."

"But Ida, quitting my job to write a book, that makes no sense. I just don't think I can do it. I don't. It's not me."

"You know this better than most. Life is too short not to do what makes you happy. Do you want to be on your deathbed saying, 'I shoulda, woulda, coulda'?" Ida inched her body closer to Emilie and continued. "One day, after my Sol died, I called Max and said, 'I want to go skydiving.' He said, 'Ma? What? You're seventy-two. Are you crazy? You'll break your neck.' And I said, 'No, I'm not crazy. I just don't want to die without knowing what it feels like to jump out of a plane.' Death of a loved one makes you see life as a gift and makes you want to do things you never thought you would."

"I know. I appreciate how precious life is. But this is different. I like to eat. I need a paycheck. I need that security."

"So, this may be none of my business, and you can tell me to shut up if you want to. Did that husband leave you any life insurance?"

"Yes, some."

"Well, there you go. It sounds like a gift from Rob. So, you don't have the four-dollar-a-day coffees, and you stop buying designer shoes. The point is, you can do it if you want to. It's not hard to do what you want, what you enjoy. It's hard to keep doing what makes you miserable."

• • •

When Emilie got home, she poured herself a glass of wine and drew a bath. As the sweet taste of chardonnay passed her lips, it hit the spot. She smiled. She placed the wineglass on the side of the bathtub. Naked, she looked at herself in the mirror. She twisted her body so she could see every angle. *Not too bad for a middle-aged old lady,* she thought. She moved in to get a closer look at her face. There were wrinkles in the corners of her eyes that she hadn't noticed before, and her brow was creased with worry lines—remnants of pain. The past eighteen months had been hard—at times unbearable. Maybe Ida was right. She was a survivor, and that was something to be proud of. She thought briefly about quitting her job. Could she do that? The thought was terrifying. Maybe she could sell her house. The equity could sustain her for a few years.

She slipped into the bathtub, careful not to disturb the wineglass, and let the indulgent bubbles cover her body. The water was warm, and the smell of the lavender was so relaxing. She took a sip of the wine and slipped her body deeper into the tub. Maybe her story could help people. She always wished there was a guide for widows. Maybe Rob's death and her life could have meaning.

35

In the middle of the next week, Dr. Jeffries smiled as he opened his office door. "Emilie, come on in."

She walked in and took her usual place on the couch. Crossing her legs, she smiled at her shiny, navy, three-inch, patent leather platform shoes—her "power" heels gave her the confidence she needed. Only a woman would know shoes could have that power.

After taking a deep breath, she looked up at Dr. Jeffries, who was smiling broadly. "So, I went to that restaurant in Ellicott City you told me about," he said.

Emilie quickly looked away; the look of excitement on his face was going to make telling him more difficult. But she didn't want to drag out the conversation. She took another deep breath and exhaled slowly. "Oh, you did. Good. I hope you liked it."

The truth was, the last few sessions had felt more like coffee with an acquaintance, only without the coffee—and at thirty dollars a co-pay, it was an expensive outing. The sessions didn't feel like therapy at all. Dr. Jeffries had even opened up to her with an occasional anecdotal story, giving her a glimpse of his personal life. After four of these "non-sessions," it was time to move on.

"Okay, good. Hmm. I've got some great news for you," she said. She paused to choose her words.

Dr. Jeffries leaned forward. "Go on." His smile noted he was hanging on her every word.

"Well, I think I'm cured!" She raised her hands, mimicking a "hallelujah."

Dr. Jeffries's smile faded quickly. "Okay. What exactly does 'cured' mean to you?"

"I feel ready to move on. I miss Rob, and I always will, but I feel better now. I feel good. I'm happy. I don't think I need to come here anymore."

Dr. Jeffries adjusted his glasses. "I see."

"I guess I owe it all to you," she added, trying to ease out of the conversation. "A lot of what you had to say to me, I found helpful. I really am okay with my life now. I even went to a speed dating event. It was hard, but I did it. And honestly, it was easier than dating was a few months ago. The point is, I think I have accepted Rob's death as part of my life. And even though sometimes it sucks, sometimes it doesn't." She ended her mini-speech with ta-da hands—just like she'd rehearsed at home . . . many, many times.

Dr. Jeffries nodded, but still looked a little bit stunned.

"My friend Ida, she's really been helpful in repeating the same things you say—that I have been through something that would cripple most people emotionally. And it's true. I haven't really appreciated that. That being said, being widowed doesn't define me, it's just an awful chapter in what has been an otherwise happy life. I know I'm a strong person. I can appreciate that now."

Dr. Jeffries cleared his throat and looked away. "Well, I'm glad I could be helpful to you. That's what all therapists want to hear." He turned his focus toward her. "I hope you don't find this inappropriate, but I'm going to miss our sessions."

Emilie smiled. "Thanks. I'll bet you say that to all your patients." She waved her hand dismissively.

"No. No. Really, I don't." He was very serious. "I hope you'll keep in touch. Let me know how things are going."

She was a little caught off guard, but then quickly disregarded her initial reaction by rationalizing that most therapists probably want to know how their patients are doing. "Sure, I will," Emilie lied a little, hoping that her eyes gave no hint of the deception because she wasn't sure how the "keeping in touch" would work. Friend him on Facebook? Um, that seemed weird to have your therapist "like" posts that were meant for friends. And what if he didn't "like" something? What would that mean?

She diverted her eyes because surely a therapist was skilled at detecting attempts to avoid the truth. And said, "Sure, let's keep in touch." Then she made a mental note to send him a Christmas card.

The two stared at each other for what seemed like minutes until Emilie finally said, "Well, okay then. I think I'll be going. Thank you. I really mean that. Thank you. I don't think I'd be where I am today if it weren't for your help. I really appreciate it." She pulled out the check from her wallet, already made out for her co-pay, stood up and handed it to him. "So, it looks like you have about forty-five minutes of free time," she said with a smile and a nervous giggle.

Dr. Jeffries stood up and approached her. He reached for the check and cupped her hand with his. Squeezing her hand, he said, "Thank you. It has been a real pleasure working with you. You owe yourself a lot of credit for all the hard work you did." He let go of her hand and looked her in the eye as he rubbed his graying goatee. "Would it be okay if I gave you a hug?"

"Sure," Emilie said.

• • •

When she arrived at work the next morning, it was a little after nine—a full hour past her usual time. When it came to her job, the passion was gone. And she had little desire to try to find her lacking motivation.

Walking by *A Nut*, who was on her cell phone, Emilie heard her say, "hold on." This gesture startled Emilie somewhat. Interrupting a personal call was very un-*A Nut*-like. "Carl said he wanted to see you as soon as you got in."

"What? Do you know what it's about?"

A Nut shrugged and shook her head no. Without another word, she turned away, put the phone back to her ear, and hit the hold button. "Okay, sorry about that . . . I'm back. No, it's a summer blouse. Sleeveless."

Emilie went into her office and put down her purse and briefcase. She paused. Dealing with Carl was the last thing she was in the mood to do. She grabbed a pad of paper and a pencil and walked to his office next door to hers.

Carl was on the phone as she entered. He cradled the receiver in between his three chins and his shoulder and looked up at her. Holding one finger up, he mouthed "one minute" and pointed to the chair in front of his desk. Emilie did as instructed.

"So, we're thinking of painting the sunroom yellow, but I'm afraid that will be too bright."

Emilie stood up and said in a low, whispery voice, "Why don't you call me when you're off the phone."

Carl snapped his fingers, pointed to the chair, and again motioned for her to sit down. He turned around to continue his call. "And you know, if the color is too bright, it's awfully hard to paint over."

Emilie reluctantly sat down. She twisted in her chair and tapped her pencil loudly on her notepad, hoping he'd get the hint and hang up. Finally, she heard him say with a chuckle, "All right, I'll call you later. Maybe we can have a painting party this weekend."

She mocked his laugh behind his back and faked a cough when he turned around to face her.

"We just got an assignment from Marketing. It's a joint venture with the History Channel. Some promotion of their Christopher Columbus documentary series. They want us to set up our booth at the Science Center during Columbus Day weekend and sign up new users to the premium channels," he said.

Emilie stopped taking notes and looked up. "Did you say Columbus Day?"

"Yes, October 10 through 12."

"I can't do it Columbus Day weekend. My best friend is getting married in Vermont. I'm the maid of honor. Remember? I asked for that Friday off."

Carl squinted and bit his lower lip. "Well, it seems like *you* have a problem, don't you? You can't be in two places at one time. And I need you here. You have a job to do."

"Can't *you* do it?" Emilie was surprised to hear herself ask. "I can't miss this wedding. It's important to me."

"No, I can't. My wife wants to go to Ocean City that weekend. You're just going to have to figure it out. Maybe ask your friend to get married the following weekend."

"You can't be serious," Emilie said.

Carl sighed. "Yes, I am being serious. As far as the Columbus Day event is concerned, you don't have a choice. You have to do it."

Emilie bit her thumbnail while she thought through options. Her mind quickly came to one conclusion that made the most sense. She looked Carl straight in the eye. "You're wrong . . . I do have a choice. I quit." *Oh, no, she didn't! Oh, yes, she did!* Her heart beat rapidly, and she felt her face get hot. For a second, she looked away, but then decided to face the bull head-on and stared back at him.

"What? Aren't you overreacting a bit? Don't get so emotional."

"I am being perfectly calm and rational when I say I mean it. I quit," she said.

"Hmm. Although this is against my better judgment—because I don't like to be manipulated, all right, you can have Columbus Day weekend off. Go ahead, go to your wedding. Even though it might ruin my marriage, I'll figure out something with my wife." Pressing his pen in an exaggerated way, Carl wrote in big block letters "CANCEL VACATION," on his daily to-do list.

"No, it's not about Columbus Day weekend. It's about every day before and after Columbus Day weekend. I haven't been happy for a long time. Since my husband died, I've learned a lot about myself. I know I have to look out for myself because no one else will. I'll be much happier doing something else. I'll stay until October fifth. That will give you a month to replace me."

For the first time in twelve years, she saw fear in his eyes. "Don't make any rash decisions. Why don't you take the day off to think about it? Tomorrow we can pretend this conversation never happened." His voice was even-toned, and he seemed sincere.

"Thanks, but that won't be necessary. I'll type up my letter of resignation, so you have an official document." Emilie got up and walked out. When she returned to her office, she pumped her fist in the air and smiled. With a mixture of fear but mostly happiness, she said, *You go, girl!*

• • •

The rest of the day flew by. It was amazing how much easier things were when there was an end in sight. Soon word got out—more than likely thanks to *A Nut* and her network of friends—and Emilie was the fodder of gossip again. The same people who said "That's the girl whose husband died," were now saying, "I heard she went right into his office and told that asshole off." It didn't matter to her that the retold story had become a tall tale—she was becoming a legend in the building.

Driving home, she kept replaying the look on Carl's face in her head. It was priceless. He looked like a kid who had just found out there was no Santa—shocked and dismayed. Very few people would put up with him for as long as she did. Maybe Carl would learn how to treat people . . . probably not.

She couldn't wait to tell Ida the good news, so she decided to stop by the nursing home. Ida would be proud. It was Ida who gave her the confidence to believe in herself.

When she got to Ida's room, she saw her sitting on the bed. A man who obviously was a doctor was listening to Ida's heart with a stethoscope.

Emilie knocked on the open door and slowly entered the room. "Knock, knock. Ida, you okay?"

"What? Yes. I'm fine. This is my son, Max." She pointed to the doctor. "Worries about me." She shrugged her shoulders. Raising one eyebrow, she added, "And Max, this is Emilie."

Max removed the stethoscope from his ears and flung it around his neck in that cool way that doctors do.

"So, was I right? Adorable, huh?" Ida said, nodding her head, darting her eyes between the two.

Max walked toward Emilie and reached out his hand. "Hi, Emilie. Max Goldenbaum. I've heard so much about you. Nice to finally meet you." His hand was soft, but his handshake was firm.

Emilie met his eyes and smiled. "Same here." And for the first time in about nineteen months, she felt her knees weaken and her heart melt.

36

The leaves were just beginning to change into yellow, burnt orange, and red hues on her drive to White River Junction, Vermont, for Colin's wedding. The landscape was beautiful and distracting, but the drive was longer than Emilie anticipated, making her a little antsy. The trip had been extended by a few missed turns, which were followed by a judgmental "recalculating" from "Stella," her car's GPS. If "Stella" was right—and she usually was—Emilie should arrive at the inn within the hour, giving her only a little time to change before the six o'clock rehearsal.

With the familiar rapid drumbeats announcing Springsteen's *Born to Run* filling the car as she drove deep into the mountains, Emilie began to sing in unison with Bruce. Whenever and wherever she heard the song, singing along was something she couldn't help but do. If she heard it in a public place, she would quietly—or sometimes not so quietly—hum the tune, but if she was alone, watch out! She would belt it out, word-for-word, as if she were reliving a concert experience from her younger days. She and Viv believed they were his biggest fans—south of Jersey, of course. Twenty years ago, after seeing him perform, they made a pinky swear pact to always get tickets when he was scheduled to be nearby, no matter what. But that was before life and death got in the way. It had been at least five or six years since they kept up their promise, and they had missed as many concerts. As he *and she* sang the final "whoas" of the song, Emilie decided that when she got home, she'd remind Viv of the pinky swear Springsteen pact. It was time to reinstate it.

• • •

The next morning was a perfect, crisp, New England fall day. Not a cloud in the bluest sky, which made Emilie feel relieved. Her mother, Margaret, used to say, "If it rains on your wedding day, that's how many tears you'll cry during your marriage."

After showering and putting on some jeans and a cardigan, Emilie went downstairs to the hotel's restaurant to meet Colin for a late breakfast. As she approached the small table where he was sitting, Colin stood up, took her hands in his, pulled her close, and kissed her cheek. He sat back down and said, "I just had a massage and a collagen facial at the spa. Makes me look radiant, don't you think?" He tilted his head to the side and up slightly, striking a movie star-like pose. Emilie sat down. She opened the napkin covering a plastic-coated menu and put it in her lap.

"So, I made a spa date for you at twelve thirty today. For a massage and mani-pedi. I want you to be relaxed by the time five o'clock rolls around. Here you go." He reached into his shirt pocket and pulled out a business card. "Make sure they give you Gabrielle. She's got magic fingers." He made a massaging motion with his hands.

"Thank you. That's very sweet of you." Emilie took the card and looked at it before putting it in her wallet. Being Colin's maid of honor was a much different experience than when she was Viv's. The morning of Viv's wedding was spent putting out fires and calming the bride's nerves. He wasn't the usual anxiety-filled, panic-stricken bride, but then again, he wasn't the usual bride at all.

Removing his reading glasses from their Burberry case, Colin put them on and looked down at the menu. "Pumpkin pancakes, I'll bet they're good. It says here, 'Served with pure Vermont maple syrup.' Yum!"

"Yeah. That does sound good. But I think I'm just going to have a fruit cup."

"You need something heartier. How about the cornflake and coconut crusted French toast?"

"No, I'm really not hungry," Emilie said.

Colin raised an eyebrow and looked Emilie over. "Wait a minute," he swiftly removed his glasses and stared at her. "I've seen this look before." Shaking his head, he said, "Oh, no. No. No. You're not going to starve yourself today. No way. Not on my wedding day." He paused and looked at her again. His eyes narrowed. "You're in love."

"What? Don't be silly."

"Yep, whenever you start falling for someone new, you start obsessing about how you'll look naked. Remember? You did it when you started dating what's his name?" Colin snapped his fingers several times.

"Erik. His name was Erik. And you're wrong. I was never in love with him. *And* I don't obsess about things."

Colin rolled his eyes. "To quote a very good friend of mine 'eyeroll, eyeroll, eyeroll!' Remember last February when you and I took the bus trip to New York City to see Jersey Boys? You had just started dating him. You were so weak I nearly had to carry you around. All you ate that day was a banana, a bite of my soft pretzel, and the black Jujyfruits from the box of candy I got at intermission."

"I had the flu."

Colin gave her a look that said "Don't tell me that." He took a biscuit from the basket, smothered butter on the top, and put it on

Emilie's bread plate. "Mm-hmm. Look, all I know is I don't want you passing out at my wedding. I can't hold you up. I'm gonna be kind of busy." He wiped his hands off with his napkin and took a sip of herbal tea. "If you're worried about Max seeing you naked, don't. Or at least start worrying about it tomorrow. Anyway, I think you look fine."

"Are you done lecturing me?"

"No. So it's obvious you like him. What's he like, this Max guy?"

Emilie smiled. "He's kind of perfect. He's so thoughtful and so nice. He opens doors for me and does that thing where he puts his hand on the small of my back." She reached her hand over and lightly touched Colin's side near the small of his back. "You know, kind of guiding me and protecting me as I enter a room."

"Yep, I love that thing. Go on, and . . .?"

"And what?"

"What else do you like about him? There has to be more than he's a gentleman."

"Yes, of course. He's really funny. Has very funny observations. He kind of reminds me of a mix between you and Ida. Full of life and makes me laugh."

"Good. I like a man that doesn't take life too seriously."

"Yes, so do I. And . . ." Emilie looked away briefly, almost embarrassed to say. "He's so freakin' hot." She felt her face warm up. She put her hands to her cheeks to cover them.

Colin smiled. "Got any pictures yet?"

"No, I can't say to him, 'I have to take your picture so I can send it to my friend.'"

"Sure, you can. Next time you're out with him, just ask the waitress to do it."

"No, that won't be obvious at all." Emilie shook her head.

"Here, hold on. 'Let's have the waitress take our picture so I can always remember our fourth date.'"

"I trust you'll think of something. So, what kind of kisser is he?"

"What? We've only been out on three dates."

Colin said, "And . . . so, what kind of kisser is he?"

Emilie smiled. "Actually, he's great. Real light touch, but passionate, you know?" She licked her lips, remembering how his kiss felt. "Wednesday I got so lost when he kissed me good night that I leaned in for more." She giggled. "I never do that."

"You should always lean in for more. Promise me you will—that is, if you want to. When Tony and I get back from Italy, we'll all have to go out to dinner. I want to meet the man who has swept my friend off her feet. A year from now, I will be *your* maid of honor." He took another biscuit from the basket and put it on his bread plate. "Emilie Goldenbaum," he said gesturing as if he were auditioning for the lead in *Hamlet*. "It rolls right off the tongue, doesn't it?

Emilie put her hand up in a stop sign motion. "Don't get ahead of yourself. We've only been on three dates." She then broke off a piece of the biscuit and put it in her mouth, licking the excess butter off of her fingers.

"I know you're afraid. And I also know this is easy for me to say because today is my wedding day, but actually, it *is* easy for me to say. Don't live in fear that something good must end. I know you're programmed that way because I used to be too. I'll bet Max is sitting around talking to his BFF and saying how perfect you are. Relax and enjoy it. You know you deserve someone who's as wonderful as you are. But you have to believe it. I mean, *really* believe it."

Emilie nodded. "Okay. I'll try."

• • •

Colin was right; Gabrielle did have magic fingers. Following her mani-pedi and massage, Emilie was so relaxed. She had enough time to put on makeup and dress before heading to Colin's room a little early in case he was having a last-minute freak-out. Knocking on his door, she said in a sing-songy voice, "Open up . . . it's your maid of honor . . . Time to get married!"

Colin opened the door wearing all white—white suit, white shirt, and white bow tie.

"Wow! You look amazing!" she said as she gave him a big hug.

"Wow, back atcha! Mmm, and you smell yummy. What do you have on?"

"It's called Pirouette." Emilie twirled into the room, the skirt of her dress flaring out like a prima ballerina. "Are you ready?"

"Yep. I am sooo excited. Not at all nervous. You know, getting married late in life when you have all your shit together—to a man that you're crazy about, I might add—is such a good thing. I highly recommend it."

Emilie smiled.

"Okay, now, you only have two jobs. One, to pin this bouton-niere on me without sticking me, *or you*, and getting blood on my Armani suit, and two, to hold on to Tony's wedding band." Colin handed her a single miniature white calla lily and a hatpin. Emilie took the lily and pin and carefully attached them to his left lapel.

"There." She smoothed both lapels with her hands.

He reached into his pocket for a green velvet box and opened it facing her. Inside was a shiny platinum band with five small dia-monds. "Okay, here's the ring. Now don't lose it!"

"Oh! It's beautiful. Nice job." She winked. "Does yours look the same?"

He nodded.

She took the ring and hesitated, contemplating where to keep it until it was needed. Deciding against putting in her bra, because digging it out during the ceremony could not be done discreetly, she slipped it on her right thumb. She rubbed her index finger over it so she could tell what it felt like to the touch. No doubt, until it was time for the exchange, she would nervously check its status throughout the ceremony.

"And these are for you." From the table, he picked up a bouquet of three long-stemmed calla lilies, tied with a white bow that had long tails, and handed them to her.

Emilie took the flowers and brought them to her nose. "Ah. I love calla lilies. They're so underrated."

"How do I look?" Colin stood back and tugged on the bottom of his suit coat.

"You look so handsome." She smiled and then leaned forward and whispered, "I am so happy for you. Tony's a lucky man." She intertwined her arm in his and said, "C'mon, let's get you married off."

When they arrived at the staging area just inside the back of the inn behind the gardens, Emilie peeked through the French doors to catch a glimpse of the venue. The sun was about to set, creating an amber glow woven through the lattice slats of the gazebo. Most of the wooden chairs were taken, indicating the guests had arrived, and the ceremony was about to start.

Reverend Joy Brown, a tall woman with silver-gray hair, stood in the gazebo. She was wearing a black robe and a purple stole that had two bright gold crosses which fell evenly on both sides of her chest. She smiled broadly as she clutched a white Bible in her hands. The Unitarian pastor Colin had found on Wedding Wire seemed genuinely honored to preside over their nuptials, even though she hadn't met Colin and Tony until the rehearsal yesterday.

Emilie looked back at Colin, who had begun to pace and wring his hands.

"Remember when I said I wasn't nervous? Well, I lied. I think I'm gonna throw up." He reached his hand out to the doorframe and steadied himself. His breathing became loud and fast. With his other hand, he fanned his face as little beads of sweat became noticeable.

Emilie stroked his back. "Just take a deep breath. I'll tell you what my dad said just before he walked me down the aisle." She took his right hand down from his face and squeezed it. Looking him in the eye, she leaned closer and whispered, "In just fifteen minutes, you are going to be married to a wonderful man. A man you love very much." Colin smiled and mouthed, "Thank you," and his breathing slowed down to normal. Emilie handed him a Kleenex she had tucked into her belt, and he dabbed his forehead.

When the harpist began to play Pachelbel's Canon, Reverend Brown gave the signal to Emilie, who turned to Colin and said, "Are you okay?"

He nodded. "Let's get these fifteen minutes over with."

"Okay, let's do it." She opened the door and made her way to the aisle. She felt all eyes on her as she waltz-stepped—right together, left together, making sure to step lightly so her heels would not sink into the soft ground. As she neared the gazebo, she saw Colin's Aunt Dee in the second row. Wearing a bright yellow, large-brimmed straw hat, Aunt Dee was sitting next to a very well-dressed, much older man who was hunched over and appeared to be asleep. Aunt Dee raised her eyebrow and gave Emilie a wink. Emilie smiled and winked back.

Colin's mother, sister, brother-in-law, and nephew sat in the front row. His mother smiled at Emilie, while his sister, Samantha, sat with her arms crossed and had her trademark look of annoyance on her face. His nephew, Anthony, slouched in his seat, his suit bunching up around his neck as he kicked the leg of his chair with his heel.

Emilie took her place to the right of the minister, and the music stopped.

"Please stand and face the back." Reverend Brown motioned to the end of the aisle, where Colin and Tony appeared. Tony was wearing a matching white suit and tie. He held Colin's hand as they walked down the aisle, both smiling and shifting their heads from side to side, nodding, and occasionally waving to friends and family. When they reached the gazebo, they turned and faced each other. Emilie rubbed her thumb to make sure the ring was still there.

"Friends and family, what a glorious day to celebrate Colin and Tony's union," Reverend Brown began. Almost instantly, Emilie felt a knot in her throat and her eyes well up.

• • •

When she returned to her room after dinner, she immediately kicked off her shoes and sat on the edge of the bed. Her feet ached from the heels that were too high and pointed toes that were too narrow. But they sure looked good in the pictures, she thought, rubbing her toes, trying to comfort their screams. She realized she felt a tinge of loneliness. Marriage inevitably changes people. You need your friends less and less. She was guilty of it when she was married and didn't realize it until after Rob died. She told herself to expect her friendship with Colin to change. She wouldn't blame him; she was happy for him. He deserved to find love. Everyone does.

Debating whether to remove her dress, toss it in a heap on the floor and sleep in her underwear or make the effort to put on some pajamas, she decided on the latter. She got off the bed and winced when her feet touched the carpet as she hobbled toward the bathroom. Walking by the desk, she noticed a royal blue gift bag that had not been there earlier. With her name on the envelope scrawled in Colin's almost illegible print, she eagerly tore it open.

The note read:

> My Dear Emilie,
>
> Thank you for all of your love, support, advice, and laughter. Most of all, thank you for being you. Even though I now have a husband, I will always have room in my life for my "wife."
>
> Love,
> Colin

She peeked inside the bag and saw a square navy blue box with the white Swarovski logo on it. Excited, but aware that the box contained a precious crystal item, she carefully removed it from the bag. Opening the box, she smiled when she saw two finely crafted delicate swans facing each other, their beaks touching and their necks forming a heart, swimming together on a mirrored glass lake.

37

When Emilie returned home from Vermont, she no longer had a job or a friend's wedding to distract her.

A week before, she'd signed a contract with Betty Capelli, a real estate agent whose face appeared on billboards and sides of buses in Baltimore and its suburbs. Selling the house was a scary step, but Emilie knew it was necessary financially and emotionally. It was time to start making a living at her lifelong secret passion— writing. She always enjoyed writing, and as an English major in college, she was able to parlay her love and skill into a career in PR. But writing and pitching press releases was not fulfilling. If Rob had to die to teach her the lesson of strength and resilience, then fate was indeed bittersweet, but not without reason.

She liked to write from her den because it had a floor-to-ceiling bookcase filled with the classics she loved to read in college: Hemingway, Poe, and her favorite, Jane Austen. She hoped just seeing the spines of their books would give her inspiration. Occasionally she would pick one off the shelf, leafing through its worn and dog-eared pages, and smile as she recounted the finely crafted tale each author told.

In college, Viv would often chide her when she stayed home to read rather than go barhopping with the in-crowd. For Emilie, it was more fun to escape into *Pride and Prejudice* and cheer Lizzy Bennet on as she caught the unlikely attention of one Mr. Darcy than it was to drink too much and catch the unwanted attention of a cocky frat boy.

As much as she enjoyed reading, Emilie enjoyed writing more. She reclaimed her love of writing when Dr. Jeffries suggested she keep a journal. The spiral-bound notebooks now tallied seven and helped her document, in a cathartic way, her feelings. She wasn't sure if anyone would have an interest in her journey, but she knew writing her story was beneficial to her, if no one else.

As she curled up on her newly purchased ergonomically correct chair, she wrapped her arms around her knees. Still in her warm, pink flannel pajamas, the ones with big black-and-white pandas, she playfully wiggled her toes in the hot pink woolen socks she had knitted herself, and willed words to come. A few minutes into her peaceful solitude, she was startled to hear the front door open, followed by the loud voice of Betty.

"Wait until you see the kitchen . . . to die for. If you aren't a gourmet cook now, trust me, my darlings, you will be. Let me just turn off the alarm." Beep, beep, beep, beep. "There we go."

At first, Emilie wasn't sure what to do. Betty hadn't told her she was bringing a prospective buyer today, had she? Emilie looked down at her cell phone to check to see if she had a voice mail.

Shoot.

Looking down at her pajamas, Emilie knew the reaction from Betty would be unpleasant. She searched the room for something to change into. Nothing. She got up and hid behind the room's open door, hoping against hope that she wouldn't be found.

"Was I right? Huh? All of the appliances are new. The kitchen was upgraded just before the poor woman lost her husband." Betty's Brooklyn accent was getting closer.

Emilie heard the oven door open and close. *Shoot.* Realizing she couldn't hide for much longer, she stepped out of the room and walked down the hall toward the kitchen and dining room. There, she met Betty and a young couple. "Oh, you're here." Betty looked Emilie up and down. "Did we wake you?"

"No. I was just . . .," Emilie stammered. Betty's judgmental stare made her instinctively smooth her hair with her hand. She crossed her arms, hugging her body, trying to cover up the fact that she was still in her pajamas at eleven in the morning and hoping she didn't look as ridiculous as she thought she did. "Um, I'm sorry. I've just been doing some writing. I didn't know you were bringing someone by."

"What? I called you. Left you a message earlier this morning. Remember I told you, 'Cell phone on hip' so you don't miss calls." Betty sounded as if she was scolding. Pointing toward the couple, she said, "This is Jack and Jackie Johnson. Cute, huh? Like the Kennedys, but they're Johnsons."

Emilie smiled and shook their hands. "Okay, don't mind me. I'll get out of your way." She walked over to the spare bedroom, where Puddie was napping on the bed. She picked him up and cradled him in her arms. "C'mon Puddie, let's go in the backyard for some sun."

Betty continued giving her tour. "Now one of these rooms is set up for an office or den with beautiful built-in bookcases. And the other room would be great for kids," she said, leading them down the short hallway. "It's already painted in a calming lilac color. I told you about the schools here, didn't I?"

The three entered the spare room as Emilie and Puddie walked out. Emilie could hear Mrs. Johnson say, "I love it. It'd be perfect for a nursery." Emilie closed her eyes. Those were the same words she whispered to Rob when they walked through the house eight years ago. Eight years was so long ago. A lifetime.

38

Within twenty-four hours of seeing the house, the Johnsons made an offer equal to the listing price, and Emilie accepted it. She then began the tedious task of packing up what was her past. So many memories—good and bad. It was hard to believe a house could have so much power, yet it did. She knew it was time to move on, time to make new memories.

She found herself a cute one-bedroom apartment in a gated community within walking distance of a park and a coffee shop that made fresh bagels daily. Downsizing from three bedrooms to one meant there were lots of belongings to sort through. She systematically divided things into "keep," "donate," and "throw away" piles.

The last room to sort out was her walk-in closet. Once a his and hers shared space, it was now filled with her clothes only. As she reviewed hangers of dresses, pants, and blouses, some rarely worn and long forgotten, she came upon Rob's leather bomber jacket—the one he wore the night she met him. Soon after his death, she had given his clothes to charity. Somehow, this jacket had gone unnoticed, hiding among her clothes. She ran her hands on the smooth brown leather and closed her eyes. She could see him wearing it—one of his most beloved possessions. She took the jacket off the hanger and held it close to breathe it in. She thought she'd smell his scent—Hugo Boss cologne and a hint of an occasional cigar, but she didn't. The jacket smelled only like real leather and nothing more. She put the jacket on. The sleeves dangled well below her fingertips, and the waistband was mid-thigh. Then she took it off, smiled, and threw it in the "donate" pile.

With all the clothes sorted into appropriate piles, Emilie stepped away from the closet to make sure nothing was left behind. Thinking she had done a thorough job, she was slightly annoyed to see something wadded up in the back, left-hand corner of the top shelf. Not wanting to bother with getting a chair, she stood on tippy toes, took a hanger, and stretched her arm until it ached and was finally able to poke it. With short flicking motions, she moved it closer to the edge of the shelf. By touch only, she still couldn't tell what it was. With one final fling, she moved back to catch the object when it fell. As it flew off the shelf, it hit her on the chest, and she grabbed it as it bounced. It was a purple Crown Royal bag. Surprised to see it, she opened the golden tassels to reveal a small plastic bag of Rob's ashes. Emilie smiled, closed the bag back up, and gently placed it in the "keep" pile.

EPILOGUE

When Emilie arrived at the Book Nook on Main Street in Ellicott City, she was greeted with a life-size cardboard cutout of herself, which stood next to the table loaded with copies of *New Normal … A Widow's Guide*. Never in her wildest dreams did she think her book would take off, but she was, of course, relieved, and glad that it did. It turned out Ida had a few friends in the publishing industry who knew a few friends, who knew a few friends until finally contact was made with a publisher that specialized in nonfiction literature, and memoirs in particular. After reading Emilie's manuscript, he agreed to take a chance on the "quirky young widow," as he liked to call her.

With a line starting to form for signed copies, Colin gave Emilie a bear hug. "Gosh, I'm so proud of you! You go, girl!" He kissed her on the cheek and squeezed her hands. Emilie took her place seated at the book display table. One by one, admirers posed with her in selfies, offered a few words of sympathy and told her their own grief accounts.

Near the end of the ninety-minute session, a man approached the table. "Can you make it out to Erik? That's Erik with a 'k.'"

Emilie looked up to see her old boyfriend, the one that broke her heart, standing in front of her. She smiled and said, "Wow! I can't believe you're here."

"Yeah, I know. I read about it in the *Sun*. I almost didn't come.

I wasn't sure what to say to you. I still feel bad about the way I ended things. I was a jerk. I'm really sorry. I have always wanted you to know that."

"Gee, I guess your phone doesn't work?"

"I know, I could have called, but one month became two months, and then soon a year had gone by. And now, what's it been? About three years?"

"Yeah, time flies, doesn't it?"

"Yes." Erik's smile faded. "You probably don't realize this, but you're the one that got away."

"Hmm. That's interesting. Yeah, I really couldn't tell that I meant that much to you when you broke up with me over the phone."

"I know. I deserve that."

"No, what you deserve is what I wrote about you in chapter thirteen."

Erik's face reddened slightly. "Thanks for changing my name. I would've never lived it down if you didn't. For a long time, I was convinced I was going to hell. You know, for breaking up with a widow."

"You aren't out of the woods yet." Emilie laughed.

Erik smiled and seemed relieved. "Will you let me make it up to you? I know this is weird, but would you like to go out again sometime?"

"Thanks, but I really don't think that's a good idea."

"Yeah, you're probably right." He looked a little hurt.

"It's not that." She started to explain. There was so much to say, but she couldn't get the words out. The truth was, for months after he broke up with her, she longed for him to call. If this encounter would have taken place three years earlier, she would have rushed into his arms and kissed him passionately, tussled his curly hair and teased him about the giant mistake he had made. A lot had happened in three years. And she knew her life was unfolding exactly as it was meant to. She was happier now than she had ever been.

Emilie took the book from him. She opened it and flipped the pages until she got to the one with the title and smoothed the cover down with her hand.

His glance fixated on the diamond band on the ring finger on her left hand. "Oh, I see," he said. His lips curled into a slight smile.

She nodded as she smiled back. "I wish you the best."

He nodded and said, "Me too."

She picked up a black sharpie and wrote on the title page:

To Erik,

Thank you for helping me find my New Normal.

Emilie Goldenbaum

Acknowledgments

There are so many people I want to thank who helped me in my journey to be an author and create my own new normal.

First and foremost, I can't thank the staff at Apprentice House Press enough. I am grateful that you have given my story a home. A special thanks to Riley, Natalie, and Sienna for working closely with me to ensure my vision came to life.

To Deborah Jayne, thank you for suggesting I send my manuscript to Apprentice House. I am grateful every day that I reached out to you.

To my editor, Kimberly Hunt of Revision Division, thanks for catching the typos and for your helpful edits.

To Harrison Demchick at the Writer's Ally, sometimes feedback is hard to swallow. Your feedback made me a better writer.

To Deliah, Susan, and Lisa—my writing buddies--I am inspired by your talent and confidence. Thanks for all the good advice, honest feedback, and the many years of friendship.

To Jen--thank you for believing in me early on—the book club meeting was fun, and it gave me courage to keep plugging along.

To Heidi—probably the most well-read Paris: thanks for being a beta reader. Hopefully, I can count on your critique for many, many more books.

To Trice and Megan—thanks for the many years of support and mutual Bravo-fandom.

To my dearest friends, Elaine, Joan, Gabrielle, Bibi, and Diane—I know you see yourselves in some of the characters in this book. That's because you have been such an integral part of my life. We've shared lots of laughs and tears. All of you make my world a better place.

To Nita, the sister I choose, thank you for your love and support through the decades. I would have crumbled years ago if you weren't there to provide great advice and a soft shoulder to lean on.

To Stephanie and Ari--thank you for accepting me into your lives without hesitation.

And most of all, to Kevin--thank you for the encouragement and for loving me every day. I never thought my new normal could be so amazing.

About the Author

Michelle Paris is a Maryland writer who believes laughter can heal the heart. Her debut novel, New Normal, is loosely based on her own experience as a young widow. Her personal story of overcoming grief was featured on the front page of the *Wall Street Journal*. And her essays about grief and mid-life dating have appeared in multiple editions of the *Chicken Soup for the Soul* inspirational book series as well as in other media outlets. She is a member of the Women's Fiction Writers Association and the Maryland Writer's Association. Currently, Michelle is enjoying chapter two of her life with her new husband, Kevin, who keeps her from being a cat lady—but only on a technicality. For more information, visit www. michelleparisauthor.com.

Apprentice
House Press
Loyola University Maryland

Apprentice House is the country's only campus-based, student-staffed book publishing company. Directed by professors and industry professionals, it is a nonprofit activity of the Communication Department at Loyola University Maryland.

Using state-of-the-art technology and an experiential learning model of education, Apprentice House publishes books in untraditional ways. This dual responsibility as publishers and educators creates an unprecedented collaborative environment among faculty and students, while teaching tomorrow's editors, designers, and marketers.

Eclectic and provocative, Apprentice House titles intend to entertain as well as spark dialogue on a variety of topics. Financial contributions to sustain the press's work are welcomed. Contributions are tax deductible to the fullest extent allowed by the IRS.

To learn more about Apprentice House books or to obtain submission guidelines, please visit www.apprenticehouse.com.

Apprentice House
Communication Department
Loyola University Maryland
4501 N. Charles Street
Baltimore, MD 21210
410-617-5265
info@apprenticehouse.com
www.apprenticehouse.com

CPSIA information can be obtained
at www.ICGtesting.com
Printed in the USA
BVHW052023040423
661748BV00006B/8